Blood Alley

By the Author

The Serpent Club (1999)

Miami Twilight (2001)

Tom Coffey

Blood Alley

The Toby Press

Blood Alley
First Edition, 2008

The Toby Press LLC
POB 8531, New Milford, ct. 06676–8531, USA
& POB 2455, London W1A 5WY, England

www.tobypress.com

This is a work of fiction. The characters, incidents, and dialogues are products of the author's imagination and are not to be construed as real. Any resemblance to actual events or persons, living or dead is entirely coincidental.

ISBN 978 1 59264 223 6, *hardcover*

A CIP catalogue record for this title is available from the British Library

Typeset in Garamond by Koren Publishing Services

Printed and bound in the United States

To my parents

"It was the richest of cities, with some of the
most dismal slums. It was elegant and it was scruffy.
It was vociferously democratic, but also decidedly oligarchal.
It was all things to all classes."
—Jan Morris, *Manhattan '45*

Prologue

Years ago I became an eccentric. Almost a recluse. My hair is longer than it should be. Stubble crowds my face. I have the distracted manner a man obtains when he limits his human contacts to the minimum he needs to survive.

I live in the desert. I moved here because I liked the landscape: brown and arid, stretching forever, shimmering so much in the summer heat I no longer knew what was real.

It is now the first decade of a century I never expected to see. I have been tired of life for a long time, but I am afraid of facing what comes next.

I brought one thing with me from my previous existence: a photograph taken on the only night I ever moved past the feeling that I was destined to stare at all the best places in the world with my face pressed against the window. For a few hours I had a taste of what it was like to dance and laugh and act carefree, and to believe that nights like these would go on forever.

The picture shows a man and a woman who seem impossibly young. They're sitting together at a club. The man wears a tuxedo in which he appears ill at ease. His eyes gaze directly into the camera. He is trying to smile. The woman is in a sleeveless dress. Her head is turned slightly. Perhaps someone just out of camera range has caught her attention. Even in black-and-white I can tell that her makeup has been applied perfectly; her eyebrows have been plucked and arched, her nails filed and manicured. Although she is seated, she conveys passion and energy and most of all the gleeful air of a girl who knows that nothing bad will happen to her, no matter how much trouble she brings to those she knows.

Several years back, when I thought I detected hints of green at the horizon, I told myself my mind had taken to conjuring things. It was the price I paid for solitude. But the green became deeper and more pronounced, sprouting incongruously against the dead tones that nature intended. As the weeks and months went on, I detected the sun glimmering off the skeletons of multistory buildings. At night, the artificial glow of electricity began to keep me awake. At times I hear the drone of traffic, the angry whir of lawnmowers, the shrieking and splashing of children in swimming pools.

A few days ago a dark-skinned man came to my door. I heard the knock and looked through the cracks in my blinds, which I usually keep closed in the middle of the day. It is a habit I acquired when I moved here, so long ago, when there was so much to hide from.

He wore a navy blue suit, striped red tie and suspenders. Daylight gleamed off his white shirt. Anyone who looked at him too long would go blind.

At first I imagined he was Death. I've often heard He can have a pleasing appearance.

I opened the door.

"Sir!"

I nodded. He introduced himself with the exuberance of youth and extended his hand.

I waited.

He asked if I'd ever thought of selling my home.

I shook my head.

He said he worked for the Something Something Real Estate Company, which was prepared to offer me a significant amount of money—right now, upfront, no questions asked and all cash if I preferred—if I was willing to shed my property.

I said nothing.

He smiled.

I pushed the door closed and went inside, then listened to some bebop on a record player I bought years ago at a swap meet. The music made me think of her—of the way she laughed and the way she smoked, and most of all, the way she always looked only at herself in the mirror.

Chapter one

The dead girl lay beneath me. The pale yellow streetlamps shed just enough light to let me see her feet and legs clearly. Black heels and flesh-colored stockings faded into a dark form that curled into a fetal position. I wanted to look away, but I was here to observe. I blew on my fingers to warm them and began to take notes.

Finkel turned on his flashlight.

"This is aces," he said.

She had sustained two bullet wounds, one in her forehead and the other in her midsection. Purplish bruises circled her neck. She wore a dark blue dress and a sleek, unbuttoned overcoat that I guessed was cashmere.

An open handbag lay a few feet from her body. Almost comically, her hat had remained on her head.

It was the middle of November in 1946. The war had been over for more than a year. With rationing at an end, people were buying whatever they could afford, although I suspected I was looking at a Manhattan society girl who was never denied anything.

She appeared to be in her twenties. The hair I could see was red, with permed curls that fell to her shoulders. Her features were pretty but too thin, as if she ate only half a meal a day. Her eyes were hazel and had the troubled glaze of a tortured soul who was, at last, at peace.

A smooth line of blood tracked down the alley toward the street. I wondered if I had stepped in it.

Finkel said he needed stuff from his car. This was gonna make a swell pitcher. He gave me his flashlight and told me not to move anything until he came back. Then he hurried away, threading through stacks of wooden crates stacked ten feet over his head.

I was left alone with the colored man who had called the city desk not more than fifteen minutes earlier. On the phone he said he was the night watchman at a warehouse on East 45th. That put him in Blood Alley, a grimy stretch of slaughterhouses, breweries and tenements wedged along the East River between the affluent enclaves of Tudor City and Beekman Place.

The watchman had told me that he found a body while he was making his rounds. He said he knew we liked to run pictures of that sort of thing. If we steered a little money his way, he'd tell us exactly where she was.

I was a rewrite man who was supposed to stay in the office. But nothing else was happening, so McCracken, the night editor, told me to take some petty cash and head to the scene with Finkel. His pictures would make the story, if there was one.

I hopped a bit from the cold as I wondered how such a proper-looking girl could have ended up in this part of the city. I asked the colored man if he had called the cops yet. He shook his head.

"What are you waiting for, Mr.—?" I realized I didn't have his name. I shoved Finkel's flashlight under my arm and tried to scratch some more notes, but I could barely see the lines on the paper, much less what I was writing.

"Anderson. William Anderson."

"You prefer William? No nickname?"

"They're undignified. When a man loses his dignity, he's no longer a man." He paused, then smiled a bit. I saw a flash of a gold tooth. "We did talk about some money before, didn't we?"

I had grabbed a fistful of bills from a metal box inside the top drawer at the desk where the copyboys sat. I had shoved the dough in my pants, but I didn't know how much I had or should offer.

I removed a crumpled greenback from my pocket. I used Finkel's flashlight to see what it was.

Twenty bucks.

"That'll do," Anderson said as he snatched the money.

I heard Finkel approaching. He was carrying a makeup kit, a pair of nylons and a woman's hat. His camera was a Speed Graphic about half as big as he was.

I asked what he was doing.

"My props," he said. "They make my pitchers look good."

I told him I thought we should call the police.

"They'll just louse it up." He pointed his stubby fingers toward the dead girl. "Get rid of that," he said, gesturing toward her pillbox hat.

I said we shouldn't disturb anything.

"You one of those by-the-book guys?" Finkel asked.

I said nothing. I'd never been to a crime scene before, but Finkel seemed to live at them.

"Listen up, Grimes. Lemme tell you something about by-the-book guys in newspapers." He paused, as if waiting for a drumroll. "At the end of the week, that book gets 'em fired."

William Anderson was smiling a bit, no doubt amused by the bickering white men. "Let the man work," he said to me.

Anderson removed the dead girl's hat and tossed it behind a trashcan. I pointed the flashlight toward her face while Finkel fluffed out the hat he'd brought. He let it drop to the ground inches from her head. The wide-brimmed job was bigger than the hat she'd been wearing, so it would show up better in a photo. The picture itself would be more dramatic if the hat seemed to have fallen from her body.

Finkel scattered the lipsticks near the open handbag, then looked over the scene like an artist trying to figure out if his painting needed an extra dash. Nodding, he bent down and unscrewed the caps of two of the lipsticks and flicked them near her. Finally he took the nylons and slipped them halfway into the handbag.

"Why are you doing that?" I asked.

"Every dame I ever met carries nylons in her bag."

The dead girl struck me as the type who could afford stockings that rarely got torn. "I don't think she's like any dame you ever met," I said.

"Blow off, Grimes. I know how to make a good pitcher."

He spread his short legs (he was barely five feet tall), stood over her body and pointed the camera straight down. I heard a popping sound, followed by a flash that turned everything in front of me into blobs of purple and blue. When my vision cleared, I saw Finkel crouching close to her head. His camera stopped about a foot from her right ear. This time I covered my face with my hands.

Finkel walked a few feet away from the body, sprawled himself on the ground and pointed his Speed Graphic. The flash lit the night a third time. He clambered on top of a tin trashcan and shot her again before walking behind the body to take one more.

We all heard the sound at the same time: a faint wail that turned piercing within seconds. Finkel let out the longest string of profanity I'd heard since I got out of the Army. "Fucking cops," he said. "They'll take the nylons. And the lipsticks. They'll say they're evidence, but they'll just give 'em to their girlfriends."

He started shoving his stuff into his pockets. I pointed to the hat he had placed near the girl's body.

"What about that?" I asked.

"Shit! Oh shit!"

"Better take it with you."

"You're finally using your noodle, Grimes."

The noise from the siren bounced between the brick walls of the warehouses, pushing everything out of my head except a desire for calm and quiet. Now it was my turn to display the extent of my vocabulary. I covered my ears and swore the way we all did back in Italy when the German guns started up.

Finkel turned to Anderson and waved the hat around. "I'm in a jam," he said. "Where can I stash this?"

Anderson motioned for Finkel to follow. They headed toward the far end of the alley. I began to go with them. Finkel gave me a sharp look of disappointment.

"You are the stupidest goddamn rookie in the history of newspapers," Finkel said. "You ain't never covered a crime before, have you?"

McCracken had sent me out because I was the most expendable body in the newsroom. I was still on probation. I'd never had a byline and didn't even have a press tag.

"Go through her bag," Finkel said. "Get an ID."

"But the cops—"

"Don't be afraid of the cops. Be afraid of McCracken. He'll give you the bum's rush if you don't know who that dame is when you get back to the office."

Anderson led Finkel into the shadows. The siren stopped. I got on my knees, turned the dead girl's bag upright and plunged my hand into it, running through her carry-around possessions: a brush, a comb, a small nail file. Finally my fingers swept over something that felt like leather. I brought out a purse that was six inches wide, which I slid inside my coat. I stood up just as the high beam of a powerful light settled on my face.

I squinted deeply. Two dark forms that I assumed were cops stood near the street.

"Hands up! Back away from her!"

I was alone in an alley in one of the worst parts of New York, standing over a dead girl whose purse was in my possession. Finkel was right: I was the stupidest goddamn rookie in the history of newspapers.

"We're looking for a nigger. Where are you hiding him?"

I figured he was talking about Anderson. I wondered how the police knew about him already.

Before I could say anything, another voice spoke up, in tones that were younger and softer.

"Wait a minute. I know this guy."

I tried to see who it was, but the light was so bright all I could discern were blobs caressing nightsticks.

"Is that you, Grimes?"

"Yeah. Who are you?"

"Joey Valentine."

After a few seconds, recognition crashed through: one of the kids in our East Side neighborhood near the 59th Street Bridge, the token Italian in an Irish area. We used to take turns beating him up. But now he was the one with force behind him, and I was afraid he'd use the wrappings of authority to extract revenge.

"You were a straight arrow," he said. "I never figured you were the type to help kill a hooker. Or even use one."

"She's not a hooker."

"Ain't no other dames in this part of town."

"I'm a newshawk, Joey. With the *Examiner*."

"Where's your tag?"

"I don't have one." I felt like I was back in fifth grade, unprepared for the pop quiz the nuns had sprung on us. "A guy called us about a body, so I came here with a snapper to check it out. They're around here somewhere."

"This is hinky all around," the guy next to Valentine said. "Where's the nigger?"

William Anderson had phoned in a tip. It wouldn't be right to give him up.

The cops were close now. Valentine pointed the beam into my eyes while his partner slapped his nightstick onto his open palm.

"We got a call," Valentine's partner said. "They told us if we came to this alley, we'd find a dead girl. They said a nigger killed her, and we'd find him, too."

I wanted to tell the cop he was wrong. Anderson had struck me as a sneak, not a killer.

"Now I figure you're in on it, too," Valentine's partner said. "So I'm gonna ask you a question. And this is the last time I'll be nice." He paused. The light was in my eyes. My temples throbbed with pain and tension. "Where's the spook?"

I couldn't think, so I asked Valentine, "Can you guys stop shining that thing right in my face?"

The next thing I felt was the heavy wooden end of a nightstick being driven into my solar plexus. I doubled over and started sinking. My breathing became short and erratic.

"Talk to me, wiseguy. Where's the nigger?"

All I could do was gasp. Then I heard a loud cracking noise that sounded like a cherry bomb going off inside my head. I wound up facedown on the pavement.

"Stand up."

I wanted to move. My arms and legs refused to respond.

"C'mon. I hit you soft. Like I'd hit a girl."

I shifted my weight to my hands and knees. I tried to settle my feet underneath me, but I felt myself wobbling. I could barely open my eyes. Blood trickled down my face. Valentine walked behind me and forced my hands together before nipping my wrists.

"We better search him," he said.

And then I heard Finkel's voice, high-pitched and whiny and the most beautiful sound that had ever reached my ears. "Hey! What're you guys doing?"

The cops kept their grip on me. All my extremities needed blood. I wanted to break free. I would reach my hands into their holsters and take their guns. Then I'd bash the pistols against their goddamned skulls until they were as stiff and unmoving as the girl who had drawn us here.

I reminded myself that the war was over. I'd been trained to kill, but I needed to stop thinking like that.

"Who are you?" Valentine's partner asked.

"Name's Finkel. What precinct you guys from?"

They mumbled something that sounded like "The Three-O."

"Ain't Tom Grady the captain there?"

They mumbled again. It sounded as if they were saying yes.

"I take pitchers for the *Examiner.* Grady's a great guy. Give him my say-so."

"He's never said nothin' 'bout a guy named Finkel."

"Met him in Forty-One down on the docks. They found some mug named Moretti on a fishhook. I told Tom to stand next to him and make like he was looking for clues. Came out real good. Helped him make lieutenant."

The cops loosened their grip. Now I was afraid they'd release me too fast and I'd fall in a heap.

"Where's the nigger?" Valentine's partner asked.

Finkel cupped his hand to his ear. "What's that? Sometimes I don't hear so good."

I resisted the urge to shake my head at his con job. I once saw Finkel charge across the newsroom in indignation when McCracken uttered an under-the-breath comment about a photo he considered lackluster.

"There's a nigger here," the cop said. "Where is he?"

Finkel walked out of the shadows. He was rubbing his Speed Graphic as if it were a good-luck charm.

"I got an idea for a pitcher." He motioned toward the body. "Why don't you guys go over there? Make like you just got here and you're lookin' for evidence." Finkel waved his free arm toward me. "Better let him go, though."

"Why?" Valentine asked.

"'Cause he can't take down what you're sayin' if his hands are tied behind his back."

The cuffs were unsnapped. I swung my arms around and wiggled my fingers. I felt blood rushing back.

Valentine and his partner marched over to the dead girl. They stopped beside her body and looked down with expressions that mirrored her lifeless features. I took out my notepad.

"You better make us look good," Valentine's partner said.

"I'll put you up real high. What's your name?"

"McMahon. First name Horace."

"Waddya think about this?"

"We'll find the lug. We always do."

Finkel snapped a shot. The night lit up again, and the flash allowed the cops to notice the colored man who had been standing in the shadows.

McMahon took a few steps toward him. "Well, well, well. Seems like we found the nigger."

Finkel jerked his thumb. "This guy? He's a shlemiel."

"Let him talk for himself. Who are you?"

Anderson stood a little straighter. "My name is William Anderson. I'm the night watchman."

"Why are these newshawks here?"

"I called them."

"Why'd you do that, boy?"

"I'm not a boy."

McMahon stopped inches from the colored man. He kept stroking his nightstick.

"Did you say something?"

"I said I'm not a boy. I like to be—"

McMahon shoved Anderson against a wall, then pressed his nightstick against the colored man's neck. Anderson's eyes bulged. He raised his hands to push the nightstick away, but McMahon rammed his knee into the colored man's crotch. Anderson tried to fall, but he couldn't. Instead he let out a sound I had hoped I'd never hear again: the rattling gasp of life leaving a man.

I turned to Valentine and said, "Do something, for Christ's sake."

He looked at me sharply. For a second I thought he was recalling all the beatings he had absorbed on the playground, and regarded this as a form of long-overdue payback. Finally he walked toward McMahon and said a few words into his partner's ear. McMahon looked surprised, as if he'd forgotten anyone else was around, before pulling his nightstick back.

As Anderson collapsed, his arms and legs flailed in directions I hadn't known existed. Valentine moved in and kicked him in his midsection. Then McMahon brought the heel of his shoe down on the colored man's nose.

Finkel leaned toward me and whispered, "You got that thing?" I whispered back that I'd taken a small purse from the dead girl's bag. Finkel nodded, as if that was good enough, then shouted, "Hey!" in a voice that could have cut through a battleship plate.

The cops paused in their beating of Anderson.

"Can we get outta here?" Finkel asked. He told the cops that if we got back to the office in time, the pitchers could make the final edition.

McMahon told us to scram. Valentine jerked his thumb toward me and said, "I still think we should search him."

I fought the urge to run away. I had to stay rock still. If they searched me they'd find the purse, but I needed them to think I was just a nosy newspaperman with nothing to hide.

"He's a boob," McMahon said. "Let's run the nigger in."

A few minutes later I was a passenger in Finkel's car, a '38 Packard that was bigger than my apartment. The hogs-hair carpet was three times deeper than the cheap rug I'd laid out in my living room. My back sank into brushed wool upholstery.

"That wasn't right," I said.

Finkel asked what I was talking about.

"What they're doing to that colored man. He didn't kill that girl."

Finkel waved me off as if I were a fly buzzing around his sandwich. "Don't worry about him. Worry about yourself."

"But they've got nothing, right?" I was trying to reassure myself. "No evidence. They'll hafta let him go."

Finkel didn't reply. Instead he switched on a police siren that he'd attached to the hood of the car to blow traffic out of the way. As we hurtled west on 45th we almost clipped one of the columns supporting the Third Avenue El. That was the boundary: the squat tenements of Blood Alley disappeared, and the heights of Midtown began to surround us. In skyscraper Manhattan the lights glowed till morning, as if every floor of every building was prepared for a party. Behind us, even though it was a chilly November night that hinted at a bleak winter, I could still smell the offal from the slaughterhouses that lined the river.

I took the dead girl's purse out of my jacket and snapped it open. Inside I found thirty-seven dollars in cash, a compact for makeup, and a business card for a lawyer on East 14th Street named Howard Munzer. On the back of the card was a handwritten note, in a feminine script, that said: "Stork Club at 7. Regarding Manley."

There was no driver's license. I searched the folds and crannies for a sign of who this woman had been, but there was no identification at all. Finally, in something close to desperation, I opened the compact. To my surprise, there was no makeup in it, only a battered scrap of paper that held a picture that could have been her. She was hatless, and her hair was longer and straighter, but the thin features matched the ones I'd just seen. The piece of paper said "Turtle Bay Settlement House" and, in small type, the words "Effective August 1944." It gave her name as Amanda Price.

Finkel parked in a no standing zone outside the *Examiner* building, a twelve-story job near Sixth that had gargoyles over the entrance. As we rushed into the lobby, he said we didn't have time to wait for the elevator. The operator was probably asleep somewhere near the roof. So we ran up four flights to the newsroom.

Fluorescent lights beat down on a black-and-white linoleum floor that hadn't been mopped since the twenties. The room was open and vast, almost a city block long, but it was almost impossible to wend through the maze of desks that had been shoved together in a way that maximized the number of books, magazines and papers that could be piled to the ceiling. Although it was close to two A.M. and the place was almost deserted, tobacco smoke clung to everything. Near the coffee urn, two mice devoured crumbs that had dropped from a half-eaten danish.

Finkel threaded his way to the photo lab. The only copyboy still on duty was leaning back in a chair near the city desk. His eyes were closed. His mouth was wide open. When I shook him on the shoulder, bloodshot eyes fluttered open. He insisted he wasn't asleep. I told him to check the clips for any stories that mentioned a girl named Amanda Price. Then I headed for the conference room. As I approached I heard the hard shouts of men who had just surrendered money they couldn't afford to lose.

I rapped on the door and leaned on the frame, just as I had before the war, a million years ago, when I was the copyboy struggling to stay awake in the small hours.

"What's the dope?" McCracken asked.

I told him what I had.

"Amanda Price," he said in the wondering-out-loud tones of a sportswriter trying to remember the details of a big fight fifteen years ago. He looked at O'Shea, the copy desk chief, who was supposed to know something about everything.

"Could be one of the Price sisters," O'Shea said.

"Find out if that's the case, Grimes," McCracken said.

I had no idea who the Price sisters were, but these men always regarded ignorance as weakness. I hoped I'd find the answer at my desk, but when I reached it there was no sign of the copyboy or the clips, so I called the Turtle Bay Settlement House. The phone rang a long time.

"Hello?" It was a scratchy voice that sounded drugged with disappointment. I couldn't tell if it belonged to a man or a woman. I identified myself and asked if the person knew Amanda Price. Through the static-ridden connection I heard the labored breathing of someone who smoked too much and slept too little.

"What happened?"

Some newspapermen felt that when calamities occurred, it was still best to tell people everything was fine. That way they'd keep talking. But I thought it was important to tell the truth. I'd been lied to all my life.

"Who am I talking to?" I asked.

"Terry."

"Is that a first name, a last name—"

"Just call me Terry."

The copyboy dropped two pale green envelopes on my desk. One was bursting with news clips while the other one had only a few, so I opened the thick one, which was dirty with fingerprint smudges.

The first picture I saw was of a blonde in a dark evening dress. It looked like the type of shot that usually ran on our gossip page.

"That's the dead girl's sister," the copyboy yelled into my free ear. "Her name's Sylvia. I thought you might want it."

I heard a panicky sound in my other ear. "What is it?"

"I'm afraid—" I said, and then I stopped. Despite my beliefs, I couldn't utter the word I needed.

After a few long seconds Terry said, in a flat voice that seemed to know everything, "She's dead, isn't she?"

"Her body was found about an hour ago. Is there anything about her—"

"She used to come around. Volunteer."

"Was she—"

"I knew it would turn out this way."

I heard muffled words, as if someone was talking to the person on the other end of the phone. I started shouting into the mouthpiece for Terry to clarify the remarks, but then I heard a click that meant the line had gone dead.

I resisted the urge to swear, but I did snap the pencil I'd been holding in two. It sounded like a rifle shot echoing around the newsroom, and I almost ducked under my desk.

Finkel broke my thoughts as he trotted toward the conference room, waving a batch of photos.

"Gonna show 'em the snaps, Grimes. Aces. Just like I told ya."

I shook open the slim envelope that contained our clips about Amanda Price. There were a half-dozen, most of them yellow and gray with age. I arranged them on my desk in chronological order. The first was dated 1938 and featured a picture of a good-looking girl in an expensive dress serving food at a soup kitchen. With the self-consciousness of youth, she extended a bowl toward an unshaven man. I noticed something in her eyes that seemed both haunted and distant, as if she was ashamed of the gilded circumstances of her life. It looked like the same girl I'd seen dead in the alley, but in the photo she seemed less gaunt.

The story said that after her debut at the Waldorf-Astoria, sixteen-year-old Amanda Price had insisted on helping some of New York City's least fortunate. She was described as being a student at Spence and the oldest daughter of Harrington Price, the businessman and philanthropist.

I turned to the copyboy and told him to get the clips on Harrington Price.

"Who's he?"

"The dead girl's father."

"You should be interested in her sister."

I called the conference room. McCracken picked up on the

first ring. I told him the victim was one of the Price sisters. Within seconds, five half-drunk editors stumbled into the newsroom. They were followed by Finkel, who kept saying: "Aces, right? Aces."

"We gotta change the wood." McCracken was directing loud, staccato bursts to Moskowitz, the makeup editor, who had to make sure the Linotype operators actually did what we told them. "Call the pressroom and see if anybody's awake. If they're not awake, go down there and kick the foreman in the ass."

Moskowitz was a short man whose gut preceded him into a room by several seconds. He had a smooth, round face, and I wondered if he ever shaved. His eyes lit with astonishment. "We're gonna tear up the paper for this?"

"It's the best thing we've got."

"What about Jimmy Walker?"

The former mayor had just died. His obit was leading the paper. The old rogue had been an icon of the Jazz Age, as big a symbol of New York in the twenties as Babe Ruth or the Ziegfeld girls, most of whom he'd slept with.

"Don't worry about that, Moskowitz. His times are coming back." McCracken's eyes sparkled; like most journalists, he delighted in the shortcomings of the human race. "The people of this good city have had enough reform to last a lifetime, and now its politics are in the hands of grifters, as the good Lord intended."

"But Walker was a big deal. Now we're giving him the brush-off. It isn't square."

"Finkel took some fine snaps the *Daily News* doesn't have. Let's make them chase our tail for a change."

McCracken turned to O'Shea, who'd have to write the headlines and captions. "I wanna take out page three. Don't worry about what's there right now. It's crap. I can't believe we're asking people to pay two cents for it."

Finally McCracken looked at me. "How many words you got?"

"Four hundred." I was guessing.

"You've got ten minutes to make it sing like a canary."

I kept looking back at the clips while I wrote. At the age of nineteen, while a student at Sarah Lawrence, Amanda Price organized a charity ball for two orphanages in the Bronx. *Life* magazine named her one of the Outstanding Young Women in America. Our next article had a picture of her in a USO uniform. It described how, once a week without fail, Miss Price led a group of college girls on morale-boosting visits to the wounded servicemen in a military hospital on Staten Island. She looked even fuller in the uniform—an attractive girl who was filling out. It was hard to reconcile this picture with her rail-thin corpse.

Behind me I heard McCracken shouting that somebody at this godforsaken newspaper had to have a phone number for Harrington Price.

The last clip about her startled me. It had appeared on the society page only a few months before. We ran a picture, of course. Her cheeks were hollowed. Her eyes had grown huge, as if she were haunted by demons. Underneath the picture was a small item that said she had been in the hospital for a while, but now she was feeling better.

I incorporated as much of this material as I could in the four hundred words I'd given myself. When I ripped the last take out of my Royal, I yelled, "Copy!" and threw the sheets at the clerk, who grabbed them while he dropped the Harrington Price clips on my desk.

The envelope smelled musty, as if nothing had been removed for years. Whatever Price did, he did it undisturbed.

As I leaned back in my chair, I wondered if I should ask McCracken for a byline. He handed them out as if they were heirlooms.

"Grimes!" McCracken's face was purple. "We need something from Harrington Price. See if you can find him. You've got three minutes."

I had to get hold of a businessman and philanthropist in the middle of the night, but I had no idea what his number was. I told the copyboy to reach Gracie Paquette, our main gossip columnist. There was a ninety-nine percent chance she was at the Stork Club. Within seconds I was talking to a middle-aged woman who was trilling over the sounds of people who'd had several drinks too many.

I told her I needed to call Harrington Price.

"What has Sylvia done now?"

"It's about Amanda."

"Mousy thing. What happened?"

"She's dead."

I heard a thud that indicated the phone was being placed on a table. In the background I could make out laughter and clinking glasses. A few seconds later, Gracie gave me a number to call.

I told her I needed something. She said she didn't have time. She was trying to get Spencer Tracy's attention. I went ahead anyway and asked, "Was Amanda there earlier tonight?"

"I haven't seen her here in years."

That made sense. A girl who devoted so many hours to volunteering wouldn't have time to go to the Stork Club, which could be a full-time career in itself. Then there was the long stint in the hospital. All of this made the note I'd found in her purse more puzzling.

I hung up and called the number Gracie had given me. I stopped counting after twenty rings and almost dropped the phone in surprise when I heard the word "hello."

I asked if this was Mr. Price.

"Perhaps." He sounded alert, like a man who was used to having his sleep interrupted.

McCracken was shouting in the background. He wanted to know if I had anything yet.

"I'm sorry to call you at this hour, Mr. Price. It's about your daughter."

"Young man, whatever you do with Sylvia is fine with me. I long ago gave up trying to—"

"It's about Amanda."

There was no response except for sharp, clear breathing. Although I could not see Harrington Price, I suspected I had his complete attention.

"My name is Patrick Grimes. I'm with the *Examiner*."

"You said something about Amanda."

"I did, Mr. Price. I'm sorry I have to tell you this." I paused. I told myself I was doing only what was necessary. "Your daughter was found in an alley on East 45th Street shortly after midnight. She'd been shot. I'm afraid she...I'm afraid she's..." Once again, I could not say the word, but Harrington Price knew what it was because the next sound was a familiar one, although I thought it belonged to my past. It was the worst sound of all—not of bombs crashing or bullets whining or even the moaning of people who were dying of hideous wounds, but the wail of a human being who had lost the most precious thing in the world.

"Please, Mr. Price, can you tell me something about your daughter?"

No response.

"Then let me ask you a question: why was a girl like her in that part of town at that time of night?"

Harrington Price's emotional heaves stopped. They were replaced by the dry but hard breath of a man who was determined to stay in control at all times.

"Let Amanda rest in peace, young man. It would be the best thing for everyone, especially yourself."

Then I heard the click that told me I'd been hung up on.

I rolled two more pieces of paper into my Royal and typed a paragraph about the reaction of a father I described as firm but upset. I could use only one direct quotation: "Let Amanda rest in peace."

"Where should this go?" O'Shea yelled after the copyboy had dropped the insert in front of him.

"Up high."

I heard the sound of paper being ripped apart as O'Shea used his sharp metal ruler to tear my story into pieces. Even from where I was sitting, I could smell the glue he used as he attached the insert to the appropriate spot. O'Shea always used a lot of glue.

McCracken stopped at my desk, looked down and said, "Tell me about this fella who found the body."

"Night watchman. Colored guy. They took him in, but he seemed on the up and up."

"They arrest him, or just haul him in for questioning?"

"I dunno."

"Find out."

"I don't see how they can arrest him. There's no evidence."

McCracken chuckled. "You'd be amazed, my young mick friend," he said.

"At what?"

"What the police can accomplish when they set their minds to it."

Most of the stories in our Harrington Price file were pro forma bits that detailed donations he had made to museums, libraries and the Metropolitan Opera. One article mentioned that he was at work by seven-thirty every morning at his office at 79 Wall Street.

I tossed that file aside and opened the one on Sylvia Price, which was twice as thick as her father's. After a few seconds I decided I should pay more attention to our gossip pages. The girl was a frequent presence in Gracie's column—a regular at the Stork Club, El Morocco and the Copacabana, although she also seemed to return frequently from Palm Beach, where her mother spent the winters. Sylvia's name had been attached to many men. She'd been engaged to a few of them. Gracie almost always called her vivacious and took care to note her blonde good looks.

I hadn't known any blondes while I was growing up. Like so many things I saw in the movies, I hadn't believed they existed, but longed for one anyway.

A news story that was dated only a month before intimated that Sylvia's latest fiancé, a man named George Stavros, was closer to the mob boss Frank Costello than a respectable person should be.

The most recent article about her said that one night, while her fiancé was driving down Fifth Avenue, Sylvia Price grabbed the wheel of the Cadillac that Stavros was steering. The car cut across a lane of traffic and crashed into the Central Park Zoo. Three sheep, two goats and a monkey escaped from their cages and headed south toward the Plaza.

The police said nobody was at fault. No charges would be pressed. The girl was just high-spirited.

I put the clips aside. It was a few minutes before three. I could hear the presses clacking and shaking on the ground floor as they spewed out the final edition.

The copyboy walked in with a stack of papers under his arm. He asked where everybody was. I jerked my thumb in the direction of Lunney's, the bar across the street. He extended the papers to me, so I grabbed them. When I walked outside I had to dodge the delivery trucks that always screeched away before the drivers even looked to see if anyone was coming.

Despite the cold blasts near Lunney's front door, McCracken and the rest were sitting at the closest table, as if they couldn't waste thirty seconds of drinking by walking to the back. I tossed the papers in front of them. The wood was a screamer:

SOCIALITE FOUND DEAD

I pointed out that Amanda Price had not been a socialite. McCracken said nobody would buy the paper if the wood said:

DO-GOODER FOUND DEAD

I got a beer at the bar and sat down. McCracken rolled his eyes when he saw my choice of beverage. He had grown up on the hardscrabble plains of west Texas, a part of the country where men prided themselves on always drinking hard liquor.

"I changed something in your story, my young mick friend."

I wasn't surprised. "What was it?" I asked.

"You called the watchman by his formal Christian name," McCracken said. "William Anderson."

"He said that's what he preferred."

"That may be what he prefers, but I prefer to call him Willie. Willie Anderson."

"He told me he didn't like nicknames."

"That's all right. He's just a nigger."

This prompted alcohol-induced laughs from the men at the table.

"By the way," McCracken asked, "how much you give him?"

I gulped. "A double sawbuck."

For the first time all night, he seemed genuinely upset at something that had occurred. "Jesus H. Christ, Grimes. The *New York Examiner* prints newspapers, not money."

I walked home up Third Avenue. Pawnbrokers straggled to their shops, sliding in keys and lifting the shades in their windows. A Philco for two bucks caught my eye. I needed a new radio to listen to Walter Winchell on Sunday night.

The surroundings seemed stark, but I enjoyed my strolls on the sidewalk under the El. I felt shielded from the world even as the trains rumbled above me. During the day I admired the ladder pattern the tracks' shadows created. At night I embraced the feeling of being in a place that felt separate from the city around it.

A diner was open at 60th. I thought about getting some eggs and juice. A couple of girls who looked like they'd been out all night asked if I wanted to have a good time.

Of course I did. But not with them.

Women were a mystery to me. Almost all of them seemed as brittle as eggshells, and whenever I was around one I was afraid of doing something wrong. I knew I was supposed to settle down with a nice girl, but I imagined marriage as always being one step away from igniting a land mine.

Still, I was twenty-three years old and couldn't stop my thoughts from being what they were. When I fantasized about the kind of girl I really wanted, my mind conjured a dish who liked to laugh and drink and tell me she never paid any attention to her priests.

I turned right on 64th. I lived in a row of tenements between Second and Third. I'd grown up in this neighborhood. It never seemed to change.

When I reached the building I lived in, I put my key in the lock and climbed to the third floor. The stairway lights were out, so

I stumbled a couple of times on the landings. A few of my neighbors had complained to the landlord. He'd told them to move if they didn't like it. Of course there was a housing shortage, so good luck finding a place.

The smell of brewing coffee filled the halls. I heard arguments resuming from the night before.

Inside my apartment I went to the icebox and took out a bottle of orangeade before removing a glass from the cupboard. The juice tasted sweet. It cleansed my mouth.

I rubbed a little soap over the glass and ran it under the faucet in the kitchen sink, then dried the glass with a towel and put it in the dish drainer. Mother had always told me that you never got something completely dry with a towel. God's own breath had to finish the work.

The apartment I'd grown up in was much like this one. When I was alone in it I often thought about Mother. She had died during the war while I was fighting in Italy. I never said good-bye. I guessed I was supposed to feel guilty, but considering the way she had treated me, and the way I felt about her, I figured things had worked out for the best.

I pulled the Murphy bed down from the wall and made sure the metal legs landed on the floor, not on my feet. I stripped to my underwear and picked up the copy of the paper I'd carried home from Lunney's. I hadn't read it while I was drinking, so I opened the pages as I propped myself up in bed.

The headline was big and bold. Finkel's photographs were splashed around. My article ran for what seemed like a reasonable length, but for a while I didn't read a word because I couldn't get past the top:

My first byline.

I finally got through the story and nodded at all the elements I and my colleagues had patched in: the description of the alley ("Any rats?" O'Shea had asked me. "Sure," I replied, and the phrase "rat-infested" was in the third paragraph), the quote from the cops, the reactions from the dead girl's father and her former co-worker at the settlement house.

Above all I heard McCracken's voice, his tone threading the line between hectoring and mentoring, as he looked over his hand during one of the card games he liked to play on nights when things were slow.

"Don't be afraid to ask questions, my young mick friend. That's what we do for a living. Above all else, don't be afraid to sound stupid. Because inevitably, the stupidest question is the one you don't ask."

And so, as I went over the article, I realized I hadn't asked Officers McMahon and Valentine the most significant question of all:

Who called you?

Chapter two

I got to the office, as I usually did, a little before the start of my regular shift at six P.M. I sat in my chair and pulled out a notepad and fixed my eyes on the four-sided clock that stood ten feet high in the middle of the newsroom. I was always ready to work exactly when I was supposed to. Mother used to tell us it took God only six days to create the universe, so there was no excuse ever for anyone to be late.

McCracken loomed over me. His thin lips were on the verge of disappearing.

"The cops still have Willie Anderson," he said. "They've been going at him since they brought him in."

"What's that supposed to mean?"

"It means they're gonna get a confession out of him. And when they do, that'll be the wood. So stay on the ball."

I still had high school ideas about justice and due process, so I uttered a protest that sounded feeble as soon as it came out: "But he didn't do it."

McCracken shook his head. "C'mon, Grimes. He's a shifty nigger. He must've done *something*." He took a few steps away, then paused. "You did swell work last night, Grimes. We were the only paper with the story. The *Daily News* is playing catch-up, but I intend to stay in front."

I began to see this story as one of those rare instances when self-interest meshed with doing right. If William Anderson was going to be arrested, my reporting could set him free. I almost felt as if there was an angel on my shoulder as I dialed the number for the Turtle Bay Settlement House. My call was answered on the thirteenth ring.

"Is Terry there?"

"Who?" a man replied.

"Terry," I said.

"There's nobody named Terry here." He sounded like a guy whose main enjoyment in life came from intimidating people who were weaker than he was.

"The person who works there late at night," I said. "I'm a friend."

"I don't know what you're talking about, pal."

I heard a click.

I tossed the receiver down and leaned back in my chair. For the first time since I started working at the *Examiner*, I felt as if the office was a cage. There was only so much you do could without visiting a place in person.

I'd never met Higgins, our lead police reporter on the night shift. A few of my colleagues had told me that he looked like a cop himself: large and beefy, his face perpetually red from booze and anger. We did all our work together over the phone, and we argued a lot, so McCracken kept teaming us up in the belief that tension between reporter and rewrite man led to copy that crackled.

I called Higgins's desk at the police bureau at ten after eight. I asked if he had anything. Deadline for the first edition was twenty minutes away.

"C'mon, kid, gimme some time."

"McCracken wants it now."

"Tell him to blow."

I heard Higgins swallow something that I assumed contained

alcohol. Some newspapermen worked better when they were drinking, but Higgins wasn't one of them.

"The cops still have Anderson," he said. "Downtown."

"No confession?"

His voice rose. "I woulda told ya."

My voice climbed in response. "How long before there is one?"

"I talked to the lieutenant. He says the spook will sing before midnight."

McCracken swooped by and hovered over my shoulder. I had started to type before I hung up. I hoped McCracken liked the style; I certainly disliked what I was writing.

"City cops investigating the murder of socialite Amanda Price spent all day yesterday grilling Willie Anderson, the night watchman who found her body.

"Police sources said they were confident of getting a confession from Anderson, who quickly emerged as the prime suspect..."

McCracken swore a few times as he hurried away. I heard him bellowing, "We've gotta change the wood."

Higgins called just after eleven. I signaled across the room to McCracken, who was resting his feet on the heavy oak desk in his glass cage of an office. He appeared at my side before I began typing.

According to the confession signed by Willie Anderson, Amanda Price had been walking by herself along East 45th Street shortly before midnight. Anderson was making his rounds. He asked her for the time. He claimed his watch had stopped. She told him it was almost twelve. He asked what a fine lady like her was doing in this part of town. He kept eyeing her handbag. It gleamed under the streetlights. He began to fantasize about the riches it contained—gold and silver, pearls strung together, hundreds of dollars in cash.

He felt he had no control over what he was doing. A voice inside commanded him to act. He was powerless as he reached out and grabbed her. She screamed. It didn't matter. The sound just rattled off the sides of the warehouses and abattoirs. He started to choke her—the autopsy revealed the marks on her neck, her windpipe was crushed—but then he remembered the gun he carried with him on his rounds.

I listened to this story with increasing incredulity. My profession dictated that I remain neutral, dispassionate, and above all objective, but everything I was hearing screamed falsehood, even if I couldn't prove it.

"Was Anderson supposed to carry a gun?" I asked.

"I'm getting to that," Higgins said.

Anderson dragged Amanda Price into the alley. He wanted to get away from the street. He reached into his waistband and removed the .22-caliber he always kept within reach. While the girl begged for her life, he shot her twice.

Willie Anderson wasn't authorized to carry a weapon. But it was a tough part of town.

I asked Higgins how the girl could beg for her life if her windpipe was crushed.

"What are you?" he asked. "A smart-ass?"

"This sounds like a cop-concocted fantasy."

"Her windpipe was partially crushed," Higgins said with the gathering-momentum air of a guy who was confident he could wing it. "The words gasped out. Put that in the story. 'Gasping, her last words escaped her.' That's good writing."

Behind me I heard McCracken on the phone with the pressroom. He told the foreman to hold everything. We were changing the wood.

I wasn't done with Higgins: "And they're saying he shot her in the alley. But I saw blood trailing from the street to the spot where her body was found."

"Do you wanna know what's in the goddamn confession or don't you? That's what we're gonna put in the paper. Not what you think happened."

I hated it when he was right. I said nothing, and he continued with the story.

After he shot her, Anderson went through the dead girl's bag and removed a number of items, including her purse. He realized he needed a cover story, so he hid the purse and his gun in the trash. He knew the garbagemen didn't come around until six, and he thought he'd have plenty of time to pick up the stuff he'd hidden.

When he had arranged the scene to his satisfaction, William Anderson called the *New York Examiner* and told the kid who answered the phone that he had discovered a body.

But an alert citizen had made a call to the police. Officers McMahon and Valentine responded. They'd been told to look for a male Negro who seemed suspicious, and Anderson's story struck them as queer.

I wrote up the story, swallowing my convictions with every word. But I kept thinking that if any section of Manhattan could be described as desolate, it was Blood Alley. Its streets were often deserted after dark. I wondered who the alert citizen could have been, or if the cops had dreamed him up, too.

After we closed the midnight edition O'Shea asked me what was wrong. I said I was swell. O'Shea said I should cut the crap; I looked like a guy who had swallowed a gallon of castor oil. Perched on the edge of the copy desk, my legs dangling toward the floor, I told him, "The cops are railroading William Anderson, and we're letting them get away with it."

"I do not believe it."

It was McCracken's voice, a millimeter behind me. I wondered if he had the ability to materialize like a malevolent spirit whenever somebody in the newsroom said something he disagreed with.

"I do not believe that a good, honest, God-fearing white man is upset because the coppers have nailed a nigger."

I wanted to reply, but just then we heard the sound of small running feet and the squeak of worn shoes on the floor. Finkel was red-faced with excitement and breathlessness. His Speed Graphic bumped against his hip.

McCracken asked if he'd gotten any good snaps at the perp walk.

"Only the best," Finkel said.

McCracken followed him into the photo lab. A minute later the phone on the copy desk rang, and I heard O'Shea taking orders for yet another front page. Higgins called me with a feed that described police leading Anderson into Central Booking as photographers swarmed. I wrote an insert and sent it to the desk.

After a while O'Shea, Moskowitz and the rest of the late-night crew filtered out to Lunney's. But I waited. I wanted to see the picture for myself, before newsprint blurred the edges of what Finkel had seen.

McCracken walked into his office shortly after two. He reached into his bottom drawer and poured a big tumbler of Jim Beam that he knocked back in one flip. I lingered just outside his door.

"What are you still doing here, Grimes?"

"I wanna see it."

McCracken poured himself more bourbon and extended the bottle. I shook my head. He told me, "You'll never be a good newspaperman until you start drinking to excess."

"I wanna see it."

McCracken said he had just spent more time than he cared to in a strange place called Finkelville. The photographer would show McCracken a picture and ask what he thought. McCracken would say it was great. Was Finkel recommending it for page one? Finkel would say he had another picture. He'd show it and ask McCracken what he thought. McCracken would give the same response. It went on like this. Finkel kept showing terrific photos, one after the other, but never made a recommendation. Finally McCracken selected one.

"What's so special about that?" Finkel asked.

"The shadows," McCracken said. "The angles. The composition."

By that point McCracken just wanted to pick a picture. So he trusted his instincts and chose the shot that seemed most dramatic.

"Yeah, it's good, ain't it?" Finkel said as he admired the print. "But what about these? What's wrong with them?"

As much as I enjoyed McCracken's stories, I was aware of how late it was. My legs felt dead. My back ached. I kept shifting my weight.

"Here it is," McCracken said at last. He took a picture resting atop a dozen pieces of scrap paper and pushed it toward me. I picked it up and held it at arm's length.

Finkel had gotten within inches of Anderson and the cops. The uniformed officers looked grimly satisfied as they crowded close to the suspect, their ham-like hands encasing his upper arms. Anderson's head lolled to one side. The cop closest to the camera had his elbow raised halfway, trying to make sure Finkel couldn't discover too much.

The picture captured the chaos and urgency of the crowd as it surged toward a man everyone regarded as a criminal. It was easy to miss the swelling around Anderson's eyes. I also noticed lumps on his temples that hadn't been there the night before.

I left the *Examiner* building a few minutes later. Instead of heading home, I kept walking east. Once I passed the El the atmosphere changed: I was surrounded by buildings that were low and dark, and the cold but thrilling current of danger charged the air. I smelled offal again, and the scent of spilled stale beer from the breweries.

I stopped on 47th Street in front of a three-story brick building. I assumed the small sign above the entrance said "TURTLE BAY SETTLEMENT," but half the letters had been smudged into unreadability.

I was doing good work on this story. McCracken had said so. I was convinced that if I kept at it, I'd get William Anderson out of jail while making a name for myself. I might even win some prizes.

The front door creaked open. I stepped into a foyer lit by a single bare bulb that dangled at the end of a wire. On either side of me, hallways stretched into darkness.

I thought there might be a bell on the front desk like the ones I'd seen in the movies, where Cary Grant would summon a buffoon of a clerk. But there was no bell, and as far as I could tell there was nothing behind the desk except a door that looked as if it had been painted shut.

I heard a shout that was muffled quickly. It seemed to come from the hallway to my left. I took a few quick strides and stopped in an open doorframe.

"What do you want?"

A delicate-looking man, no more than five foot four and dressed entirely in white, stood underneath the bare bulb. He looked like an orderly. I sensed he was the kind of guy whose veins held ice water instead of blood.

"I'm looking for someone," I said. "Terry."

"Terry who?"

I shrugged and stepped toward the man. Although I was seven inches taller and forty pounds heavier, I felt that I was the one who had to be careful.

"Just Terry," I said. "It's someone I know. Someone who works here."

He shook his head. "Nobody named Terry works here."

"Are you sure? I called last night and we talked."

His eyes flashed, as if he'd just discovered the answer to a question that had been bothering him all day.

"Nobody named Terry works here," he said. "Nobody named Terry has ever worked here."

"I must have been misinformed."

I could have asked about Amanda Price and the work she had done here or mentioned the shout I'd heard down the hall, but the leer on the man's face was unnerving. He glanced to his right. His smile grew wider. I sensed he was about to summon someone who would not be interested in talking to me, and my years in combat had made me sensitive to dangerous situations.

I spun around and went out the door. I told myself to walk quickly, but not to run.

I was close to Second Avenue when I heard a door crash open. What sounded like two pairs of footsteps hurried onto the street. I wanted to hail a cab, but none were around. So I kept heading west, toward the El, before turning north.

From a doorway I heard a girl's voice asking why I was running away. The bars were having last call. I thought for a moment of slipping into one, solely for sanctuary, but those places were darker than the street.

A ferocious roar overhead crowded out every thought. For a few seconds I was conscious only of the screech and rattle of a train making its way uptown. When it faded I heard the footsteps again, only a few feet behind.

I thought about looking back, but I was afraid they'd rush me. So I kept my eyes focused ahead as I hunched my shoulders and thrust my hands deep in my pockets in an imitation of the bums Mother had always told me I'd join.

Another roar began: an El heading downtown.

I did not turn my head, but I knew I had to get across Third. I couldn't lead them back to my place.

I told myself not to tense. I could not tip off what I was about to do. Back in Italy, whenever the shooting started the noncoms would always shout at us to stay calm and keep our butts close to the ground. The guys who got rattled were the guys who got their heads blown off.

As the noise of the train got louder, I charged out between the Studebakers and Buicks parked trunk to hood. My peripheral vision caught lights coming down the avenue.

I could not slow down. I could not stop.

I ran across the street and squinted as something blinding passed in front of my eyes. I heard tires squealing and horns honking and the shouts of men who were angered because something unexpected had happened.

The train was pulling in. I took the steps three at a time. As I climbed my breath grew short. Sweat beaded on my face. I reached into my pocket for a nickel and shoved it in the wooden turnstile as the train stopped and the doors opened. I looked into the stationhouse and saw a low fire glowing in the potbellied stove. I thought of how nice it would be to linger, but then I heard two pairs of footsteps racing up the stairs.

I ran through an open door on the train and threw myself down on a hard rattan seat. Slowly, almost imperceptibly, the elevated's ancient doors began to slide together.

"Wait!"

I recognized the deep, angry voice from a phone conversation earlier in the night, a mocking tone telling me that I didn't know what I was talking about.

"Just wait a minute, goddammit!"

As the doors inched toward shutting, all the air left my lungs. My heart ended up somewhere beyond my grasp. Now I remembered the worst times of all in the war—when the wind died and the birds grew quiet and the sky itself seemed devoid of life. In that moment we knew the long German guns would find us, and there was nothing we could do except throw dirt over ourselves and hope they'd miss.

The doors finally closed. The train pulled out. I was alone in the car and felt myself breathing again.

I leaned back and closed my eyes. I wished I had a handkerchief so I could wipe off the perspiration. I was convinced that I needed to talk to Terry, and the men who had followed me were determined to prevent it. But what bothered me most was the sense of being stuck. I had no idea where Terry was, or how we could get in contact, and I was starting to worry that the story—*my* story—would run into a series of dead ends.

I enjoyed riding the El, feeling the sensation of traveling above the streets and finding so many lives so different from my own. I especially liked passing through the Bowery, where the flophouses jammed flat against the tracks. I always looked into the windows at the grimy men in drunken sleep and imagined that my father was among them.

"He was nothing but a drunk."

Sometimes I heard Mother's voice. Sometimes she was sitting right next to me.

"You'll end up that way, too, Patrick Grimes. I have no doubt of it."

I tried to remember what had provoked her condemnation. Probably nothing. Mother was one of those strange Irish Catholics who labored to bring children into the world, then spent years telling them how awful it was.

I told myself to forget about her. It was impossible, of course. After I was drafted she said that if I left for overseas it would be the death of her. That was the only promise she'd ever made to me that she kept.

Maybe I was being harsh. I was always scrubbed and neatly dressed for school. Whenever I was sick she made homemade soup. If I was too weak, she'd feed me with a spoon. Mother was an excellent cook. If I were a glass-half-full type of person, those memories would have been the ones that lingered.

The El swung out over Coenties Slip, seemingly nothing between the tracks and the water. It was the best ride this side of the Cyclone, and I didn't have to go all the way through Brooklyn.

My father had taken me to Coney Island a few times when I was a kid before his own demons finally took control of his life. But he was always upbeat when he was around children. I remembered the day we were boarding the Cyclone. The operator stopped us, pointed at me and said, "How old is he?" Father looked right at the guy and said, "Old enough." We rode in the front car. He threw his arm around me. We went faster than I'd ever imagined human beings could go, and I recalled feeling warm inside, and mighty strange as well. At last, when the ride ended, I realized that my unfamiliar sensation was one of happiness; I had finally done something I really wanted to do.

The train reached South Ferry. I didn't feel like going home, so I boarded a boat instead. Despite the cold, I sat outside on the upper deck and looked at Ellis Island, where Mother had entered the country in a year she never chose to reveal.

In fifth grade we were studying immigration in history class. As Sister Ursula caressed the ruler she always carried, she said we should ask our grandparents about their experiences. Some of us might even have parents who had been born in another country. As I left school that day I told Sister that I thought my mom had been born in Ireland, although she didn't talk about it much. The nun told me to ask Mother about it over supper. This was a chance to discover history firsthand. In the morning I could talk about what I'd learned in class.

As Mother served us potatoes and a few chunks of beef that night, I told her what Sister Ursula had said.

Mother's reply was swift. She didn't want to talk about it. It made no difference what the nun wanted.

I told myself to persevere. The only way anybody ever found out about anything was by asking questions. So I said, "It's interesting, the way people leave everything behind and go to a new country." And I asked Mother why she came to America.

She snatched away the food in front of me and hurled it into the sink, where the plate landed with so much force I could hear it breaking. I knew what was going to happen next. I wanted to bolt from the chair and charge into the living room and out into the hallway and down the stairs that led out to a brief promise of freedom.

But I stayed where I was. I could not move. The Lord had commanded all of us to honor our parents.

Mother grabbed my wrist. She laid my hand flat on the table. I closed my eyes and turned my head, but she jerked it back.

"Open your eyes," she said.

I did.

She wielded the big metal spoon as if she were Toscanini waving his baton in front of the Philharmonic. Her eyes sparkled a bit. The corners of her mouth were turned up in an embryonic smile.

Whap!

The pain shot through the bones in my hand before charging up my arm.

Whap!

I thought about closing my eyes again, but I knew that would just make her more furious.

Whap!

My teeth were grinding. I wanted her to halt. But if I begged, she'd do it longer. The rage I usually kept hidden bubbled inside me. I thought about fighting this woman. I thought about making her stop. But I was little and she was big and it was God's will that I be punished for my transgressions, even if I didn't understand what they were.

Whap! Whap! Whap!

I finally heard her as she screamed into my ear: "Don't you ever ask me about that again!"

"I'm sorry, Mother."

"Don't you ever!"

"I didn't mean anything."

"I wish you'd never been born."

The next day at school, Sister Ursula asked what my mother had told me. I replied that she hadn't said anything, and told myself it wasn't much of a lie. Sister closed her eyes and shook her head with the kind of profound disappointment a teacher can display only toward her best pupils. She told me I'd have to do better. Then she asked Tommy O'Brien, who was sitting behind me, if he had anything to report. He took out a sheaf of papers an inch thick, and said his parents had spent the night telling him stories about all sorts of interesting things.

I snapped back to the present. I reminded myself it was impossible to change the past, much as I wanted to.

The ferryboat passed the Statue of Liberty. I'd always been told that her torch represented the light of freedom, the promise that had drawn so many people to America. It was a nice story, but I had long ago stopped believing what anyone in authority told me. Now they were spinning tales about William Anderson, and I thought maybe I had a chance to shatter one of the lies they liked to tell.

Chapter three

I got to sleep at six in the morning. I was still cold from the ferry ride. The ringing phone woke me just before noon. As I reached for it, I knocked over the box that contained the Bronze Star I'd been awarded in Italy. I hadn't wanted the medal, and resented the memories it stirred, but I'd never been able to throw it out.

I tried to speak into the receiver. All I could do was mumble.

"Is that you, Pat? It's Kathleen."

My sister lived in a railroad flat in Woodside with her husband, who worked for the Sanitation Department. I tried to remember his name. Kathleen asked if I was all right.

"I'm swell," I said. "You woke me up."

"Those crazy hours," she said in a scolding voice that reminded me of the nuns. "Can't you find something better?"

"I don't mind."

My sister's voice softened. Unlike the nuns, she hated to encounter hostility. "I've read those stories," she said. "The ones with your name on them. It's a good thing they caught that guy, huh?"

"I guess so."

Kathleen called me about once a week. She was three years

older than I was and she didn't have any children and she was married to Dan. That was the guy's name: Dan Ryan. They'd gotten married while I was away in the war.

"How's Dan?" I asked.

"Fine," she said. Then she asked if I was free on Sunday. My first instinct was to find out what she wanted, but I said nothing. Kathleen told me that she wanted to have a nice Sunday dinner, just the three of us: me and her and Dan. Before I had fully realized it, I agreed to go.

She gulped before plowing ahead in a scratchy voice: "Those stories you're doing. They really bug me."

"Why?"

"That coon. They bother me."

"Why?"

"They're animals. All of them."

I didn't reply. What could I say?

"Dan and I have been talking about it," Kathleen said. "We've gotta get out of the city. It's dirty and it's noisy and there are too many coloreds and now the Puerto Ricans are moving in. They're animals, too. I'm scared all the time. How are we supposed to live with them?"

"I don't know." I hoped I sounded weary. "I guess we'll just have to find a way."

My sister's voice stiffened. Sometimes she sounded as hard as Mother. "That's no answer," she said.

Amanda Price's funeral service was conducted that afternoon at Trinity Church. I decided to check it out even though it was on my own time. There was a chance I might learn or observe something.

I took the El to Hanover Square, then walked up to Wall Street. I turned west at the Morgan Bank and tried to blend with the Financial District workers as I strode past Federal Hall and the Stock Exchange. But I felt the weight of the money and history around me, so I kept slowing down to stare at the buildings. Clerks, brokers and message boys brushed past. A few asked what my problem was.

It was darker on the street than it should have been. The downtown towers cast long shadows over everything. Back when the city was young, there was an informal rule that no building could rise above the spire of Trinity Church. But in the end, as always happens, the interests of Mammon trumped those of God.

I stopped on the sidewalk outside the church's entrance on lower Broadway. The Price family had lived in New York a long time, but had never shifted its place of worship uptown. I blew on my hands. The wind was raw, rushing in right off the harbor. It was getting colder every minute.

I walked up to the door. I wanted to enter, but my legs refused to move. And then I realized why: as I grew up, the nuns and the priests and Mother had impressed upon me the knowledge that I was a son of the one true church, and entering a place where a false religion was practiced was the greatest blasphemy a believer could commit.

I peered inside. The dark wood and stained glass were familiar to me. So were the sounds of organ music. I took note of the sparse number of people scattered among the pews. Up near the altar, a closed casket was covered with flowers. I heard the mumblings of a cleric, but no sounds of crying. It struck me as odd that acceptance, not grief, was the reaction to Amanda Price's death among the people closest to her.

When I pulled my head back, I bumped into Dietrich, our top dayside photographer. Tall and lean, he was the only man on the staff with a full beard, an aspiring bohemian who was determined to look a bit shabby. He looked at me as if he thought he should know who I was. Since our schedules were different, we'd met only a few times. I reintroduced myself. He asked if I was working the story. I shook my head.

"Curiosity, mostly," I said. "I was there when they found the girl's body. Me and Finkel."

Dietrich glanced down, around and up. He said the bell tower would be the best place to take a picture, but he doubted he'd be able to get up there.

I asked if he was religious. Dietrich said he'd never seen the point. It was like believing in spooks.

"Religion is like anything else," I told him. "Money talks."

I poked my head into the vestibule. Standing off to the side was a colored man leaning on a broom. He wore a gray shirt and gray pants. If it weren't for his tufts of white hair, he would have faded into the wall.

"Excuse me."

My whisper sounded fierce. I hoped nobody inside could hear me. Pushing his broom, the colored man took a few steps toward me. I jerked my thumb at Dietrich and said: "My friend here is a photographer. He'd like to get into the bell tower to take a few pictures."

The colored man shook his head. He said he doubted it was possible. Only authorized people were allowed up there.

"We'd make a contribution, of course," I said. "For the church."

I removed my wallet and took out a fin. The colored man grabbed it. He said he thought he could do something. It was awfully generous of us. For the church and all.

They left me standing there. A few minutes later the music grew deeper and more solemn. The few people inside rose to their feet and reached for their coats and purses. I caught the godly smell of incense. I heard words that tried to sound uplifting.

I trotted toward Broadway, past the wrought-iron fence that surrounded the church and its graveyard. A hearse idled at the curb. Behind it was a black limousine. When I looked back toward the church, I saw a man pushing the casket along the walkway. Five other men, all of them burly, walked beside the vessel that contained Amanda Price's remains. As the men fanned out on the sidewalk, two of them raised their hands to restrain the pedestrians who wanted to pass by.

I stood on my toes. I had to see. Sylvia Price and her mother, both dressed in black, walked slowly toward Broadway. They stood at least a yard apart. Harrington Price remained on the church steps. He was talking to the minister. He wore a charcoal gray business suit.

With a swift, clean jerk, the pallbearers loaded the casket into the hearse. Sylvia Price and her mother entered the limousine behind it through separate doors. When the cars took off, pedestrians once again took over the sidewalk. The whole scene was curious. This was the only funeral I'd ever seen that struck me as businesslike.

I lingered at the fence. The minister said something to Harrington Price, who threw back his head and laughed. The two men shook hands. Price then walked briskly toward the street. I was tempted to call out to ask for a comment, but I remembered our tense conversation the night of the murder. So I just watched him as he walked. His head was erect, his back ramrod straight. His arms swung ever so slightly. He crossed Broadway against the light. Then he strode down Wall Street, looking for all the world like the man who owned it.

After the funeral I went back to my apartment for a quick flop. William Anderson was still in jail and I was concerned that goons were following me around. I needed somebody in my corner and thought about Joey Valentine, once the target of my boyhood fists and insults, now a cop. Although the members of the New York Police Department were notorious for being lazy and easily bought off, and even though our last encounter had been anything but friendly, helping to crack a case like this might do him some good.

I made a detour on my way to work, stopping at the apartment where Valentine lived with his mother. It was a third-floor warren on East 65th that never saw the sun. A patch of missing plaster on the wall revealed termite-eaten woodwork underneath.

I knocked hard on the door a few times. From inside, I could smell tomato sauce cooking.

I hadn't called. I was hoping my unexpected appearance might surprise him into doing what was right.

"Who's there?" It was Valentine.

"Grimes. Pat Grimes."

The response came from a woman's voice that was sharp and shrill, full of a lifetime of anger and disappointment. It reminded me of Mother, and I wondered if every woman in the world turned out like that.

"Is that one of your bum friends?"

"No, Ma. It's a guy I went to school with."

"I don't remember no Pat Grimes."

"He went away, Ma. To the war."

"Fighting for strangers. Goddamn ridiculous. Get rid of him, Joey."

The door opened, but Valentine did not remove the chain. I saw half his face, which was fleshing out in a condition I called Policeman's Bloat.

"You heard my ma. Beat it."

"I wanna talk about the colored guy."

Valentine glanced backward. The sauce smelled good.

"I've got questions, Valentine. This whole thing stinks."

Valentine scrunched his face in an attempt to look hard. "What are you talking about? We have a confession."

"How'd you get it?"

"We brought in our best guy—a detective named Koenig. When that guy walks into a room, if he looked at me the wrong way, I'd confess, too."

From a place deep within the apartment, Valentine's mother asked if he'd gotten rid of that bum yet.

"So what did Koenig do?"

"He let the nigger talk. Koenig made him describe the scene. The shine told us what he said he found. But it didn't jibe. We know what the scene really looked like because your guy took those pictures."

Valentine listed the things that had appeared near her body, but that William Anderson had failed to mention: the lipsticks and the nylons, as well as the hat that had fallen a few feet from Amanda Price's head. Those items were nowhere to be found, and the reason was obvious: he was trying to steal them.

"But he knew we'd taken pictures of all that stuff." My voice was rising with righteous indignation. "He was right there with us, helping Finkel. And why would the guy steal lipsticks and nylons, for God's sake?"

"Give 'em to some nigger dame, I guess."

Valentine's mother announced that dinner was ready. He started to close the door on me, but I reached my hand through the narrow opening and grabbed his shirt.

"All those things—the lipsticks, the nylons, the hat—they were props." My voice had the urgency only truth can provide. "I shouldn't tell you this, but Finkel carries them around and plants them at crime scenes. They make his pictures look better."

Valentine shoved my hand away and filled the doorframe. If our faces were any closer, we'd have been kissing.

"You do that on the street," he said, "and you're looking at time in the joint. I'm not some little goombah kid you and your mick buddies can pick on anymore. I'm a fucking police officer."

I wanted to tell him to do his job and catch the right criminal, but I was teetering on the edge of serious trouble.

"Now blow," Valentine said.

At work that night I tried to think of my next move. When things got slow I opened the top drawer of my desk and looked at the sequence—two letters, four digits—that Gracie had given me two nights before. I had failed with the police. Now I needed help from higher up. When I picked up the phone, the world went silent except for the sound of the rotary dial spinning and slipping.

"Hello."

It was a girl's voice, vibrant and singsongy. I said I was looking for Harrington Price.

"Oh."

That short word conveyed a powerful sense of surprise and disappointment, as if the girl was sure every call coming into the place was for her. I heard a single muffled word—"Father"—spoken in the neutral way somebody would discuss the weather.

"Yes?"

The voice was deep, with the gloss that comes from a lifetime of after-dinner brandy and fine cigars. He sounded like a man who was trying to sound both wary and in control of every situation, even when he received an unanticipated call on his private line.

"We spoke a couple of nights ago, Mr. Price. My name is Patrick Grimes."

I waited a second. In my neighborhood, an unsolicited call from someone you wanted to avoid usually provoked a stream of epithets followed by the sound of a line going dead. But I heard nothing. Harrington Price came from a world where it was fine to treat people with cruelty as long as you displayed good manners.

"We have nothing further to discuss, young man."

"I think we do, sir."

After I was discharged from the Army I had vowed to never call another man "sir." Harrington Price must have sensed how low I was groveling, because his voice adopted the tone of moderate curiosity that I was sure he used at the Harvard Club when he was talking to his fellow alums about a good spot to vacation this year.

"What do you mean by that?"

"It's about Amanda."

"The police caught the fellow. What else is there?"

"I'm privy to some information I'd like to share with you."

"You can't do it over the phone?"

"I have to show you."

"Can you do it now?"

"I'm at work. I can't leave. We could do it tomorrow. I know you work at 79 Wall Street and I could just drop by whenever it's—"

"That's out of the question."

I licked my lips. My hands were sweaty. My breath came in bursts. I remembered how anxious I felt in Italy whenever I was about to run out from a protected position.

"What time do you start work, young man?"

"Six o'clock, sir."

"Morning or night?"

I thought this was a curious question, but then I realized that a man like Harrington Price might very well be behind his desk, steaming cup of coffee within reach, by six o'clock every morning.

"Night, sir."

There was a pause. I could have sworn I heard wheels spinning. And then he said: "Come here at five-thirty. I'll give you ten minutes."

* * *

McCracken swung his feet off his desk, poured himself some Jim Beam and tapped the bottle as he looked at me. I shook my head.

"You were a goody-two-shoes even when you were a copyboy, Grimes. I don't know what got into my head to hire you when you got your discharge."

Alcohol-laced laughter crashed against the walls of McCracken's office as the clerk walked in and tossed copies of the first edition on the night editor's desk. Our hands reached for the stack. Once we checked the paper, McCracken would decide if we should tear it up or play cards.

The wood blared Mayor O'Dwyer's lament about the imminent departure of the United Nations. Bill-O said he wanted to keep it, but the city had no room or money to build a headquarters. McCracken's take was different:

GOOD RIDDANCE

"Where are they gonna go?" Moskowitz asked.

"Truman wanted to give them the Presidio in Frisco," O'Shea said. "The Europeans put the kibosh on it."

He reached into his shirt pocket and took out a cigarette, which he lit with a smoldering stub in the ashtray beside him.

"You failed to answer the question that was directed to the floor," McCracken told O'Shea, who replied that Boston and Philadelphia both had good offers on the table.

Moskowitz said he hoped New York could still make a bid. He'd hate to lose something big to a second-rate burg.

"The city wants to give them Turtle Bay," O'Shea said. "But it doesn't own the land."

I flipped through the paper, but I couldn't concentrate on the stories on the pages, or the words I was hearing around me. With the war over, deals were percolating all over town. It was hard to imagine Turtle Bay staying the way it was.

"Nice job, Grimes."

"Huh? What?" My head swiveled. I was as startled as I used

to be in Italy when the German guns began firing unexpectedly. All around I heard laughter.

McCracken took another swallow of Jim Beam. "Dietrich's picture. It turned out swell. He told me how you helped get him up there. I like a young man who can think on his feet."

"Thanks."

"I'd like you better if you drank more."

I joined the room's laughter. It was important to show I could go along with a joke. I was still on the six months' probation all new employees had to endure, and I wanted everyone to think I was a right guy.

About half past two, as I tried to stay in the shadows, I found myself at the corner of 47th and Second, occasionally peering down the block at the Turtle Bay Settlement House. My back was pressed against the grimy brick façade of the East Side Brewery. I tried to remember which brand it produced, but it was one of those places that was always changing hands.

I was aware of how ludicrous I must have looked, but I told myself I was only working on a story—a good one, something that might get me noticed. If I broke it wide open, I might start an ascent that would eventually lead to the masthead. Above all else, I reassured myself that I had not slipped into obsession. I was not trying to atone for all the wrongs I had committed, beginning with my conception in Original Sin and stretching all the way forward to the things I'd done during the war.

The settlement house was only fifty yards away, but I was afraid a walk past it would summon the goons who had followed me the night before. So I kept glancing from my hiding spot, periodically blowing on my hands in an effort to keep my fingers from tingling. I should have bought gloves to ward off the late November cold, but like everything else, they cost so much.

Ten minutes passed and a chill began to spread through my body. I didn't know what I was looking for. As I was about to leave, a pair of high beams swung into the street from First. I crouched low and shielded my eyes. The beams were attached to a long black car that rolled to a stop about halfway down the block, almost directly across the street from the settlement house. The driver's door opened. A man wearing an overcoat and a pointed cap got out and hurried over to the back door on the passenger side. He pulled open the door. A guy in a tuxedo stepped out unsteadily. He stood there a moment between the limo and the sidewalk, swaying slightly from side to side, as if he'd had three martinis too many at some swank spot in Midtown.

He held out his hand. A girl emerged. She was in a white dress and wrapped in a mink stole. Her hair was blond. It was difficult to tell for sure because of the distance and the darkness, but I could not rule out the possibility that I was once again looking at Sylvia Price.

The girl said something to the driver, who nodded and went back behind the wheel. As the limo pulled away and headed toward Second, the girl and the man accompanying her walked toward a building that looked like a warehouse.

I hid in a crevice of the brewery's wall while the limo went west on 47th. When I stepped out to look again, the man and the girl were gone.

I didn't want to go down there. But I couldn't figure out what those two were doing on a street like this.

I pushed away from the wall. I looked down at my overcoat and saw that it was covered with brick dust. When I lifted the sleeve to my nose, I caught the strong odor of stale beer. The coat would cost a fortune to clean, and money was one of the many things I did not have.

I was upset with myself, but I realized I could make my appearance work to my advantage, so I thrust my hands deep in my pockets and hoped I seemed like one of the derelicts who wandered this part of town.

When I reached the point where the limo had stopped, I slowed and looked to my left. The main door to the warehouse was huge and made of steel. It rested a few feet above the ground on a wrought-iron landing four metal steps above street level. An alley to the right of the building was wide enough for a truck.

The top floors of the warehouse were dark, but I could see slivers of light around the door. I hunched my overcoat around my shoulders and bent down a few inches, then walked up the steps. My footfalls rang so loudly I was sure everyone in the city could hear me. I pressed my ear against the door. Even through the thick barrier, I picked up faint shouts, and the sounds of music and laughter.

About twenty feet down the landing was a window with iron bars jutting out in front. Still imitating a bum, I shuffled over to it. The window had curtains, but they hadn't been pulled all the way. I straightened a bit and looked through the inch-wide gap in the middle.

The room was large, brightly lit and filled with cigarette smoke. The few people I could see were dressed in evening clothes, standing around a table with a roulette wheel on top. Many of them clutched martini glasses.

"Scram!"

The word was loud and harsh, and I recognized its source: a voice I had heard the night before commanding an elevated train to just wait a minute, goddammit.

I had assigned myself a role. I had to continue playing it. So I resisted the impulse to whirl around and confront the man behind me. Instead I bent lower and wrapped myself more tightly in my overcoat.

"Get outta here, you lug. You smell like you've been rolling in beer."

I nodded. I mumbled that I was going. I might have even said I was sorry.

Chapter four

The next night, for my meeting with Harrington Price, I dressed myself in the only suit I owned, a double-breasted job I'd bought before the war. I laced my wing tips and put on my best hat, a gray homburg that was always in danger of falling off. When I glanced in the streaky mirror over my dresser, I tried to convince myself that I looked like John Garfield.

Amanda's purse lay atop the dresser. I had kept it hidden in the bottom drawer of my desk at work for a couple of days. For a time I considered giving it to the police. Important evidence and all that. But my encounter with Valentine had convinced me that the cops would conveniently lose the thing, or alter it in a way to make William Anderson look even guiltier than he already appeared.

I had snuck the purse out of the office the night before. Now I tucked it inside my jacket, then draped my overcoat (which I'd spent an hour dusting off) around my shoulders.

On the street, a late autumn wind whipped the city from the west. The sidewalks were crowded with people returning home from work, and the air had that everything-is-possible anticipation that runs through Manhattan just after sunset. Off to the left, when I looked up a bit, I saw the graceful steel spire of the Chrysler Building.

As I walked west on 63rd, I heard two pairs of footsteps a half block behind me, with the same heavy clump I'd noticed two nights before.

I froze for a second. I told myself it couldn't be the same guys. They had no chance of finding me. The island of Manhattan held many dangers, but it also offered safety in anonymity and its countless places to hide.

I thought of spinning around to see if it was them. Instead I walked quickly toward Third, hoping I looked like a typical New Yorker in rush hour. I listened intently. The footsteps were still behind me, and they seemed to be getting closer.

I considered hailing a cab when I reached Third, but then I realized I'd be on the curb, stationary, an easy target. I whirled north and walked under the El. Its deep shadows made the early evening seem like midnight. I hurried past Clancy's, where old men were already hunched over their boilermakers. The steps behind me sounded nearer. I walked faster. Ahead was the 67th Street station, wooden and boxy and seeming to offer, at least for a moment, some sort of refuge.

I crossed against the lights. Cars honked behind me. Amanda's purse slipped inside my jacket, so I pressed my hand close against my side. I climbed the stairs two at a time and paused at the platform. Without turning around, I listened. Faintly but distinctly, I heard heavy footsteps beginning to walk up.

I paid the fare and walked along the platform. I considered heading down the other side, but Mother had always said it was a sin to waste anything, even a nickel, so I ducked into the stationhouse. The pot-bellied stove was glowing with coals. I hoped to blend with the two dozen people waiting for the next uptown train.

Two blurry figures, one tall and one short, walked slowly outside. Although their features were indistinct, I could see their fedoras turning in every direction. I lowered my head and prayed that the stained Victorian-era glass in the windows would be enough to shield me.

It was dark and warm in the stationhouse. I would have enjoyed staying there a long time.

When the door opened, I lowered my head. Two pairs of footsteps kept hitting hard on the wood floor. I wished I had a better place to hide. Sweat seeped into my undershirt.

I wondered why my questions about Terry had inspired such a severe reaction. These guys had to be tied in with the settlement house and the gambling. I had a short debate with myself about what they wanted: to give me a once-over as a warning, or was it worse than that, and did they somehow know about the purse? And, on top of all that, how the hell had they discovered where I lived?

I heard the train before I saw it, a clackety-clack that echoed back to another age, when life didn't have to move so quickly. I joined the crowd headed for the door, all the while keeping my head down and my hands in my pockets.

The train stopped. I waited for the other passengers to get off before stepping inside the car. I sat down, raised my head and looked around. At the next door down, the two men in fedoras—one tall, one short—sat together on one of the rattan seats. They stared at me. The short man had a scar on his cheek.

The doors began to slide closed. In one motion, I slipped out of the train and onto the platform. The men in fedoras seemed surprised; it took them a second to jump up, and by then the door in front of them was shutting closed. I smiled and waved.

The train doors jammed.

I saw a heavy black shoe wedged between the doors, which then jerked open with a loud squeak. The men stumbled out, but I had already begun to run.

My oxfords were clunky, and I had to keep the purse pressed close against me. I couldn't lose it. William Anderson's fate depended on my ability to get it to a place where it would become a battering ram for his freedom.

As the rear of the train passed by me, I jumped.

The leap took a second, but it seemed that I dangled much longer than that, suspended over the tracks and looking down through the latticework at the cars and the buses and the hats on the heads of the pedestrians. I saw a lot of garbage on the trainbed and the street below, and I wondered why the city didn't clean things up.

The train's rear platform was no more than two feet wide. I landed on it with a thunk. My right knee buckled and for a moment I felt myself falling, but I grabbed the latch on the train's back door, then held tight and screamed as the Third Avenue local bounced toward 76th.

Park Avenue was hushed, lined with the gray-faced residential fortresses of the privileged. At exactly five-thirty, I reached the front door of the building I wanted. A doorman blocked my way. White gloves protruded from a dark wool coat. His cap was pulled almost over his eyes.

"I'm here to see Harrington Price." My voice climbed half an octave with each word.

The doorman disappeared inside. It took him two minutes to come back out.

"Are you the man from the newspaper?"

"I am."

He stepped back inside. It took him another two minutes to return. I wondered what the problem was. I thought I was expected.

"Fifteenth floor," he said in a tone that indicated my presence was barely tolerated.

My footsteps echoed as I walked across marble tiles laid in a design that looked vaguely Egyptian. Many of these buildings had been built in the twenties, when Tutankhamen fever seized the imaginations of architects and their clients.

A gnomish man sat on a stool inside the elevator. His white gloves and gray uniform were both too big for him. We rode up in silence, for which I was grateful. When the elevator stopped, he leaned forward and pulled back the accordion gate. Then he opened the door, revealing a tall, silver-haired man in black tails.

"Come with me, Mr. Grimes."

He had a clipped British accent that sounded authentic. I followed him through a narrow room lined with cans and boxes. We were in the pantry, and it occurred to me that I was entering Harrington Price's world the same way the servants did.

In the kitchen I saw cabinets that were white and made of metal. They were the latest design. Nobody could get work like that done during the war. On a counter I saw a pop-up toaster. I reminded myself that I wanted one if I could find it at the right price. They hadn't been around long enough to be available second-hand. I also noticed that the Prices had kept their gas range, despite the government's wartime pleas to switch to electric.

"Excuse me," I said.

"Yes?" He did not slow down or turn around.

"Would it be all right if I washed my hands? They got covered with schmutz while I was riding the El."

The butler motioned toward the sink. My overcoat was dirty again as well. I tried to brush it as clean as I could. After I was done we walked down a hall lined with vases perched on antique tables, as well as paintings that would have looked at home in the Old Masters section of the Met. The butler led me into the library, lined floor to ceiling with leather-bound books. He told me to remain standing. Mr. Price would be in presently.

As I strolled around the room I wondered if Harrington Price had read any of these volumes. The collection was mainly full sets. Most of the covers looked as if they had never been cracked, although his copies of Nietzsche seemed well-worn.

Behind me the door opened, then closed. A white-haired man of sixty had entered. He was jowly, with a fleshy face, but he carried himself with the ease of a fellow born into a life of money and athleticism.

"Your favorite writer?" he asked.

"Hemingway."

He shook his head. "Newspapermen are so predictable."

I reached into my coat, took out his daughter's purse and tossed it on the table in front of me.

"Is that predictable?" I asked.

Something close to a gasp escaped Harrington Price's lips.

Within a second his face again became a mask. He reached for the handkerchief that was carefully folded into his breast pocket. I expected him to mop his face, where tiny beads of moisture had gathered on his temples despite his attempt to look impassive. Instead he used the white cloth to pick up the purse by its clasp and bring it close.

"You should give it to the police," he said softly.

"I found it at the scene. If I give it to the cops, they'll just lose it or destroy it. They have their suspect, and a story everybody is willing to believe."

He looked at me curiously, like a grandmaster trying to analyze an unexpected move on the chessboard. "You don't think I should believe it," he said at last, with the first note of uncertainty I'd heard from him.

"No, sir. I was there. I talked to William Anderson, and I saw what the cops did to him."

Price put the purse down and folded his handkerchief, which he placed back in his breast pocket before walking past me to a small cabinet with oak doors.

"What do you drink?" His voice had regained its tone of command.

"Nothing right now, sir. Thank you."

"You're a newspaperman. Who are you trying to fool?"

He poured himself a glass from a long-necked crystal decanter. I thought I smelled scotch. He lifted the drink and rocked back on his heels and drained it in one gulp. Then his eyes acquired the hard gaze of an intelligent man who realized he had overlooked some obvious points.

"Why show this to me?" he asked.

I breathed hard and told myself to stay calm. "I need your help," I said.

He looked puzzled. "Help with what?"

I plunged ahead with words I had rehearsed in front of my mirror: "I'd like to do a story that says there are questions about William Anderson's guilt. That the family has doubts. The cops said they couldn't find your daughter's purse. You could say you came in possession of it. You don't have to say how. I'd write it up and get it into the paper, and the cops would have to reopen the investigation."

He was silent a few moments. I was conscious of being in the presence of a formidable mind, one that could see around corners that I didn't even know existed. Finally he asked me a question. Perhaps it was the one thing he couldn't parse out.

"What's in it for you, young man?"

In Harrington Price's world, a person could not convey information simply because it was the right thing to do. There had to be an angle, a benefit for the guy handing out the straight dope.

"It's a helluva piece," I said. "That's all I care about."

I cared about more than that, but I couldn't let him know. I assumed that like all powerful men, Harrington Price possessed a deep and abiding contempt for altruism.

"You found the purse," he said. "I assume that means the police missed it. Why don't you just print that in your newspaper?"

"I withheld evidence. The cops would make a stink about that. I could lose my job."

Harrington Price shook his head. I sensed he had performed all his calculations and had formulated a plan.

"It's an interesting thesis, young man, but the colored man confessed. If he didn't do it, why would he admit to murdering Amanda?"

"I don't know what the cops did when they grilled him. But if you read his confession closely, it doesn't make sense."

"I'm sure the whole thing happened in a blur," Price said. "It doesn't have to make sense. What's important is his admission."

My lips were dry and cracked. I kept hoping my host would offer me a glass of water. I sensed we were at an impasse, and decided to throw a curveball.

"Who's Howard Munzer?" I asked.

Harrington Price switched his glance from the decanter to me. When his eyes returned to the booze, I knew he was going to lie.

"That's a curious question. I've never heard the name."

"He's a lawyer on East 14th Street. His business card was in your daughter's purse."

"If you already knew the answer, why did you ask me?"

"Did Amanda ever talk to you about him?"

Harrington Price seemed ready to say something, but then he stopped himself. For the first time since we began talking, he seemed excited about the possibilities of our conversation.

"Do you think he was involved in Amanda's death?" he asked in a tone that indicated he would be happy if somebody could link Howard Munzer to the murder.

"I have no idea," I said. I decided to mix up my pitches again. McCracken had always told me that keeping people off-guard was the key to a successful interview. "Who was Amanda supposed to meet at the Stork Club the night she was killed?"

"You must be thinking of Sylvia," Price said with a tone of bafflement, as if I'd just announced that Harvard was being taken over by the Jesuits. "Amanda hadn't been there in years."

I was tempted to reach into my pocket and take out the handwritten note I had found in her purse, but I suspected I would get nothing except another claim of ignorance.

Harrington Price took another sip of his drink. The only light in the room came from a bulb on the desk lamp. The windows were blocked by heavy damask curtains. I wondered what he was trying to keep out.

"Let's return to my original point," I said. "I could write up a story that says the cops overlooked evidence at the scene, and William Anderson's confession doesn't gibe with reality. I could quote you as saying you now have serious doubts about—"

Price cut me off. "I'm afraid not, young man. To be honest about it, I didn't expect you to have the gumption to show up tonight. I may have underestimated you."

I found his remark curious, and I felt myself deflating. I tried to avoid sounding petulant as I asked, "Why won't you help me?"

"I've talked to the police." His voice acquired the certitude that accompanies wealth and privilege. "I have every reason to believe their version of events."

"What did they tell you?"

"Something they're saving for the trial. I shouldn't repeat it to anyone."

I offered a prayer to the gods of indiscretion. People like to flaunt their knowledge, and I suspected even Harrington Price would be unable to resist showing a cub newshawk that he was privy to information that was unavailable to the public.

I told him I wouldn't reveal his secret to anyone.

"When the police searched the colored man," he said, "they found a twenty-dollar bill on him. Where would a creature like him get that kind of money, unless he'd stolen it from Amanda?"

I recalled William Anderson's delight in taking the bill from my hand, and chuckled at the consequences of one small, greedy act.

"What do you find so amusing?"

"I gave him that money."

His jaw moved a few seconds before he said, "You did?"

I sensed I had miscalculated. A lie would have been better. "He gave us a tip," I said. "So we gave him one."

"You gave him money," Price said. His voice was rising. "So you could take pictures of my daughter. My dead daughter."

His face was scarlet, and it wasn't from the scotch. I realized I had to try to appease him.

"It does seem awful, sir, I grant you that—"

"Get out!"

I stayed where I was. I had to continue pleading. William Anderson faced the electric chair.

Harrington Price wrenched the decanter off the shelf. As he poured more scotch, he regarded me with the burning, hateful eyes that my mother used to cast upon my father when he came home from the pub, stout on his breath and no money in his pockets. I could endure anything except the fury she used to hurl at him.

"Please don't hold this against the colored man," I said. "He was just trying to make a buck."

Harrington Price knocked back his drink and brought the glass close to his eye, as if hoping to find a drop he'd missed. "I was correct the first time," he said. "You're a worthless guttersnipe. Another cockroach from the press. Now leave my presence before I have you—"

And here he paused as he searched for exactly the word he wanted.

"—exterminated."

I backed away and looked to the side. Amanda's purse was still on the table where I'd placed it at the start of our meeting. I made a motion to grab it, but as I did Harrington Price said, "You'll leave that here, young man."

I was tempted to snatch it and run away, like the daring kids who liked to swipe stuff from stores back when I was growing up.

"I'll do you a favor," Harrington Price said.

I listened closely. I'd never had a man like Harrington Price say he'd do a favor for me.

"If you drop this matter, I'll pretend none of this ever occurred, and that I never even heard of you. Believe me, that's what I prefer. But if you remove that purse, I'll make the authorities aware of what you've done."

My head throbbed with the twin pains of confrontation and failure. The only other person who had made me feel this impotent was Mother. I reached behind me for the knob, opened the door and slipped through.

I thought the butler would be waiting outside, wearing the blank and neutral look of a man trying to pretend he had not overheard an argument. But no one was there. I lurched down the hall and into the kitchen. I figured I'd keep walking until I reached the elevator.

But then I saw something that made me stop.

Leaning into the opened icebox was a girl of about twenty, with blonde bobbed hair that stopped just above her shoulders. A gray cashmere sweater clung to her, accenting a black skirt that cost more than I made in a month. A cigarette dangled from her mouth.

This time I was definitely looking at Sylvia Price.

"I'm famished," she announced in a voice that told the world that anything that happened to her was important. "Is there anything in here? Even a piece of fruit?"

"I wouldn't know."

When she turned toward me, she blew out a cloud of smoke that escaped through lips painted somewhere on the border between pink and red. She straightened herself, closed the icebox and asked who I was.

"Patrick Grimes."

She placed herself directly in front of the entrance to the elevator. She struck me as the type of girl who had a compulsive need to learn all her companions' secrets, while hers stayed tightly wrapped inside.

"And why are you here, Patrick Grimes?"

"To see your father."

"Is this another project of his? He has many, you know."

"Could be."

She smiled. She knew she was dazzling, and she was trying to tell me up front not to fight the attraction. "I always get the men to talk," she said. "You can save both of us some time by telling me what it is right away."

"Speaking of time, Miss Price, I'm already late for work. Will you excuse me?"

I expected her to step aside, perhaps look down demurely as I passed, but she stayed where she was and gazed right at me. Her eyes were blue with hints of hazel.

"This is a ridiculous hour to be going to work," she said. "It's almost six in the evening. Are you a vampire?"

She arched her eyebrows as if she was sure she'd just said something witty. Mixed with the tobacco I picked up a flowery scent, and I knew it came from her.

"I'm not a vampire. But I like what I do."

"Which is what?"

"I work at the *Examiner*. On the night shift."

"What do you do…at the *Examiner*…on the night shift?"

"I'm a rewrite man."

She looked puzzled, then blew out more smoke. "Am I supposed to guess what that is?" she asked.

"I take information over the phone from our reporters and turn it into English so we can print it. Now if you'll pardon me, Miss Price, I must be going."

I took a step toward her, but she did not move. Instead she asked if I knew Gracie Paquette.

I flashed to the few times I had interacted with the *Examiner*'s star gossip columnist. "I've seen her in the office once or twice," I said. "And I've talked to her on the phone a few times. Other than that, it's strictly by reputation."

"What is her reputation?"

I shifted from foot to foot. I wasn't sure I wanted to keep talking. "I can't say in polite company."

She stretched her frame wider. The only way I'd get to the elevator was by running her over. "Don't you read your own newspaper? My company is anything but polite."

I could hear Mother's voice telling me it was sinful to be late and waste God's precious time, but in this girl's presence I didn't care. I grinned widely.

"What did you give Father?" she asked.

"What makes you think I gave him anything?"

"Should I be candid with you?" The line sounded practiced, as if she used it all the time, usually as a prelude to a remark that was, at best, half true.

"Please."

"I was looking for Father. The butler said he was in the library with a man. He thought you had brought something."

Her voice was smooth, with the hint of a lilt at the end. For a moment I was tempted to accept what she said.

"How would the butler know that?" I asked. "I didn't tell him why I was here."

"He eavesdrops on everything."

"Why don't you fire him?"

The hazel came up strong in her eyes, as if she couldn't believe an underling had the temerity to ask a difficult question. Finally she put one hand on her hip and used the other to remove the cigarette from her mouth.

"His faults give us something to talk about," she said.

I enjoyed the way she could concoct an explanation in an instant. I liked looking at her hair and her eyes and especially her sweater, and imagining what was underneath.

I had never talked to a girl like this before. She was everything

Mother had warned me against, so of course I wanted to stay with her as long as I could.

"I gave him your sister's purse," I said in as authoritative a voice as I could summon. "I found it at the scene where her body was found."

Sylvia Price sagged against the doorframe. I could have passed if I'd wanted.

"The police said they couldn't find it," she said in tones that were suddenly more real. "They said the killer hid it. He was hoping to come back for it later."

"Your father made me leave the purse behind in the library. Why don't you be a good girl and go get it for me?"

Sylvia laughed. It was the cackle of a young woman who was always in on the joke well ahead of everyone else. "If Father caught me in the library, he'd know I was up to something. I haven't read a book since eighth grade."

"You should try it sometime."

I stepped toward the elevator, but she shifted her weight and was directly in front of me again. We were inches apart. She ran her tongue against the back of her teeth. My breath grew quick and shallow. Sylvia's eyes were full of mirth and playfulness, as if she expected me to do something. So I reached into my pocket and took out the note I had found in her sister's purse.

"Does this mean anything to you?" I asked.

As she read the words, she scrunched her face so much her eyebrows ran together. It occurred to me that she needed glasses, but was too vain to wear them.

"That's Amanda's handwriting," she said in a soft voice. "Crimped and pinched, but precise."

"Who's Manley?"

"I'm not sure," she said, wondering aloud. "We know a family named Manley. But that can't be it."

"Why not?"

"They're in Palm Beach. All of them. At the first sign of cold weather, they bundle up and fly south like robins. Just like my mother."

The way that last word came out made me think we had at least one thing in common.

"Your mother was at the funeral," I said.

"She's back in Florida already," Sylvia replied.

"Why didn't you go with her?"

"It's warm but dull. I'd rather be here."

I decided to press her a bit. She didn't seem like a girl who minded.

"The night your sister was killed—did you see her at the Stork Club?"

Sylvia thought for a moment. "It was Monday, wasn't it?" she asked.

I nodded.

"I never go to the Stork on Monday."

"Why not?"

"I go to Swing Street. A place called the Downbeat. It's the best night for jazz."

She turned sideways, leaning her back against the doorframe. I took it as a sign that she was done with me, and I should step through. But I had one more question.

"The place where your sister's body was found. Blood Alley. Do you ever go there, Miss Price?"

Her mirth returned. I sensed I had exhausted her daily quotient of seriousness. "I venture into every part of town, Patrick Grimes," she said as she walked out of the pantry.

When I got to the office, Higgins already had a gruesome piece: a butcher in Throgs Neck had taken a meat cleaver to his wife, leaving a trail of body parts through their one-story house. He suspected her of cheating on him.

"Punch it up, Grimes."

McCracken stood over my shoulder while I turned Higgins's grunts into *Examiner*-worthy prose. The wife was "sultry," the scene "grisly," the neighbors "stunned."

"This could be the wood." McCracken clapped me on the back

and ran his bony fingers over my right shoulder before saying, "I smell perfume and cigarettes, Grimes."

I said nothing. I felt my face turning red.

"Be careful of the broads, my young mick friend. A good newspaperman has no place for them."

Shortly after eleven that night, as if McCracken had created an incident to prove his foresight, the copyboy yelled out that I had a call from a girl on line two. All the men in the newsroom stopped what they were doing and turned to stare at me as I picked up the phone to say hello.

"Patrick?"

Even through the static, I recognized the musky thrill of Sylvia Price's voice.

"Yes?"

"You sound so far away."

"I'm trying to keep my voice down."

"I thought you'd be happy to hear from me."

I lowered my voice even further. "Why are you calling?"

"What was that, Patrick? I can barely hear you."

"I'm glad you called," I said a little louder, immediately regretting both my words and my amplitude. "But I'm busy right now. I'm on deadline."

Our next deadline wasn't for an hour. Even from the first, my relationship with Sylvia Price was based on lies.

"I'm at the Stork. I have some news for you. A scoop."

She let the word draw out. I imagined her mouth forming a perfect circle. By now her lips would be colored ruby red.

"What is it?" I asked.

"Can't you at least sound interested?"

Oh, I was. I was interested because she remembered me and she had called from a place I could only dream about getting into, but most of all I was interested because of the way she made me feel.

"You could give it to Gracie," I said.

"I like you better."

I tried not to stammer. "Go ahead."

She began talking in the breathless manner of a girl who was spending an evening in the company of champagne cocktails and people she enjoyed. She had asked some of the regulars if they'd seen Amanda at the club on the night she was killed, but the idea seemed so preposterous everyone laughed. Then she asked about the Manleys and everyone said they'd been in Palm Beach for at least two weeks. Yet a few moments ago Sylvia was talking to a girl she had known at Spence and the girl said she could have sworn she'd seen Jeff Manley on Madison Avenue just the other day. She had called out to him, but he ducked into a cab. She remembered thinking his behavior was both rude and odd.

"Did your sister know Jeff Manley?" I asked.

"We all know everybody."

"Did they ever go out with each other?"

"I don't think so. Amanda hadn't had a beau for a long time." The unspoken words at the end of that sentence were, *Unlike me.*

"Did your friend see him at the club?"

"I didn't ask her. But I'm sure she would have mentioned it if she had."

I didn't know how promising this information was. But it was more than I'd had five minutes before.

"What does he do?" I asked.

"What do you mean?" Sylvia replied.

"This Jeff Manley—what does he do for a living?"

"I don't think he does anything. But I believe his father is involved in insurance."

"How old is he? What does he look like?"

"He's twenty-five or so, nearly six feet tall and a bit chubby. He's one of those quiet chaps who keeps to himself." Sylvia's voice became animated, as if she had just cracked the case herself. "Aren't they the ones who always snap?"

The first edition was in and McCracken was satisfied. O'Shea dealt a hand of five-card draw and told us that the fix was in: Philadelphia would get the United Nations, with the announcement coming in the next few days.

"Who's your source?" McCracken asked.

"A guy I know at *The Bulletin*."

"If he could tell his elbow from his asshole, he'd be working in New York instead of Philadelphia."

McCracken had made the journalistic journey from small towns in Texas to the biggest stage of all. He always made it clear that anybody with ambition, brains and talent should do the same.

Behind me I heard a rustle and rattle. I turned to see the clerk standing in the door, his bony finger pointing at me as if he were a harbinger of the Grim Reaper. This was his sign that I had a phone call, so I threw down my cards, took my money from the pot and headed for my desk.

As I sat down, I hoped I sounded annoyed as I barked out my name.

"Did I catch you at a bad time, Mr. Grimes?"

The words bordered on the fearful. They came from the person I'd heard when I first called the Turtle Bay Settlement House the night Amanda Price was murdered, a person who was devastated but not surprised to learn that the girl had been killed.

"Is this Terry?" I asked.

"It is."

"It's not a bad time. I went to the settlement house a couple of nights ago. Nobody had ever heard of you."

A long silence on the other end. And then Terry said, in a voice that seemed to come from the bottom of a well in China, "Going there may have been a mistake."

"I didn't identify myself. I said I was a friend."

Another long silence followed. I fished for a notepad in case my source decided to talk.

"I liked Amanda very much," Terry said at last. "A lost soul. I have an affinity for people like that."

"You told me that you knew she was going to die."

"That's correct."

"Why did you say that?"

"Because she said it herself. She had information about the area where we worked. Where her body was found."

"What did she know?"

"There were two incidents in particular."

"Tell me about them."

And then I heard a door slamming open and shut, followed by muffled voices and the *ching* of a cash register. In the background I heard a blaring horn followed by a low but steady siren that sounded like a fire engine. Terry was calling from a pay phone. I wondered how long the dime would hold out.

"I'm sorry," Terry said in a tone that sounded a bit too self-assured, almost like the bluffs we tried to pull in our poker games. "Something's come up. I have to go."

"Where are you?"

Nothing.

"Tell me where you are," I said. "I'll call you back."

Silence.

"Please. You've gotta stay on the line."

No response. I threw the phone down and swore a few times. I couldn't return to the settlement house. I had no idea how to find Terry. The cops were of no use, and Harrington Price had rebuffed me. His daughter was dead and buried, a colored man was charged with her murder, and everybody except me seemed content with the way the case was heading.

Chapter five

That Sunday I took the 7 train to Woodside. Manhattan faded on my way to dinner at Kathleen's. She lived in a low-rise world of wood and brick, in an apartment with walls as thin as fingernails, much like the cold-water places in which we'd grown up on the East Side. Unlike Mother, Kathleen was quiet and withdrawn, but she shared one important trait with the woman who'd given birth to us: she was determined to get her way.

When I reached her building I walked three flights up. After I knocked I heard footsteps followed by my sister's tentative voice, as if she were afraid it was the devil himself: "Who is it?"

When we were kids she stayed in her room a lot. Kathleen had a fantasy life that was difficult to disturb, and whenever I had to talk to her I stood outside her door, raised my voice and said, just as I did now, "It's me."

The lock turned. I wedged myself into the apartment and kissed my sister on the cheek. Ryan, her husband, nodded from a chair in the corner of the room as he read the sports pages in the *Daily News*. On the front page the *News* trumpeted its circulation: two million daily, four million on Sunday, twice the numbers of the paper that employed me.

Kathleen offered to take my coat. She said the food was almost ready. I sat on the sofa, which was hard and lumpy. Across from me, against the wall, was the dark maple hutch that had once belonged to Mother. Doubtless it was filled with the things that had meant so much to her: doilies, a tea set, and, most important of all, the faded baptismal certificate from a parish in Roscommon that proved she was a true and faithful Daughter of the Church.

I wished Kathleen had thrown out the hutch, or given it away. Its presence cast a darkness on the room more profound than the late afternoon shadows.

The radio was in a dome cabinet next to Ryan's chair. Sheer curtains with cheap lace fringed the window that fronted the street. Both Kathleen and her husband worked, and I wondered if they were saving their money for something better, or just barely scraping by.

Kathleen called out from way in back, asking if I wanted anything to drink with dinner. I said I'd like a beer. Ryan grunted and turned the page so loudly I thought he was angry I was drinking some of his suds. I didn't want to look at him, but I did. He asked if I could believe what the Dodgers were doing, signing this colored guy to play ball. I said I hadn't followed the story much. Ryan said it was a disgrace, letting some jigaboo replace a white man. It was going on all over. The spooks were leaving the South where they belonged. They were used to working for peanuts. Now they were taking the decent jobs away. He saw it happen all the time.

I said I hadn't really thought about it, but if the Robinson fella had ability, they ought to let him play.

Ryan turned the page with so much force I thought it was going to rip apart in his hands.

"We're being conned," Ryan said. "Ever since Roosevelt came in, we've bent over backwards helping the Jews and the coloreds, but it's only buying us trouble."

Now I wished I had that beer in my hands, if only to give me something to do.

"Like the war. I can see why we fought the Japs, but what was the point of sending our men to Europe?"

Ryan hadn't gone. He'd been declared 4-F even though he worked on a garbage truck all day. Kathleen once told me he had an eardrum injury, just like Frank Sinatra.

"We did what we were told," I said. Ice gripped my voice.

"You didn't have a choice," Ryan said. "But that cripple Roosevelt sure did. Hitler and Mussolini never lifted a finger against us, and they were fighting the Communists. Instead we ended up on the same side as Stalin. I can't believe it. At least Hitler allowed the Church."

I had seen some Germans up close. A lot of them knew English. They all talked about how much they liked America. None of them admitted to being Nazis.

As I shifted my weight on the sofa in my sister's living room, my most vivid wartime memory rushed through me. I was near the Arno, behind our own lines, my anger rising as I led a bunch of prisoners who kept smiling and laughing as they spoke a harsh language I did not understand.

I put my head in my hands. I felt cursed, like a biblical character who had tried to lead a righteous life but was doomed by the one unforgivable act he had committed.

I told myself the memory would pass. It always did. But it always came back.

From behind me I heard the soft clatter of serving dishes being placed on a table, followed by Kathleen's announcement that everything was ready.

Three settings were on the table, with beer glasses at two of them. I asked Kathleen if it mattered which one I took. She pointed to a chair that faced the kitchen. Ryan, I assumed, would sit at the head, where he and I could ignore each other while I talked to my sister.

I heard the rustle of the *News* being put down, followed by the clump of weighty male footsteps. In a soft voice that did not entirely hide the steel underneath it, Kathleen told Ryan to make sure he washed his hands before we said grace.

* * *

After dinner Ryan said he wasn't sure how it had happened, but he'd run out of butts. He knew a store that was run by kikes; the Hebes were all gonna rot in hell, but in the meantime it was convenient because they didn't care about the blue laws. As the door closed behind him I felt relieved, but then I realized I'd been left alone with Kathleen. The feeling that wormed into me was the same dread I experienced whenever I was with Mother and nobody else was around. She always seemed angry with me, although she never explained what I had done wrong.

"You look queer," Kathleen said. "What's wrong?"

"I was thinking about Mother."

"If she still upsets you, you should put her out of your mind."

I said nothing.

Kathleen went on. "I try to be kind when I think about her. She had a hard life. I realize that now. Every Sunday at Mass, when the Host is consecrated, I say a prayer for her soul."

I had given up going to church, but I decided not to mention it. Instead I reached for the coffee my sister had placed in front of me.

"There's something I wanna ask you," she said.

I told her to go ahead.

"You know we'd like to move."

"Then move. You don't have to talk to me about it."

"It's not that simple," she said. "There's a housing shortage and a lotta these places…" Her voice trailed off, as it did whenever she was discussing something she really desired. It was always up to somebody else to find the words that would please her.

"A lotta these places what?"

"There's one place we like, Pat. We like it a lot. It's out on Long Island. You should see it. It's everything we want. A house in the country."

"I've heard about it. That crazy guy Levitt. He's building a town in the middle of potato fields."

"That's just the point. There's peace and quiet. Away from all this." She waved her arm in a sweeping movement that tried to brush away the entire city.

I shrugged and said, "If that's what you want, then live in the potato fields."

"It's gonna be tough for us."

I nodded. "Saving for a house is hard."

"That's not it. Oh no, Levitt's made the whole thing cheap—if you're the right kind of a man."

"Waddya mean?"

"A veteran."

A sour blanket settled over my stomach. I realized why Kathleen had invited me to share her Sunday dinner, and why Ryan had disappeared right after dessert.

"Your husband didn't go," I said. "Those are the breaks."

We'd all been told it was our duty to serve, but plenty of guys found ways to avoid it.

"You're a veteran," she said as she fidgeted with her best cloth napkin. "Maybe you could help us."

I drummed my fingers on the table, then reached for the coffee. I took it black; the bitter taste matched my mood.

"Why don't you apply for one of those houses?" she asked.

"Because I don't wanna live in a potato field."

"You don't have to live there. Once you buy it, turn around and sell it to us."

She was staring straight at me. I knew she wanted eye contact. Instead I looked out through the back of the apartment, where a small window revealed a tenement that contained apartments exactly like this one.

My sister touched me on the wrist. I recalled a time when we were kids. We were tossing a spaldeen back and forth in the street, but it squirted into the basement of our building through a half-open window. We needed the ball, so we went to look for it. The basement was dark and drafty. We heard a clank, so we approached the sound, thinking it was the ball rattling around. But the noise came from our father, who was nestled next to the furnace underneath some cobwebs. He blinked at us at first, as if he thought we were apparitions, but then he smiled and asked what we were doing there. We got over our surprise and blurted that we were looking for a spaldeen. We didn't want to lose it. Everything cost so much. Father said we were good kids. He motioned toward us. Kathleen grabbed my hand. I had never been so close to Dad. I asked what he was doing there. When he smiled even further, we saw the gaps between the few teeth he had left. He said this would be our secret if we promised to keep it to ourselves, just the three of us. We nodded. He said it was a sin to break a promise to your father. We said we understood. Then he held a long crooked finger to his lips and told us he was hiding from Mother. Didn't we ever feel like hiding from her? We both nodded as he took a flask from his pocket and brought it to his mouth. That was when we noticed the strong sick smell of alcohol. After gulping at the tin, Father extended it toward us. He said it would be all right if we had a sip. It would be part of our secret. I took it first and thanked him and tried to drink, but the taste burned my mouth and throat and tummy. All I could manage was a swallow. Then he handed the tin to Kathleen. After a second she began coughing violently, almost puking, but I could do nothing to help because I felt rubber-legged and foggy. Everything looked bent and blurry but somehow more benign, and I realized that this was how my father saw the world.

I finally looked at my sister, now grown up with a husband and a job and undoubtedly kids in the future because she wanted to produce soldiers for Christ. Her eyes were wet with pleading.

I thought about giving her what she wanted. But then I remembered the guys I'd fought with in Italy, especially the ones I'd watched die.

"I'm sorry, Kathleen. I can't do it. It's not on the level."

Her voice rose. "Why should we suffer just because Dan wasn't in the service?"

He was a slacker and my sister was sticking up for him. My voice escalated to match hers. "Because the guys who went deserve it. You have no idea what we went through."

She bowed her head. Her shoulders heaved as she wept.

"You went away and I had to deal with Mother," she said. "I had to watch her as she wasted away and blamed everybody for what was happening to her—but especially me, just because I happened to be there." She raised her head. Her face was red with grief. "Goddammit, Pat, you owe it to me."

I told her I needed to use the bathroom. When I got there I splashed water on my face and considered crawling out the window, onto the fire escape. Instead I jammed the window up a bit and put my nose near the opening. I was desperate for a hint of air, no matter how cold. From below I heard a crying baby, followed by a raging male voice saying he busted his balls all week to keep a roof over everyone's head and all he wanted on his fucking weekend was a little peace and quiet and was that too much to ask?

My pulse slowed. My breath returned to normal. I knew I'd have to face Kathleen again and I decided I'd just thank her for a lovely meal and be on my way. I'd keep my darkest thought to myself: the old saying was right about the fruit not falling far from the tree. In her own quiet way my sister was just as manipulative as Mother had been, and at times I saw myself turning out just like Dad, smiling and trying hard to be nice, but above all else looking for a place where the world would leave me alone.

When I came out Kathleen was in the kitchen. Her hands whipped around dishes and glasses as she washed them clean before placing them in the drainer with an angry force that left them just shy of breaking.

"Do you need a hand with that?" I asked. "I can dry."

"I'm doing just fine, Pat," she said. If her words had been any more clipped, they would have been snorts.

We stood there a while. I didn't know what else to say. Finally Kathleen ended the silence: "Dan will be back any minute. It'd probably be best if you're not here."

I worked overtime that night. Higgins called about eight-fifteen.

"The Throgs Neck butcher," he told me.

"What about him?"

"He's gonna plead insanity."

"Source?"

"Cops in the Bronx. They say he's cuckoo."

"Of course he's cuckoo. He chopped her up."

"He talks to her. Out loud. A couple times a day. He says she comes into his cell. He says she takes her clothes off. He says she tells him to fuck her." Higgins emitted the guttural hack that passed for his laugh. "See if you can get that past the copy desk."

It was an interesting idea. "What does he say to her?"

"He says he's sorry. Ain't that sweet?"

"Is he faking?"

"They don't think so. They have a shrink who can spot a phony a million miles away. He swears he's never seen a guy so nutso."

"Why'd he snap?" I asked, although I thought I might know the answer.

"He was in the war," Higgins said. "In the Pacific. When he came back he couldn't get it up anymore. Which was a problem, because his wife was a slut. She was cheating on him even before he came home."

I took all this down. I wondered how I'd write it.

"Wasn't that what all you guys were afraid of?" he asked. "There you were, in some godforsaken shithole getting shot at by the Japs or the Krauts, and back home some 4-F asshole was porking your girl?"

I remembered why I couldn't stand Higgins, and asked if he had anything else.

"Yeah, wiseass, I've got something to tell you—write it up like I said."

I looked at the clock. It was only two minutes before deadline. The copy desk needed the story and O'Shea was waving his arms at me as if he were a traffic cop at Fifth and 42nd. But I couldn't just let Higgins go.

"What are you talking about?" I asked.

"Don't act dumb, kid. You know what I'm talking about."

"No, I don't. I never have any idea what you're talking about."

"That shit you threw into my story the last time—'grisly' and 'sultry' and all that crap. The broad weighed two hundred pounds, for Christ's sake."

"I'm trying to liven it up."

"You're turning it into bullshit."

"If you'd just do some fucking reporting—"

"You can't talk to me—"

"You want me to spew some incoherent shit onto a piece of paper and hope our readers can figure it out?"

"So help me God, I'm gonna go up there—"

"So now I'll just put the ramblings of some half-in-the-bag hack—"

"—and bust your face wide open—"

"—who can't even call in on time—"

"—with my own two hands—"

"—into the paper verbatim."

"—and I'll laugh while I do it."

"I need some fucking details, Higgins!" The veins in my neck were straining. Everyone was looking at me, but I couldn't stop. "I need you to tell me what's going on. You keep it all to yourself so the cops will keep talking to you, but I've gotta do something with this shit so somebody will wanna read it."

"Watch your fucking mouth, kid."

"My name is Grimes. Patrick Grimes."

I slammed down the phone and typed furiously for a minute before yanking the paper out of my machine. Then I walked into the bathroom and splashed water on my face until my skin cooled. When I opened the door, McCracken was waiting.

"Grimes, will you please tell me with whom you were having that animated conversation?"

I waited a second before saying, "Higgins."

McCracken smiled. "Good."

* * *

My phone rang just as I was about to leave. I had no idea who'd be calling at shortly before two in the morning, but then I had a flash: it was Sylvia, at a jazz club or a nightspot, with information for me and me alone.

I made my voice deeper in an attempt to sound older and more professional: "City desk. This is Grimes."

"Hello, Mr. Grimes. It's Terry."

My initial disappointment gave way to excitement. I gripped the phone tighter, as if that would somehow keep my caller on the line.

"How are you?" I asked. "Where are you?"

"I'm all right, Mr. Grimes. At least for the time being."

"Can you talk to me?"

"I don't want to do it over the phone. You can never tell who's listening."

"Then can I meet you someplace?"

"You can, Mr. Grimes. If you're willing to go to the end of the world."

Chapter six

The next afternoon I took the El to the bottom of Manhattan. I walked down from the platform to the ferry slip directly underneath. After I boarded the boat, I rode outside despite the chill. The downtown towers, so imposing up close, began to fade to a human scale. Even the Woolworth Building, for years the tallest in the world, was now a structure that managed to claw just a bit higher than its neighbors. All of them were citadels of capitalism, monuments to the furtive processes of making fortunes, and the activities inside were so secretive they seemed Masonic. It was in one of those places that Harrington Price worked; he was in the business of making money, and I understood so little of what he did that it seemed like a form of alchemy.

When I reached Staten Island I took a train, sitting uncomfortably on a straw seat in a drafty car that bumped and clattered through woods interrupted by small clusters of commercial buildings. As the ride went on the trees grew thicker, the buildings less frequent, and I felt I was in the country although I was still within city limits.

Terry had told me to get off at the Eltingville station. Only one other passenger left the train, a woman who walked to the other end of the platform. Her heels clicked loudly on the hard cracked wood.

Terry had said to take a bus. I found it difficult to believe one would ever come through so isolated a place, but I located a bus-stop sign across the street from the station, so I waited with my hands in my pockets.

A bus finally came twenty minutes later. The driver's eyes went wide with surprise when he saw he had a fare. I gave him a nickel and told him I didn't know where I was going, but I was supposed to meet someone at Arden Avenue down past Hylan Boulevard, right near the beach. The driver said I was crazy. Nobody lived there this time of year.

The trees gave way to tall grasses. Cold salt air blew in off the water. When the bus turned onto a four-lane road that looked as if it never saw traffic, the driver told me that this was my stop.

I stepped outside and crossed the street. The wind lifted tiny icicles off the bay and threw them into my face. There was no sign of any life except for the grasses, which whipped around and reached over my head.

"Mr. Grimes."

I turned full circle but saw nothing. Perhaps the wind was making me hear voices.

"Mr. Grimes!"

I turned more slowly. When I had gone three-quarters I saw a figure a few feet away wearing a dull green coat that blended into the surroundings. As the wind gusted, hard crisp blades snapped against my face. I knew I was supposed to respect nature, but at that moment I wished I had a scythe so I could take everything down to ankle level.

The person who had called my name was nearly a foot shorter than me, shaped like a pear and topped with a brown woolen hat. As I got closer and saw the face, I pegged the age at around forty. I noticed a wisp of a mustache, and lumpy protrusions that I assumed were breasts.

"Come with me. There's a path."

Terry pushed the tall blades aside. After a few steps we followed a narrow dirt lane that zigzagged through the growth. Toward the end the dune grasses became shorter. I saw several bungalows perched on short stilts only a few feet from the water line. Terry led me into the smallest one. The wind banged the flimsy door shut behind us.

Terry motioned to a small bookcase, which we pushed over to block the entrance. Even in this isolated place, precautions were necessary.

The bungalow consisted of a single room with a cot, a battered bureau, a portable heater, a sink and a stove. A large crucifix was nailed into the wall over two sagging chairs. I could see blood on Our Savior's hands and feet.

"What is this place?" I asked.

"Sanctuary," Terry said.

It was too cold to remove my coat, so I reached inside and took out my notepad. I blew on my hand to keep my fingers warm.

"What's it really called?" I asked.

"Spanish Camp," Terry replied.

The name sounded familiar. I flashed to a warning I had heard about communists from Mother and the nuns.

"Dorothy Day and the people in the Catholic Worker use it," Terry said. "Mostly as a summer retreat. They've been kind enough to let me stay here."

Left-wing Catholics. I supposed they existed, although I'd never met any.

"It's certainly out of the way," I said. "Is that what you want?"

"Why do you ask that?"

I had come all this way. I decided to say what I really thought. "You're acting like you're in physical danger."

Terry didn't reply. I thought about pressing her, but I was afraid that would drive her deeper into silence. Then my trip would prove pointless, and I'd be no closer to unraveling any of the puzzles that surrounded Amanda Price.

"Are you Catholic?" Terry asked.

I wondered why that mattered. I waited a few seconds before saying I'd been raised as one.

"Then you understand the concept of confession," Terry said.

"If you want to confess, you should find a priest."

"You'll do." Terry paced from wall to wall, as if manic energy alone would keep her warm. "What's your biggest failing, Mr. Grimes?"

"That's hard to say. I have so many."

She didn't smile. "Mine is that I lack the courage of my convictions. I should bear witness. Shout what I know from the rooftops. Put my fate in the Lord's hands. But I can't do that. I like this world too much."

She reached into the cupboard above the stove. I expected a can of coffee or box of tea, but instead I saw a cigarette bouncing nervously between fingers that were red from the cold. Terry turned on a burner and leaned over it, then puffed. The tobacco smelled fresh and warm, with the biting appeal it has when it mixes with freezing air.

"I'll start at the beginning," Terry said.

She began working at the settlement house in 1942. The place was a last-chance stop for men whose spirits had been destroyed by booze or psychosis. It welcomed anyone who wanted to stay and charged them ten cents a night. The staff did its best to help the men, but there was so much to do. Some of the ones who'd been in the war had witnessed horrors they couldn't escape.

Terry met Amanda Price in August of '44. It was a sticky night when no one could sleep. As the hours wore on the men kept screaming out. Poor fellows couldn't stop themselves. Their demons had all those dark hours to work.

Amanda was a new volunteer. She had a soft but precise way of speaking that indicated years of finishing school and elocution lessons, as well as a reserve that conveyed a sense of inbred dignity. But on that night she and Terry were so busy they barely had time to talk. Toward the end of the shift, a big man with wild hair and eyes that went in different directions stumbled into the lobby screaming that he couldn't sleep because of the bats. He'd seen them; he knew they were there; they were flying around his head; why didn't somebody stop them?

Terry reached for the phone to summon one of the attendants, but Amanda just walked over to the man, put her hand on his arm and said it would be all right. They were going to take care of the bats.

The man started to cry. He asked if she was an angel. Amanda smiled and said she wasn't, although she thanked the man for his kind thought. She said she was just a girl who liked to help.

She showed up exactly at ten every Monday, Wednesday and Friday night. She was an excellent volunteer, with an outstanding ability to calm the troubled souls who sometimes created disturbances at the settlement. Terry began to rely on her, and thought the girl was being too modest about her own abilities. But after a few months Terry noticed changes in Amanda's demeanor. She stopped wearing makeup. Her hair became dirty and unkempt, and she began replying to requests with strange non sequiturs. Terry recalled one in particular: things were slow at the desk, so she asked Amanda to check the supply room to make sure they had enough light bulbs. Amanda responded by saying she hadn't done her Christmas cards yet.

About a week later, Amanda excused herself to go to the bathroom, but she was gone so long Terry began looking for her. After a few minutes, Terry heard what sounded like weeping coming from one of the back rooms. She cracked open the door and saw Amanda sitting on the floor, in the corner, her knees tucked under her face as if she were trying to turn her body into a ball. Her knuckles were torn and bloody. Her mouth was bloody, too.

Terry turned on the light.

Amanda shrieked a single word: "No!"

Terry said it was all right. Nothing bad was going to happen. Amanda pitched a laugh that sounded almost maniacal. Terry told her to stand up and get washed. Then they'd find a doctor. Amanda shrieked two more words: "Go away!"

"Please," Terry said. "I want to help you. Please."

"Everyone always wants to help me," Amanda said. "Why don't they help the world?"

She leaped up, grabbed Terry's shirt and clawed it with bloody hands.

"Don't let them send me back," Amanda said. Her voice was

guttural; all its gloss had been stripped, and the only thing that remained was her pain.

"Back where?" Terry asked.

"The worst place you can imagine."

Amanda collapsed. Terry placed her in as comfortable a position as she could arrange before heading back to the front desk to look for Amanda's file, which contained a number to call in case of an emergency.

Terry dialed. The phone rang a long time. Finally a gruff male voice came over the line. Terry identified herself and asked if this was Amanda Price's father. The man said he was. Terry expressed all kinds of apologies, but there was no good way to say it: Amanda had suffered some kind of a seizure. The girl was resting now, but perhaps it would be best to send her to the emergency room at Bellevue. Terry knew some of the doctors there. They were a dedicated bunch who'd take good care of her.

There was a long pause. Terry thought the line had gone dead or the voice that answered the phone hadn't heard clearly. But then Terry finally heard this question: "Where are you again?"

Terry gave the address.

"Oh God. Oh my God. What is she doing there?"

Terry said Amanda was a volunteer. A wonderful girl, really.

The man regained his composure and told her to keep Amanda comfortable. This had happened before. Somebody would be over to look after her. Above all else, everybody should remain quiet. He spoke with the authority of a man who was used to being obeyed.

About fifteen minutes later, a private ambulance stopped in front of the settlement house. A doctor, a nurse and two burly men walked in waving papers that allowed them to take Amanda away.

As the weeks passed, Terry thought about her all the time. She kept asking what had happened, but nobody had an answer.

Roughly a year later, in the late autumn of '45, Terry was working by herself at the desk while a northeaster raged outside. Nobody was coming in or out. Terry was absorbed by the crossword puzzle in *The Times*. So when the front door swept open, she looked up with both shock and surprise.

Amanda stood in the doorway. Her clothes were drenched. Her hair was matted to her scalp. Behind her the rain came down like wet curtains puddling against the ground.

The girl was shivering. Terry ran across the lobby and threw an arm around her.

"Why are you here?"

"I must tell you something," Amanda said.

"We have to get you dry."

"You must listen to me."

"I will. I promise. But you have to come with me. We have to get you out of these clothes. You'll catch pneumonia."

"I'm going to die anyway."

At first Terry dismissed these words. She had heard them many times on many nights from the men in the settlement house. Like any warnings heard over and over, they had lost all their force.

Terry led Amanda to the room just off the lobby and told her to take off her clothes. The girl just sat on the edge of the desk, unmoving and unblinking. Terry started to unbutton Amanda's blouse. It seemed like a violation, but she didn't resist. All her clothes were soaked, even her lingerie, so Terry took off Amanda's bra and panties, then wrapped a towel around her. Amanda shook so badly she seemed on the verge of convulsions. Terry noticed how emaciated she was—sticklike legs, skeletal arms with protruding elbows, shriveled breasts sinking toward her navel.

"Do you ever eat?" Terry asked.

"Why should I?"

"I'll get you something. What would you like?"

"Nothing."

"How about some soup? A nice bowl of hot soup."

"It doesn't matter. They're going to kill me."

The matter-of-factness in Amanda's voice made Terry stop. It seemed as if the girl had left her body and was watching her own slow, inexorable execution.

Terry left the room and rang the kitchen to ask for a big bowl of chicken noodle. An attendant brought it to her a few minutes later. Once he was out of sight Terry reentered the room Amanda was in.

The girl had thrown the towel to the floor and was chopping her hair with a pair of scissors.

"What are you doing?" Terry asked.

"They hate me. They all hate me."

"Nobody hates you. Put the scissors down."

"They hate me, they hate me, they hate me."

Terry placed the soup on top of a filing cabinet, and, arm outstretched, walked toward the girl. The tearing sound of clip clip clip filled the room as Amanda's red hair fell to the floor. She kept repeating, as if in a trance: "Hate me, hate me, they all hate me."

Terry stopped a foot away. She picked up the towel and tried to put it back over Amanda, who shook it off. Terry reached for the scissors. Amanda pulled them tight against her body.

"No, no, no, no. Mine, mine, mine, mine."

"Please, Amanda, give me the scissors."

"Noooooooooooooo!"

Her voice had become an otherworldly wail. Terry wondered what the girl was seeing. Her hand sought Amanda's. The scissors felt heavy. Amanda had wrapped her fingers around them. Terry yanked the scissors loose.

"Noooooooo! Noooooooooo! Noooooooooooo!"

Terry picked up the towel again and draped it around the girl's shoulders. Gradually, as if apathy were overcoming her last bits of desperate energy, Amanda's wails subsided. Terry grabbed the soup, dipped a spoon into the bowl and extended it toward the girl's mouth. At first the broth dribbled down her chin, but after a few attempts she began to accept the offering. Her cheeks gained a bit of color. She said she had always liked chicken noodle.

Terry fetched some discarded clothes from a closet. Ragged but dry, they were too big for Amanda, so Terry rolled up the sleeves and cuffs and tried to beat the dust out of them. She kept apologizing for their condition, but Amanda said she didn't mind. She was tired of the things she had. At least these clothes were honest.

Terry helped Amanda get dressed while talking gently to her, almost speaking singsong nonsense, as if the girl were a toddler who needed her hand held. Finally, when Amanda was clothed and breathing normally, Terry said, "We should get you home, dear."

Amanda began shaking again. Her face splotched red.

"Nooo. Noooo. Nooooo. Noooooo!"

"What is it?" Terry asked. "What are you afraid of?"

Their faces were inches apart. Amanda's eyes were aflame. Terry stood behind the girl and tried to massage her back and shoulders in an attempt to relax her, but it was like rubbing bone.

"Why did you come here tonight, Amanda?"

"I had to tell someone."

"Tell someone what?"

"What's going to happen."

"And what's that, dear?"

"It's all going to end."

Terry had heard words like these before, apocalyptic bursts from unwashed men with hollow eyes. But by now Amanda seemed composed, almost serene, and Terry believed the girl was trying to be lucid.

"What's going to end?"

"This place. Everything."

"What do you mean?

"There are plans. The city. Gangsters. I wasn't supposed to know, but Father..."

She stopped and put her hands over her mouth, like a child who has let a secret slip.

"What about your father?"

"He has things in mind. So do his friends."

"What do you mean?"

"But they needed money. That sweet little girl..."

Amanda put her hands over her eyes.

"What girl?" Terry asked. "What are you talking about?"

"They killed her! Why did they have to kill her?"

Terry wondered exactly what Amanda was trying to tell her. She wanted to hide her in the settlement house until she could speak coherently.

But then they both heard it: a sharp noise echoing around the lobby, as if somebody had dropped a metal pot on a tile floor.

"They're after me," Amanda said. "I know they're after me."

Terry peered into the lobby. Standing only a few feet away was the same doctor who had been at the settlement house that awful night more than a year earlier. The doctor was flanked by the same two men. The same nurse held a vial and a needle. As Terry walked toward them, she offered a silent prayer that Amanda would stay quiet and find a place to conceal herself.

"Where is she?" the doctor asked.

"Excuse me?" Terry said.

"Amanda Price. She's a sick girl. Where is she?"

Terry shook her head. "I don't understand."

It felt as if nobody in the room was breathing. It felt as if there was no air in the place at all.

The doctor pointed at the door behind Terry. "What's in there?" he asked.

"It's a storage room. With files and things. It's a mess."

"Mind if we look?"

"No. But I should get permission. I'll have to find the night supervisor."

The doctor's face turned crimson. He said they did not have time for this.

The large men flanking the doctor walked slowly around the front desk. Their eyes locked into Terry's. Finally one of them shoved her aside and put his hand on the knob.

And then they all heard a terrible hissing sound, as if a ninety-pound cat had been left behind in the room. The men were bleeding and shouting and taking the Lord's name in vain as Amanda scratched their faces and screamed:

"Noooooooooooooooooo!"

Terry stopped talking. She let another plume of smoke escape toward the ceiling. I realized I had almost stepped out of my body, as if I was hardly present in a waterside bungalow on Staten Island in the waning weeks of 1946. Instead I felt I was with them, more than twelve months earlier, at the Turtle Bay Settlement House.

"The rest is a blur," Terry said. "I wish I could recount it exactly."

"They took her away," I said.

"Yeah."

"That's the important thing."

I rubbed my hands over my face and told myself I had to focus. William Anderson's life was at stake. I had to get everything right.

"Did you ever see Amanda again?"

Terry shook her head.

"Who owns the settlement house?"

"If you find out, let me know. When I started, I asked that question a lot. I was always told 'The Foundation.' After a while, I stopped asking."

"If you don't know who owns it, then who runs it?"

"Managers come and go. Nobody pays much attention. The operation plods along in its own peculiar form of inertia."

Finding out who owned the settlement house and the property it occupied would require at least one tedious trip through the municipal bureaucracy, but I was confident I could locate the information. What I didn't know and wanted desperately to find out was this:

"Why do you suppose Amanda was back in Blood Alley that night?"

Terry stopped pacing. She stared straight at me. I had never seen anyone who looked so worn and tired, not even in the war.

"I don't know."

"Was she trying to see you?"

"Maybe. But I hadn't talked to her in more than a year."

"Was she trying to meet somebody else?"

"That could be."

"Who? For what purpose?"

Terry looked at her cigarette, which had burned down almost to its filter. "There are some things I can't tell you. Even now. I'm sorry."

"Why don't you work there anymore?"

"They know I was friendly with Amanda."

"So?"

"When you called me that night, as soon as I hung up the phone, the night supervisor was standing right over me. He hardly ever checks the front desk. There are always far more urgent crises."

"He a small fella? About five and a half feet, looks like a ghost?"

"That's the one."

"He said he never heard of you."

Terry shook her head and let a long plume of cigarette smoke rise toward the ceiling. "I must have looked awful. He asked me what happened. I should have lied. But instead I told him that Amanda was dead. He nodded, like it was something he'd been expecting to hear. And then he said: 'I guess we can all forget about her. And if you have any sense, that's exactly what you'll do.'"

"But they're not sure you will," I said.

"I decided it was best not to find out."

"They've sent goons out from there to follow me."

"It's a rough place. Some rough guys work there."

I waited a few seconds. I wanted to take the interview in a different direction. "They've charged a man with the crime," I said.

"I know. I've been reading the papers."

"I don't think he did it."

"I'm sure he didn't."

"Then who did?"

"I can't answer that."

"Because you're afraid? Or because you don't know?"

"A little of both."

I tried another tack.

"I think she met somebody named Manley at the Stork Club earlier that night."

"Is that why she was all dolled up? I was glad to read that. I hope she had at least a few good hours…"

"The name Manley doesn't mean anything to you? She never spoke about someone named Manley?"

With a casual flick of the finger, Terry's cigarette joined a mound of others in an ashtray beside the chair. She shook her head.

"How about a man named Howard Munzer?"

Terry raised the tips of her index fingers and let her chin rest on them. She looked beyond me, at the crucifix on the wall, as if she were hoping for guidance.

"That name rings a bell. Is he a lawyer?"

I nodded my head.

"You should call him."

"Why?"

"She called him an honest man. That was the highest compliment Amanda paid anyone."

"What did she talk about with him?"

"He'll have to tell you."

I suspected I had received all the information Terry felt like dispensing, and it was going to take me a long time to return to Manhattan. But I had to find out one other thing. It was trivial to the story, but it was essential to me. I tried to keep the anxiety out of my voice as I asked: "Amanda had a sister. Her name is Sylvia. Did she ever talk about her?"

Something flashed in Terry's eyes. Perhaps it was a memory of words Amanda had once said, or else an insight into my true purpose in asking the question. Maybe it was just the weak winter sunlight breaking into the room for a moment. Whatever the reason, after the flash, Terry's eyes became hooded and clouded.

"She did talk about Sylvia."

"What did she say?"

"That she had tried to save her, but she was too far gone."

I picked up the path through the tall grasses that Terry had led me through less than an hour before. Within minutes, I was standing at a bus stop, hopping a bit in an effort to warm myself. It was three in the afternoon. I figured I had plenty of time to make it back before work.

Suddenly all the air rushed out of my lungs. Something was crushing my windpipe. I gasped and flailed and felt myself being hauled into the grass. My legs left the ground. I kicked out at open air.

I had fought men hand-to-hand in the war, grappling to the death in Tuscan mud, so I remembered what to do: I lunged forward and fell to the ground. A heavy mass went over my back. I felt it land a few feet in front of me.

I sucked in wind-whipped air and tried to size up the man who had jumped me. All I could see was glare. The form in front of me sprang for my throat. I rolled away and thought to run, but my legs were still too weak. I reached for his face and knocked his head back to the ground. His fedora flew off as I wrapped my fingers around his neck. I had a flash of recognition: one of the guys who had followed me onto the 67th Street platform of the Third Avenue El.

He shoved me away. I landed on my back. A bolt of pain sliced up my spine. I assumed he had a gun, so I sprang up and wrapped my arms around him. We rolled on the ground. I gouged at his eyes, felt a savage joy as he screamed. Then I bit through his glove. Blood spurted into my mouth. He screamed again. He said I was a goddamn animal.

He did not know what I was capable of. He was unaware of the deaths I had caused in the war. I knew that combat turned men into beasts, and I felt my dark impulses sweeping aside the civilized veneer I presented to the world.

I saw the glint of a police-issue revolver. He pointed it at my face before sliding his finger over the trigger. I kicked him in the knee and bit down on his thumb. He bellowed in pain as the gun slipped from his hand. When he reached for it, I socked him in the face. He fell like a sack of stones. For a second he didn't move.

I grabbed the gun, then raised myself to my feet. The revolver felt heavy, although both my hands were wrapped around it.

"Who sent you?" My words panted out. "Who are you working for? How the fuck do you keep finding me?"

He was a couple of inches taller than I was and sturdily built, with gray hair beginning to thin. His features looked Italian, but I didn't jump to a conclusion. McCracken always told me that the news business was based on facts, not assumptions.

"Gimme the gun." It was more like a bark than a sentence.

"I asked you some questions."

"Gimme the fucking gun, you fairy."

"Why are you calling me that?"

"All McCracken's boys are fairies."

In my exhaustion, the gun felt like it weighed a hundred pounds. The wind was colder than anything that had ever rubbed against me.

"How do you know McCracken?"

"We know everything. And we know all about you."

"You don't know a thing about me."

"We knew you'd get here sooner or later. We've been watching this place. And now we're taking care of that weirdo in the bungalow."

Terry wouldn't stand a chance against hoodlums, and this guy always had a partner. I tightened my finger around the trigger.

"A nancy boy like you shouldn't be playing with guns," he said. "Give it to me."

I considered my next action. It seemed as if the world had gone mute, and I was left in absolute solitude, with nothing to distract me from my thoughts. This had happened to me only once before: in Tuscany, as I led some prisoners away from the battle line.

"Besides your partner, who knows you're here?" I asked.

He looked at me strangely, as if he'd overheard me talking to myself. Then his eyes bugged a bit as he realized the meaning behind my question. He lunged forward, but I squeezed the trigger before he reached me.

The gun jumped a bit, but I knew I was on target. The smoke scattered in seconds. I saw his fallen body sprawled at my feet. His right eye was smashed in, but there was no exit wound. The bullet must have lodged in his brain.

The wind was to my back. It had blown his blood spatter away. I opened my coat and put the gun inside. Then I bent down and grabbed him under the armpits and dragged him farther from the road. When I could see nothing except tall grass, I let the corpse rest on the ground.

I ran my hands through his coat pockets. At first I felt only lint, but way in back I touched the bulky leather of a man's wallet. I pulled it out and flipped through its contents. He was carrying close to two hundred dollars in cash and had cards for all the swank places—El Morocco, the Copacabana, Toots Shor's, the Stork Club. His driver's license gave his name as Peter Cangelosi, with an address in Brooklyn. I took the license, then gave the money to the air. I figured those bills were his wages for killing me.

I took out the revolver as I headed back toward the water. When the grass thinned I spotted the bungalows about fifty yards to the north. I crept toward them, listening for man-made sounds. I heard none. Only minutes had passed, but they seemed like weeks as I snuck up the steps to the bungalow where Terry and I had talked. When I looked in, there was no sign of a recent human presence in the room. Even the ashtray was empty. I went back out and scanned all around but saw nothing. Finally I called out Terry's name, and kept calling it, shouting into the wind even as I knew there would be no answer.

Chapter seven

I had killed a man. I told myself it was self-defense. There was no reason to feel remorse. Still I was haunted by the look in his eyes that I remembered from the war: the vacant glance bordering on terror that overcame everyone as life ebbed away.

On the ferry ride back to Manhattan, I felt colder than I had all day. I sat outside anyway because my stomach was churning. I jumped up and leaned over the side. I wanted to vomit, to expel everything bad inside me, but all I could summon were dry heaves.

I thought about going home and staying there. I could call the office and say I'd suddenly taken ill. I was sorry. I was sure I'd be better tomorrow. But my apartment offered no sanctuary, and my trip to Staten Island had left me with more questions than I'd had before. The only way I could start getting answers was by going to work.

When I walked into the newsroom I tried to keep my voice steady as I asked the copyboy to get all our clips on a guy named Peter Cangelosi. A few minutes later, a file much thicker than I expected was dropped in front of me. I put the clips inside my jacket as nonchalantly as I could while I walked toward the men's room. I was five feet from the door when I heard McCracken calling my name.

My feet felt stuck in hardening concrete. For a moment I flashed to the body I'd left in the dunes. I wanted to ask McCracken why the man I had just killed knew who he was, but an inquiry like that could lead too easily to the unraveling of everything I had done.

"You look like hell, Grimes," McCracken said as he approached me.

I told him I didn't feel so hot.

"Go home if you're sick."

I told him I'd rather stay.

"Suit yourself. Then I've got something to ask you."

For some reason I figured he'd demand the Cangelosi file. All the workers on the night side thought McCracken knew everything about everyone.

"How long are you gonna be in there?" McCracken asked, pointing to the bathroom.

I told him I wasn't sure. I really wasn't feeling well.

"Make it snappy. I've got an assignment for you."

All the stalls were empty. I chose the one farthest from the door and locked myself in. I hung my jacket on a peg, took out the file and sat on the seat. I lowered my pants in case McCracken came in to spy.

The most recent clips in Cangelosi's file were dated to the fall of 1944, when the *New York Examiner* ran a number of stories that described how the NYPD had dismissed Sergeant Peter Cangelosi after an internal investigation proved he had taken money to protect gambling dens and slot machines operating almost openly in Blood Alley. The stories implied that those outfits were controlled by Frank Costello.

I tried to make a connection. Amanda had said something about gangsters to Terry. It was possible that she had discovered something about Cangelosi and perhaps even Costello while volunteering at the settlement house.

Undoubtedly, his partner would realize that Cangelosi had gone missing. He could search the grasses near the bungalows, but that was a tough piece of real estate and it might take weeks to find the body. On the other hand, if he figured out what had happened, he just might leave the body there. Stories about Cangelosi's death could attract attention to people who wanted to keep things hidden.

The door to the bathroom blew open. McCracken called out, "Christ Almighty, Grimes, did you fall in?"

"Just a minute," I yelled back.

There were more clips, many more, but I had to stuff the pieces of yellowing paper back in their envelope and then shove the envelope deep into the inside pocket of my jacket. Before I left the stall, I made sure to flush.

"You wanna play Boy Reporter?" McCracken asked as soon as I reentered the newsroom.

"Waddya mean?" My voice sounded weak.

"I've been thinking about that nigger. The one who killed Amanda Price."

I wanted to tell McCracken that the colored guy hadn't done it. I was convinced that William Anderson was being set up to make the whole thing go away. But I didn't trust McCracken enough to tell him what I thought.

"What about him?" I asked.

"I can get you in. For a one-to-one."

I knew I sounded suspicious, but I had to ask: "Why?"

"For the same reason I do anything, Grimes: I wanna move copies of the *New York Examiner* off the newsstands. I wanna get close to the *Daily News*." He rubbed his slender fingers against my shoulder blade. "I also wanna see what you can do, my young mick friend."

He walked toward his glass cage and, I figured, his third or fourth shot of Jim Beam since his shift began. I glided toward my desk, but stopped by the copyboy just long enough to dump the Cangelosi clips in the metal tray he used as his inbox. I asked him to bring them back to the paper's morgue right away.

The next day, I took the El downtown. As we bounced past Gramercy Park I kept looking back at the Metropolitan Life Building. Its elegant top reminded me of the towers I had seen in Italy, graceful structures that soared over the carnage being wrought on the ground.

I went over the instructions McCracken had given me: I was to meet a guy named Pugliese who would take me to an out-of-the-way room where I'd talk to William Anderson. McCracken said he wanted a straightforward account of how Anderson had murdered Amanda Price. He already knew what he wanted the wood to say:

HER KILLER SPEAKS

McCracken said a byline on a story like this would make people notice. He emphasized that he didn't want any sob-sister shit.

I got out at City Hall and walked over to Centre Street. Amid all the drab buildings the city had built to house its municipal operations, the Tombs was the dreariest. It sagged, as if it were ready to ooze into the East River. As I approached I caught the stench of unwashed men. Inside, the building was a warren of dark cubbyholes. Sitting behind the front desk was a clerk who looked bored but angry. As I glanced around I saw guards slouching against the walls, their hands stroking nightsticks.

I told the clerk I was looking for a man named Pugliese. He asked if Pugliese was expecting me. I said I thought he was. The guard sighed like a worker who hated to do anything, then opened a blue-bound directory, picked up the phone and said, "Some palooka is here."

A steel door off to the side opened a minute later. The frame was filled by a guy whose neck bulged over his collar. His arms were close to bursting through his coat. His stomach jutted out a foot, and his doughy face was mottled with red splotches. He mopped his forehead with a handkerchief that looked damp with sweat. Even before he spoke, I heard his wheezing.

"You Grimes?"

I nodded. He motioned for me to follow. We walked through dingy, narrow corridors. The walls were concrete, but every few seconds we passed by a series of steel bars that let the prisoners' sounds escape. I heard the echoes of a man screaming about what he was going to do to that cunt, that bitch, that whore once he got outta this joint.

As we climbed a flight of stairs, Pugliese's wheezes grew louder. I asked how he knew McCracken. He said they met at a bar. Then he coughed in a spasm that frightened me. This guy was going to die soon.

We stopped at a grimy door that he pushed open before stepping into a room that contained a desk, two folding chairs, no windows and years' worth of dust. Pugliese told me to wait. When he left, I sat at the desk and took out my notepad. The bare walls were painted in a faded institutional green. I figured this was a forgotten office, overlooked when the organization chart was redrawn. But then I saw something on the far wall. At first I thought it was paint flaking off, but when I walked over I saw reddish brown spots that I picked at with my fingernails. I remembered where I had seen this kind of color before: in Italy, after a battle just north of the Arno, when I walked through a church the Germans had fortified. Bodies had been sprawled across the floor. Behind them were the dark stains of dried blood, splattered into the wall as if they were part of a ghastly fresco.

I was startled by footsteps in the hallway. I hurried back to the desk. Pugliese's brawny arm was wrapped around William Anderson, whose hands were cuffed. The colored man's knees kept buckling, but Pugliese's hold was strong. Anderson's eyes were puffy, almost swollen shut, and I saw scabs along his hairline. Pugliese threw him into a chair. Anderson toppled off. His head hit the floor with a crack. Pugliese kicked the chair upright, picked up Anderson and dumped him back in.

"C'mon, ya stupid nigger. Tell him what ya told us. Tell him ya did it."

Anderson nodded and closed his eyes. I sensed that keeping them open, even for a second, required more energy than he possessed.

Pugliese slammed his hand into the back of Anderson's head. The colored man fell to the floor again. The rising and falling of his chest provided the only sign he was alive.

"You talk to this guy," Pugliese shouted. "You tell him the truth. The fucking truth, you dumb nigger."

I thought I saw Anderson nod. Pugliese picked him off the floor, then wrenched Anderson's arms behind him and snapped the cuffs.

The colored man was sitting only a few feet from me. His head was tilted so far it brushed against his left shoulder. His tongue lolled listlessly against the side of his mouth.

Pugliese left the room, but I suspected he would wait only a few feet away. I imagined him pressing a fleshy ear to the keyhole, so I kept my voice as low as I could as I asked Anderson, "Do you remember me?"

An eyelid flickered. Anderson was acknowledging me for the first time since he'd been dragged into the room.

"Did you do it?" I asked.

Anderson rolled up his right eyelid all the way. A thin film of water covered his brown eye.

"What do you think?" he asked softly.

"What I think doesn't matter. Did you kill Amanda Price?"

There are times when it seems as if all the air rushes out of a room, when the temperature starts to climb and inhaling the oxygen you need becomes almost impossible. At moments like these all your senses are heightened—you can hear and see and smell everything in the world as the seconds slink by, one by one, and you wonder why you can't live your entire life with that degree of awareness.

Finally William Anderson sighed, shook his head and mouthed the word 'no'.

"Then why did you confess?"

Anderson blinked rapidly. A bit of life crept into his voice. "You remember what those cops did to me in the alley?" he asked.

I nodded. Of course I remembered.

"Compared to what happened later, they were playing patty-cake."

"Then tell me about it."

Soon after detectives arrived to examine the alley where William Anderson had discovered Amanda Price's body, Patrolmen Valentine and McMahon shoved him into the back of their squad car and started pounding him in the midsection with their sticks and fists, demanding to know why he had killed the girl. They never relented. He had no chance to respond. By the time they arrived at the stationhouse, Anderson's ribs and abdomen were so sore he felt like crying out in pain every time he breathed. After he was booked and fingerprinted, the deskbound cops took turns throwing him down the stairs.

The next thing Anderson remembered was waking up in a small room devoid of light. He lay on a thin mattress. He could see a bulb in a socket on the wall beside him. When he tried to sit up, he realized his wrists and ankles were strapped to a metal bed.

He was left there a long time. He had no idea how many hours passed, or whether it was night or day. At one point he awoke with a powerful urge to go to the bathroom. He wanted to get up, but he realized he couldn't, so he cried out, trying to get the attention of people he could not see. Nobody came in, or even answered. Finally he had to let go, and he felt his pants fill with piss and shit.

That was when he heard the door creak open. A patch of illumination slanted across the floor.

"What's that I smell?"

Anderson tried to say he was sorry. He'd held it in for as long as he could.

"I know what it smells like. I've smelled it before."

The bulb on the wall beside him glowed on. Anderson turned his head away.

"It smells like a nigger."

Looming over him was a man he estimated at more than six feet tall, with a broad chest, an ample belly and a shiny head that gleamed like glass.

"Do you know who I am?"

Anderson's mouth refused to make words. All he could do was move his head from side to side.

"I'm everything you've ever been afraid of."

Anderson heard a chair being scraped across the floor. A bulky form settled beside him.

"Why'd you do it?"

Anderson shook his head. His throat croaked. His mouth was dry. But he was able to push out the words, "I didn't."

"Didn't what?"

"The lady. It wasn't me."

And then Anderson became unaware of everything except the searing kind of pain that obliterates a man's senses. He wasn't sure at first what the man had done, but something began swelling around his mouth. It felt as if two of his teeth had come loose.

"I am a detective in the New York City Police Department," the man said. "I will not let some nigger make a fool of me."

Anderson managed to open an eye. His vision was blurry, but he could see that the man was holding a baseball bat.

Anderson tried to say that he didn't want to make a fool of anyone, but before he could talk the detective shouted: "We know what happened! We know why you had that twenty-dollar bill in your pocket! You stole it from her!"

Anderson tried to tell the man that he'd received the money from one of the fellows from the newspaper, but it did no good. The detective did not listen. He just kept on beating Anderson with the bat. It went on for a while, but the blows grew more perfunctory until the detective finally dropped the weapon to the ground.

"Christ," he said, "why does it always come to this?"

Anderson was puzzled as he heard the detective unbuckling his belt and lowering his pants. But a moment later Anderson was choking and gasping, then screaming, "Sweet Mother of Mercy," as the detective's urine and excrement smothered his face, slid off his chin, ran onto his neck and chest and arms. A few seconds later, Anderson felt soiled toilet paper being rubbed against his face.

"That's it for now," the detective said. "But I'm gonna keep coming here. Two, three times a day. Until you sign."

At that point, Anderson wanted only to be left alone. He was willing to sign anything. So he did.

When Anderson stopped talking, I tried to focus on his situation and what I could do about it. The man's life was at stake, but I felt I was going into battle with no ammunition. I could try once again to tell the police about how Anderson came into possession of a twenty-dollar bill, but my encounter with Valentine had convinced me it would be useless to tell the truth to anyone in the NYPD.

I asked Anderson if he'd seen a lawyer. He shook his head. I asked if he knew when his trial would start. He said that during one of the beatings that were regularly administered in this place, a guard had told him that before they fried his black ass, they were going to haul it into court on January 10, a Friday. They figured they'd need only a day to wrap it up. Then everyone could enjoy the weekend.

I looked into Anderson's eyes, which were clouded with the despair that descends upon people when horrible things occur for no reason. He asked what was going to happen to him. I wanted to tell him that everything was going to work out, but I knew he'd only laugh at me.

"I don't know," I said. Even to my own ears, my voice sounded like it was coming from the end of a mile-long tunnel.

I took the El back uptown. It was already night. I idly looked into the windows of the walk-ups as the train passed by. It was easy to imagine Peter Cangelosi living in a place much like one of these. On many days, right around this time, he probably walked into the kitchen while his wife stirred a big pot on the stove. He'd ask what she was making for dinner. Sauce stained the apron over her housedress.

I closed my eyes. Cangelosi's death was only the latest one I'd caused. I'd been defending myself against him, but I wondered if that excuse ever grew tiresome to the one who will judge us all. Although I no longer believed in the catechism, I suspected there would be a final accounting, and I imagined my ghost at the pearly gates, trying to explain my actions, my words increasingly hollow and unconvincing.

There were so many actions to atone for. I had not been blameless in the war. I could shift the culpability onto my superiors, but I had made my choices willingly, perhaps even enthusiastically. Now I was haunted by dead staring faces looking up at me from the Tuscan mud. Cangelosi had joined them in my mind. But if I could prove he was involved in the murder of Amanda Price and the efforts to frame William Anderson, perhaps I'd help my chances of gaining at least a small measure of absolution.

I tried to think about my interview with Anderson. Nothing he said gave me any insight into who had killed Amanda Price. And although Koenig was the detective who had beaten the confession out of the colored man, I couldn't be sure if he was crooked or merely wanted to get a high-profile murder case out of the way.

When I got to the newsroom I felt nervous. I figured McCracken would ask what I had, and I'd have to tell him it was sob-sister shit. But I was surprised by the scene I encountered. Most of the dayside staff was still around. Every phone was ringing. The place was so crowded I couldn't walk more than a few feet without bumping into someone. Dozens of reporters and editors shouted to make themselves heard. McCracken's voice carried above them all as he yelled that for just once in his life he'd like to work for a paper that wasn't caught flat-footed whenever news broke.

O'Shea sat in his usual slot in the center of the copy desk, surrounded by empty chairs that would eventually be filled by the rim rats who worked for him. His feet were up. He looked around with the frown of a newsman who knew that his night was going to be long, but not particularly exciting. Everybody else was typing away like monkeys, so I asked him what was going on.

"It's a good thing I like you," he said. His voice sounded icy. He usually didn't get this angry until we had blown deadline.

I decided to keep quiet. I knew more was coming.

"If McCracken heard you ask a question like that, on a day like this, he'd probably let off a string of nasty remarks about your ancestry."

I told O'Shea I'd been busy all day. I was working on something. O'Shea swung his feet off the desk.

"Then write it up, Grimes. This is a newspaper."

I returned to my desk and watched frenetic bursts all over the newsroom—jangling telephones and clacking typewriters, the sounds of paper being ripped up and tossed away, the cries of "Copy!" that I remembered from my days before the war, when I was the one who had to jump at the sound of that word. I breathed deeply and smelled the glue that the editors smeared on the copy paper as they tore stories apart and rearranged them to their liking. I imagined that I would grow old doing this.

From overheard snippets of conversations, I pieced together the cause of the commotion: at the last possible minute, the Rockefellers had ridden in like the cavalry, buying up eighteen acres along the East River in Turtle Bay, then donating the land to the United Nations for its new headquarters.

As I typed out the tale of my encounter with William Anderson, McCracken called my name from halfway across the room. I looked up as he asked, "Did you see that nigger this afternoon?"

"I did."

"He tell you anything worthwhile?"

"He's back to saying he didn't do it."

"Nuts!"

"He said some interesting things."

"I don't have time. Not now. There's too much going on."

"I'm sorry," I said. "But he's got a different story now."

McCracken dropped his voice to its professorial level and patted my shoulder. I almost told him to cut it out. "When you've been in this business long enough," he told me, "you'll learn how to make them say what you want them to say."

* * *

Finkel hurried across the newsroom just before deadline for the final.

"Got a good one, got a good one, got a good one."

He disappeared into McCracken's office. In a moment the light snapped on. McCracken looked intently at a picture on his desk. Then he strode toward me while waving the print.

"I think we've got something here, Grimes."

In the foreground was a man. At least I thought it was a man. It was difficult to tell because there were two bullet holes in his left temple and his face was drenched with blood. His eyes were open.

His tongue stuck out. His head leaned against the steering wheel of a car that looked like a Cadillac. His fedora was set at a rakish angle that must have been Finkel's doing. In the background, a couple of adolescent boys were smiling.

The car had been parked in front of the Turtle Bay Settlement House on East 47th Street. Finkel said a cop had told him the dead guy's name was Horwitz. That was the only thing he knew.

"Ya gonna run the pitcher? Huh? Ya gonna run it?"

"What do you say, Grimes? You think the *Daily News* will have this snap?"

"It's aces," I said. "What are we gonna do with it?"

McCracken told me to get Higgins on the phone. He'd have to ask the cops for information about the victim and the scene. McCracken chuckled, mostly to himself, as he said he doubted the Rockefellers had plunked down all that dough for the United Nations site just so gunsels would have a place to ply their trade.

I rang Higgins. No answer. I called out to McCracken, who was already huddled with Moskowitz on the other side of the newsroom. I assumed they were figuring out where the story would run.

"Higgins isn't there," I said.

McCracken's back straightened. Even from across the room, I could see his face flushing crimson. He looked like he was about to say something, but instead of speaking he hurled the grease pencil in his hand against the wall, where it made an angry red mark.

"Call the cops yourself, Grimes. See if you can find anything."

I called the precinct but the desk sergeant said he didn't know nuttin' 'bout nuttin'. I asked to talk to his supervisor and he said he was the fucking supervisor. I said we had a picture of a dead guy named Horwitz in a Cadillac parked in front of the Turtle Bay Settlement House. We were going to run it and it would look bad for the NYPD if we said the cops didn't know anything about the murder. The desk sergeant hesitated, then said they usually talked to Higgins about stuff like this. I said Higgins wasn't the only reporter in the world. The desk sergeant took my number and said somebody would get back to me.

When I hung up, McCracken was standing over my shoulder. I told him what I had, which wasn't much.

"I tried to get Higgins myself," McCracken said quietly. "No luck. I suspect he gave himself a slide tonight and didn't bother to check in with anybody."

McCracken tapped his fingers on the edge of my desk, as if he were telegraphing himself a message. I sensed he was going to keep talking, and decided against interrupting.

"I don't mind that he's a drunk mick," McCracken said. "This business would fall apart if we got rid of all the Irish alkies who work in it." Then he slammed his open palm on my desk. Everything on it hopped two inches. "What I cannot abide is an unreliable drunk mick."

My phone rang. McCracken grabbed the receiver and shoved it into my hand. When I identified myself, the voice that came back at me was deep and gruff.

"This is Detective Koenig."

I wondered what it had been like for William Anderson, alone in a room with those tones in his ears for hours.

"You wanna know about some mug named Horwitz."

"That's right. We have a picture."

"Are you sure you wanna know? These are trouble boys. They play rough."

I thought of Cangelosi, and what might happen when his fate became known.

I told Koenig I could take it. I'd seen worse in the war.

The dead man was named Irving Horwitz, nickname Chick, age thirty-eight, with a history of arrests for gambling and numbers running. I asked if there were any convictions and Koenig said yes, two, both for minor charges. The second time, Horwitz spent six months upstate.

Everyone knew who ran gambling in the city, so I asked the obvious question: did Horwitz work for Frank Costello?

Koenig said he didn't.

"Then who did he work for?"

"He made his bones with Dutch Schultz. You remember what happened to him."

Back in the thirties, the Dutchman was cut down by a chopper squad in Newark. The top gangland guys had gotten nervous when they heard he wanted to rub out Dewey back when he was a rackets buster.

"That was a long time ago," I pointed out. "What did Horwitz do after that?"

"Running his own gang. But we also hear he was tied in with Bugsy Siegel."

Siegel, too, had been connected to the Dutchman. After Schultz was killed, Siegel relocated to the West Coast, where he became the mob's man in Hollywood. I wondered why a dropper in New York would target one of Bugsy's guys. Off the top of my head, I couldn't think of a reason.

In a voice that screamed impatience, Koenig asked me if there was anything else. He was a busy man.

I was questioning the detective who had beaten William Anderson. Despite my reservations about telling the truth to the cops, I was tempted to explain why they had found a twenty-dollar bill on William Anderson. The explanation may not have proved his innocence, but it was at least exculpatory.

I thought about it a little more. Most of the cops in the city took money from Costello, and the dead guy I was calling about had been found across the street from a gambling joint. Now I had one of those epiphanies that are a staple of the movies, but rarely occur in real life: if Chick Horwitz was running the place, but he wasn't working for Costello, it was more than likely that one of Costello's underlings had rubbed him out. And the NYPD would be more than happy to look the other way. In fact, the one thing that would set off alarms through the vast underworld that actually ran New York was a lot of questions from a tabloid newshawk who wasn't in on the game.

I decided to play another angle.

"The timing's kinda strange, don'tcha think?" I asked.

I heard Koenig bristling. "Waddya mean?"

"This guy's found dead in Turtle Bay the day the Rockefellers donate all that land to the United Nations. It's almost like somebody's trying to send a message."

"It's nothing like that, son," Koenig said. "The two events have nothing to do with each other."

"How can you be so sure?"

"You some kind of wiseass?"

His vehemence surprised me. I thought my question was legitimate.

"I'll tell you why I'm sure, you punk," Koenig said. "Because it's my fucking job to know these things."

And then I heard him hang up.

It was later than I wanted. As I left the building I thought I'd head toward Third and ride the El home. But after a couple of steps I felt familiar bony fingers on my shoulder. My night was a long way from being over.

"And just where are you going, my young mick friend?"

"Bed."

"You got a girl lined up?"

"I was gonna go to sleep. Alone."

"Then you have no excuse. Your next stop is Lunney's."

McCracken clapped his hand on my back. Flakes of snow and city grit swirled under the streetlamps. In a gesture to the Christmas season, a shrub with a scrawny string of red and green lights was leaning to the right in the bar's window. McCracken and I sat on wobbly barstools covered with torn green vinyl. The bartender put a tall glass in front of my boss and filled it with a few pieces of ice and a long pull of bourbon before spritzing it with water. Then he pointed at me. I asked for a Rheingold.

"For God's sake, Grimes, in a place like this you're supposed to *drink*," McCracken said as he tilted his head and knocked back half his bourbon.

I said I liked beer. The bartender put a mug in front of me.

McCracken said his young friend would have some Jameson's as well.

"Everybody who works for newspapers is a nut job," McCracken said as the barkeep set up a shot glass in front of me. "I've known hundreds of people over the years. Maybe thousands. And all of them—every single one—has had some kind of problem that explains why they went into a line of work that would drive Carrie Nation into the arms of my good friend Jim Beam. So what is it with you?"

I sipped my beer. I told him he should guess.

"You drink, but you're not a drunk. You don't like boys, but you don't seem like a pussy hound. I heard you had a rough war, but there's gotta be more to it than that."

McCracken wanted something from me. But I wasn't giving up my secrets. I had yet to reach that point.

"I'm just a guy," I said. "I like the work."

"You are a bit antisocial."

"You might be right."

"Now I get it. You don't like dealing with people too much, do you?"

For the first time since we entered the bar, I turned toward him. "That's why my deal now is so good. On rewrite, I don't spend much time talking to the public."

"Can't say I blame you for feeling that way," McCracken said as he knocked back the other half of his bourbon. He pointed at my tumbler and asked, "Are you gonna drink that hootch or just admire it all night?"

I held the shot glass as if it contained something rancid. I closed my eyes and almost gagged as it snaked down my throat. It settled in my stomach, where it burned like a low flame. I gulped some beer to erase both the taste and the image of my father that Jameson's always produced.

"He'll have another," McCracken said to the bartender, who put a shot in front of me before I even put my beer glass down.

"What do you think of cops?" McCracken asked me. "New York's Finest. The best police force money can buy."

"Assholes," I said, thinking of Koenig.

McCracken nodded as he drank some more bourbon. "They spend twenty years on the public teat," he said, "with all the graft they can get, plus the kind of pension we mere mortals will never see, and they still think they're doing us a favor by showing up for work every day."

I took a few more sips of beer. I sensed McCracken was coming to a point, and wondered what it was.

"I'm thinking of making you a legman, Grimes."

I turned to him in surprise.

"I want you to cover cops. On the night shift. You'll be working the same hours, but you'll be in the pressroom in Police Headquarters instead of the office."

"That's Higgins's beat," I said.

"Not if I say it isn't." McCracken finished his bourbon. The bartender appeared with a refill as soon as his empty glass touched the counter. "Tonight was the straw that broke this camel's hump. I will tolerate just about anything, Grimes: drinking to excess, gambling away church money, getting caught in bed with a live man or a dead woman." He looked at me out of the corner of his eye, which was alive with a dark kind of mirth. "I'll even tolerate nigger-loving Yankees." Then he slammed his drink on the bar. "The one thing I will not tolerate is laziness. That loafing sonuvabitch gets beat on too many stories."

"It's hard to see how this is a promotion," I said. "Rewrite is usually a step up from being a legman."

McCracken shook his head. "This is the top beat at the paper. Higgins can't find his dick without directions, and he gets the wood half the time. On top of that, his stories are bylined. Unlike most of yours, my young mick friend."

"Did you give me a byline on that story about William Anderson?"

McCracken's face darkened. "I had the copy desk chop it in half and ran it in next to an ad for the Automat on page thirty-three. No, I did not give you a goddamn byline."

"Just because he wouldn't say what you wanted him to."

McCracken smiled. He seemed bemused by the way our drinking session was going. "I like your moxie, Grimes. A guy with your kind of drive will get the wood almost every day. You'll be noticed all over the city. Okay, you did come up short talking to Willie Anderson this afternoon. But at least you tried. And you came back nice with the dead kike in the Cadillac."

I thought back to the image of Chick Horwitz, awash in his own blood outside the settlement house. I kept trying to make a connection between his death and the announcement about the United Nations.

"Something's going on in that mick brain of yours," McCracken said. "Better let it out, Grimes."

"That guy Horwitz," I said. "Why'd they leave him in Turtle Bay?"

"It's a good place for it," McCracken said. "The place is a dump."

"Then why are the Rockefellers buying all that land and donating it?"

McCracken hung his head, as if I were a bright student who was having trouble learning an obvious lesson. "Money will take care of all the problems in Blood Alley," he said. "Money solves everything."

"But Blood Alley's been awful since forever."

McCracken drummed his fingers on the bar, a sure sign of impatience. "Remember what Midtown looked like before Rockefeller Center?" he asked.

I tried to recall. I was just a kid. "Vaguely," I said.

"Let me remind you. Then as now, Fifth Avenue was the grandest street in America, if not the world. Sixth Avenue, on the other hand, was a slum lined with brothels and speakeasies." He bit his lower lip. For a second I thought his eyes misted over. "God, I miss those days."

Now it was my turn to sound impatient. "What's your point?" I asked.

"The Rockefellers spent a ton of money," he said. "They got

the Sixth Avenue El knocked down. Now the area is beautiful, and all the property in it is worth umpteen times more than it was just fifteen years ago." McCracken swallowed some more bourbon. I had the feeling it was helping him think. "The Rockefellers' money will change Blood Alley, Grimes. Probably quicker than you think."

I tried to shoehorn what McCracken had told me into what I knew, but figuring out real estate angles was several levels above my ability to make sense of financial shenanigans. Still, from somewhere deep in my mind I remembered that the Rockefellers had purchased their Midtown tract from Columbia University, and some officials there later regretted not hanging on to some of the land as it soared in value.

"Let's return to the topic of money, Grimes," McCracken said to me. Our eyes were directly level. I had the feeling he was trying to look past them, down into the darkest part of me, where I kept my worst secret. Every once in a while I felt it bubbling up, but I always managed to put it back in a box I wanted to keep locked forever.

"If you take Higgins's job," McCracken said, "I'll make sure your probation period ends early, and I'll steer an extra ten bucks a week your way."

I squirmed on the stool. A warm tingle ran up my back as I told him I was interested.

"But there is a problem," McCracken said.

I leaned toward him.

"Trust," he said. He put his hand on my shoulder and pressed his mouth against my ear. "I need to trust you."

I could smell the bourbon on his breath, could feel the stubble of a cheek that hadn't been shaved since morning. The touch gave me the creeps, so I pulled my head back, reached for the bar and grabbed the tumbler of Jameson. I drank it in one gulp. This time the fire in my throat was duller. Everything in Lunney's began to get blurry.

"I want you to tell me something," McCracken said. "I want you to tell me something about yourself nobody knows."

I motioned to the barkeep. My brain felt loopy. "I don't like Jameson," I said.

"That's not good enough."

I wrapped my fingers around the shot glass and poured booze into my mouth. Then I picked up my beer and took a few swigs and mumbled into my glass. McCracken leaned even closer to me.

"I didn't catch that, Grimes."

I turned to him and shouted: "I hated my mother. I'm glad she's dead."

McCracken arched his back, as if the force of my words had almost blown him off his stool. Then he shook his head.

"That's not good enough, either. Lots of boys hate their mamas."

I finished my beer and yelled to the barkeep that I wanted another round. For a second I considered turning the question on McCracken and saying something like:

Yesterday I killed a guy. His name was Cangelosi. He was a crooked cop until he got bounced off the force. He mentioned your name. He seemed to know who you were. So why should I trust you?

My mind didn't stop with Cangelosi. It kept racing all the way back to the moment I began being wary of people who demanded trust. Late one night, when I was a seven-year-old boy having trouble falling asleep, I stood at the living room window staring at the street, when my dad walked in from the hall that led to the room he shared with Mother. He seemed surprised to see me. I could smell the Jameson on his breath. I wondered where he had gotten it. He patted me on the head. I asked where he was going. He said he needed a bit of air. I must have looked at him dubiously because he leaned close to me and said, in his grand way with a hint of a brogue that implied the pot of gold was just a bit out of reach, "Don't you trust your father?"

Then he slipped into the darkness and out of my life.

"She drove him out," I said.

"You're babbling, Grimes. If you're gonna survive in the news business, you've gotta hold your liquor."

I held up the shot glass, which was full again. "My dad drank this stuff. Gallons of it. That's why I avoid it."

McCracken nodded approvingly. "He was a drunk."

I downed the Jameson. It didn't bother me anymore. "Now you sound like Mother." The booze had eroded the defenses I had built, stone by stone, over the years. I felt a wave of blind anger rising. This time I rammed the glass on the bar so hard it shattered. Blood spurted from my hand. McCracken yelled, "Jesus Christ!" The barkeep hurried over and wrapped my hand in a dishtowel to stanch the bleeding. I kept shouting through it all, like a man who had finally let Lucifer seize control of his soul.

"She hated all of us. Me and my sister and Dad. She kept telling us how worthless we were and how we were all gonna rot in hell, but she saved most of it for Dad. Lord knows what she said to him when we weren't there. And finally he had enough. He just walked out. For a long time I hated him for doing it, but finally I understood. And when I got my draft notice, I was happy—I was the only happy draftee in the United States of America—because it meant I could get away from her. And she said—"

Here I adopted the soft brogue she used, and I was surprised at how much I sounded like her.

"'You can't go, Patrick. It'll be the death of me.' And I looked at her as I left that apartment. I had my duffel bag slung over my shoulder. She was crying. It was the only time in my life I'd seen her cry. And I said, and I meant it with every fiber of my being, 'I don't care.'"

I reached for the Rheingold with my free hand and drained it. I felt McCracken and the barkeep both looking at me, but I refused to make eye contact. I kept staring ahead, at the hundreds of bottles lined behind the bar. I wanted to drink them all.

Chapter eight

I eyed the phone a long time. I was afraid of how she'd respond. She lived less than two miles away, but the distance between us seemed infinite. My hand shook as I dialed a number I had committed to memory. I heard ring after ring. I imagined the sound reverberating through splendid rooms.

Then came the voice I wanted, slightly out of breath but confident of life's possibilities, a voice filled with cigarette smoke and champagne. It was the voice of a girl who knew she would never be lonely, because all her hellos were given to people who wanted her company.

"Miss Price?"

"Yes?"

"It's Patrick Grimes. From the *Examiner*."

A pause. The world had stopped. I needed to tell myself to breathe. My worst fear was about to be confirmed: she didn't remember me. I'd describe who I was and how we'd met and she'd have no recollection whatsoever.

"How *are* you?!" she exclaimed with theatrical exuberance.

I tried to put confidence back in my words. "I'm fine, Miss Price. How are you?"

"I've been meaning to call you. I'm dreadfully sorry. I've been so busy. I wanted to warn you about Jeff Manley."

Manley. A friend of the Prices. Perhaps he'd been at the Stork Club with Amanda the night she died.

"Is he armed and dangerous?" I asked.

"It's a dead end, copper," she said, mimicking Barbara Stanwyck. "He's been in Florida since October. That friend of mine saw one of his cousins. He isn't named Manley at all, although they do bear a strong resemblance."

"Must be the inbreeding," I said.

"I'll do you a favor, Patrick Grimes, and ignore that remark. Why did you call me?"

"To be honest—"

"I hate honesty. Try deception. It's much more civilized."

I told her I wanted to ask a favor, but I didn't feel comfortable doing it over the phone. I said I'd like to ask her in person if we could arrange a place and a time. It would take only a few minutes.

As soon as I sat at my desk that night I motioned toward the copyboy and asked for our clips on Detective Walter Koenig. Then I did my best to avoid making eye contact with McCracken. Because of my outburst the night before, I was convinced he was going to rescind his offer to make me a legman. Since I was still on probation, he had the power to kick me out of the newsroom and into the street.

I told myself I'd just have to do my job better. All my life I'd been told that succeeding through hard work was the American way. Everything would be fine if I cracked open a big story.

In a few minutes the copyboy dumped a thick file in front of me. As I thumbed through the articles, I ascertained that Walter Koenig had received numerous citations for outstanding service. I couldn't figure out why we wasted space detailing all of them until I realized that Higgins must have insisted they get into print. That way he could keep the detective primed as a source.

Several articles from the fall of 1942 made me stop. They concerned a crime I had forgotten: the kidnapping and murder of a three-year-old girl named Lara Van Duzer. A Blood Alley vagrant named Anthony Mancini had confessed to it. When I found out he had been arrested by Patrolman Peter Cangelosi, I began to read more intently.

According to the stories, one day in August of that year Mancini broke into the Van Duzers' town house near Gramercy Park with the intention of robbing it. But when he saw the girl walking in the hall, apparently having trouble getting to sleep, he ripped a page from a notebook and scrawled a ransom demand. Clamping his hand over the girl's mouth, he started to drag her away. As he took her down the stairs to the ground floor, the girl wriggled free, fell down the rest of the steps and broke her neck.

Anthony Mancini gathered Lara in his arms, took her to the East River and threw her in. When the Van Duzers contacted him, he said in his confession, he was tempted to tell them the truth. But the temptation of money proved greater. They lived in such a nice place.

Mancini demanded a hundred thousand dollars. The note told the Van Duzers that their daughter would be killed if the police and press were notified.

By indirect communication—crumpled pages dropped in telephone booths, blinds open and drawn at prearranged times, cryptic classifieds in the *Examiner*—the Van Duzers told the kidnapper they were trying to raise the funds.

Although they tried to keep up pretenses by summering in Newport, the Van Duzers were not as wealthy as the kidnapper assumed. It was an old money family, but from my reading I sensed that in this generation, the bills had come due.

It took the Van Duzers a fortnight to collect the ransom. They left a suitcase full of cash in a garbage can near Blood Alley. They were told that Lara would be delivered to their doorstep within an hour.

They waited. They waited past midnight and stayed awake until the sun crept up, and still they waited, the hours sliding by and their hopes crumbling. When they realized that their daughter was not coming home, that their money was gone and most likely she was, too, they finally contacted the police.

There were questions, of course, many of them raised in the press once the case went public: How did the kidnapper get into the house? Weren't the doors locked? Why wasn't anybody inside awakened or disturbed? Why were there no signs of a struggle as Lara Van Duzer was abducted?

And then came a break: the suitcase was found. Patrolman Peter Cangelosi, walking on foot near Blood Alley, noticed a sleeping derelict whose head was resting on an expensive piece of luggage. The cop took in the bum, name of Anthony Mancini, for questioning.

At first he denied knowing anything; he had never heard of Lara Van Duzer and he had no idea what the police were talking about. But after the Van Duzers identified the suitcase as theirs, the police checked out Mancini's room in a flophouse in Blood Alley. Two thousand dollars in small bills were hidden around, and Mancini confessed to Detective Walter Koenig, who was hailed in an editorial in the *Examiner* as a savior and protector of the City of New York.

At his trial, Mancini said that Koenig had coerced his confession. The vagrant also claimed that the money had been planted in his room. But the jurors convicted him after the judge told them they could not disregard his confession. So Anthony Mancini died in the electric chair at Sing Sing on April 28, 1944. The *Examiner*'s story noted that Koenig was a witness to the execution.

As I waited for Sylvia outside the Central Park Zoo I thought about all the times I went to the place when I was a kid. I rarely had the money for admission, so I'd try to catch glimpses of the animals as I hung around the entrance. The balloon men would ask if I wanted anything, anything at all—c'mon, kid, it's only a penny, how 'bout helpin' me out here—but I always shook my head and said no. If they were insistent I'd tell them to stop bothering me.

Sometimes I'd see Al Smith walking from his building on the other side of Fifth, cigar clenched in his mouth and bowler clamped to his head. He'd stride with purpose through the gate while the workers called out a welcome to the hale fellow they still called Governor.

Smith was dead now. So much of that world was dead.

I stuck my hands in my pockets. A cold wind whipped into my face so I turned a 180, but the East Side buildings snapped the air back. The guys with balloons were still there. So was a vendor selling peanuts, popcorn and pretzels from a cart that looked like a Good Humor man's. I figured that during the summer he sold ice cream, but it was hard to imagine it would ever get warm again.

"You have a devilish streak, Patrick Grimes. Suggesting this place."

Sylvia's voice was breathless and carefree. I turned to face her. The flush in her cheeks was deeper than rouge. I could smell a perfume that was scented with roses. Her full-length mink caused my jaw to swing open a bit.

"What do you mean, Miss Price?"

"The last time I was here, it was in all the newspapers. Especially yours."

I told her that I recalled an article about a couple of sheep finding themselves suddenly free and deciding to head for the Plaza. "That's pretty smart for sheep," I said.

Sylvia laughed and touched my wrist. Her fingers felt as if they were wrapped in ermine.

"I should be angry. But I find you amusing."

"I was going to suggest a walk through the zoo, but if the animals see that coat, they might get upset."

Sylvia flashed a look that lasted only a second, but in her eyes I saw something harder and more streetwise than a girl who'd been to finishing school should possess. Then she must have remembered that ladies of her station did not look at anyone that way. Her eyes reacquired their sheen of civility.

"Do you like art, Patrick Grimes?"

"Sometimes."

"We'll go to a place I like. I want to see your reaction."

As we turned south, the wind calmed down—for her, I supposed.

"I've been talking to people about your sister," I said. "I've learned about her…" My voice trailed off. The right word was elusive. I finally came up with "troubles."

Sylvia frowned, but I couldn't tell if she was upset or merely annoyed. "Then you know more than I do. We weren't close."

"Why was that?"

"I thought you wanted a favor, not an interview."

There was so much I wanted to know. I wanted to find out where Amanda had been institutionalized and what had happened there. I wanted to describe what she had said about Blood Alley and ask Sylvia if this made any sense to her. Above all, I wanted to know why Amanda's murder seemed to have had so little effect on the people who should have cared the most.

"Fair enough," I said. "I'm gonna be straight with you."

Sylvia Price was walking neither quickly nor slowly, but with the perfectly measured gait of a girl who had been taught never to rush or dawdle.

"I have to get into the Stork Club."

"Why?"

"I'm a newspaperman. I have to ask questions."

I told myself that I had to save William Anderson. I couldn't walk away from this story. It felt as if my soul was at stake.

"Why don't you just go there and present yourself and traipse inside?"

"Come on, Miss Price, they'd never let me in."

Cold mirth filled her eyes. She brought her fingers to her mouth, as if to choke off her reaction, before saying, "You're right. They wouldn't."

"But you go there all the time."

"Three times a week," she said in a la-de-da way. "Sometimes four. Occasionally five."

"You can get me in."

"How? I can't write you a pass. This isn't the Army, Patrick Grimes."

"You'll go the Stork Club as usual, and I'll escort you."

This time Sylvia couldn't contain herself; she threw back her head and laughed so loudly the few people strolling along Fifth slowed down. We must have made an incongruous sight, the man in the battered cloth overcoat with the girl in the mink.

"I'm serious, Miss Price. It's the only way I can get in."

"Out of the question," she said as if she were dismissing a servant's request for a raise. "I'm engaged to be married. Word would get around if I showed up with another man."

I was tempted to say that scruples like that had never stopped her before.

"Take your fiancé if you like. I don't care. Tell everyone I'm your cousin from Milwaukee and you're showing me the town."

She adopted a tone of mock grievance. "I don't know anyone from Milwaukee and wouldn't admit it if I did."

We turned west on 57th. The wind picked up again on the wide street. I found myself raising my voice.

"Then say I'm from Boston. Or San Francisco. Someplace that appeals to you."

"I adore San Francisco."

For years I had tried to wean myself from the habit of pleading—to the Almighty for mercy, to the priests for absolution, to the nuns for relief and to Mother for understanding. But now, as Sylvia Price smiled condescendingly, I could think of no other way to behave.

"Please, Miss Price. At least think it over."

We stopped in front of a nondescript building five stories high. Sylvia looked up at the top floors and put her hand to her chin in the classic manner of a woman trying to think about something that mattered deeply to her.

"While I think it over," she said, "we'll go in here."

"Why?"

"Because I want to shock you."

We rode to the fourth floor in a gleaming brass elevator that opened into a gallery named Art of This Century. A man in a faded sweater cried out, "Sylvia!" and rushed forward to kiss her on both cheeks.

I found myself staring at concave walls the color of the ocean.

Over our heads were objects that hung in defiance of gravity. Sculptures of twisted metal reminded me of the wreckage I had seen in the war, but what captured my eye was a series of large canvases filled with lines and curves and splashes, explosions of color, as if the artist made no effort to control what he was doing.

Sylvia was engaging me in some kind of test. Whatever this exam was, it was vitally important that I pass it.

She pointed to the paintings and asked if I liked them. When I said that I did, she asked why. I thought for a second and replied, "Because they look the way I feel."

"Father hates all of it," she said. "He calls it trash. Father's disapproval of anything makes me embrace it."

I was standing next to a girl I'd been thinking about for weeks. My heart was pounding so loudly I was sure she could hear it. In as disinterested a tone as I could muster, I asked her how she had met Stavros.

I sensed her looking at me. I kept my eyes on the paintings.

"That's a curious question," she said.

"I'm a curious man."

She turned her gaze upward. I sensed her lips twisting into a pout.

"I could shock you again. Shock you to the core of your being."

"Go ahead."

"I was gambling. In a place on 47th Street. Near the East River."

I was on the verge of blurting out that I knew the place she was talking about and she'd better tell me all about it, but I decided it was too early in the game to play that particular card.

"Imagine that," Sylvia said. "Engaged in an illegal activity. What's more, I was by myself. An unescorted woman in a den of sin and vice. Do I shock you now?"

"Were you drinking?"

"Of course."

"So then what happened? You saw Stavros at the roulette wheel and your heart fluttered?"

"Now you sound cynical."

"I'm not cynical. I'm realistic."

"It's a fine line."

The man in the faded sweater waved at the painting that was closest to us. His hair was long and lank on top. He kept brushing it out of his eyes. "Jackson's latest," he said. "What do you think?"

Sylvia said she loved it. She was tempted to purchase it even though Father would probably hurl it out the window.

"And what do you think?"

He was addressing me, although I had the feeling Sylvia was somehow pulling his strings.

"It's good," I said. "Who's it by?"

"His name is Pollock. Have you heard of him?"

I shook my head.

"Do you know anything at all about art?"

"I saw a lot in Italy, during the war."

"I spent a lot of time in Italy. Before the war."

He sounded like a guy who was determined to prove he knew more than you did. I looked at him and said, as matter-of-factly as I could, "We bombed everything you'd recognize to smithereens. Sorry."

He looked at me in a way that made me shiver. For the first time in my life, I was aware of being the object of a man's desire. He turned to Sylvia.

"You've been holding out on me. Who is this fellow you dragged in here?"

Sylvia smiled at him and then at me. I sensed she was thinking hard and fast, finally reaching a decision about my request.

"This is my Cousin Matthew," she said. "From Portland, Oregon."

The man extended his hand, which was soft and clammy. He asked if this was my first time in New York. I said it was. He asked how I liked it. I said it was swell. Then he turned to Sylvia and asked if she had any plans for me.

"As a matter of fact, I do."

"Please tell."

"Before he goes back where he belongs, I'm going to take him to the Stork Club."

Sylvia and I looked at a few more artworks and made arrangements to go to the Stork Club the following Monday. As soon as we left the gallery, she said "Too-de-loo" and hurried off to an engagement at the Oak Room. I had time to spare, so I walked down Fifth. Traffic crawled both ways. Boxy DeSotos and LaSalles were trailed by even more gigantic buses. It was impossible to see to the other side of the avenue. Traffic cops' whistles cut above all the other noise. Around me, well-dressed women in heels and hats toted shopping bags past the most expensive stores in the city.

I stopped on 51st. I remembered halting at the same spot with my father a long time ago. I had pointed at the spires atop St. Patrick's and asked him why they were so tall. My dad lifted me with big rough hands. He put me on his shoulders. He told me they built the cathedral so high because they wanted to make it easy for the Almighty to reach down and touch His people.

My gaze dropped back to the street. I was not blessed with faith but cursed by skepticism, and I suspected that everything I'd ever heard about God's love was a lie. I did, however, retain great respect for His wrath.

I tried to remember when my belief was destroyed. But I could not pinpoint the moment. Was it in Italy, the first time I shot a man? Perhaps it had occurred in training, when I did not object to the idea of killing for my country. Or did it happen earlier, far earlier, during one of Mother's random acts of cruelty? Sometimes they blurred together in my mind, but the overwhelming feeling I had during those hours was wishing that this woman and her God would go away forever.

Opening the heavy oak door to St. Patrick's required all my strength. Inside, the space was smaller than my memory. A hush filled the air as the faithful ebbed toward the altar and back.

I joined the line for the confessional, bowed my head and tried to formulate a prayer. Nothing came. So I recalled the words that rushed out of me when I was a boy who slipped through the heavy purple curtain and found the kneeler in the darkest place in the world, so dark it must have resembled the worst part of my soul:

"Bless me Father, for I have sinned, it has been many years since my last confession."

An old woman clutching a rosary tripped over the bottom of the curtain as she left the booth. She steadied herself before shuffling toward the altar.

I had committed so many sins I couldn't remember them all. I had lied and taken the Lord's name in vain. I coveted a woman who belonged to another man. I had not kept the Lord's day holy, had dishonored my father and mother. Worst of all, I had killed men, lots of them, and some deep pit in my character responded to my actions with rationalizations instead of remorse. I needed forgiveness for these sins, but particularly for that one incident I could not shake, the act that seemed like the crux of my life. It had happened in Tuscany, when I stared into a bunch of dead eyes and understood just how depraved human beings could be.

I was at the head of the line. My breath came in quick and shallow bursts. Then the curtain fluttered. A heavyset woman lumbered out. My feet carried me across the floor. I hesitated a second before putting my hand on the soft velvet and pushing it to the right.

It was black inside. I stuck out my hand and felt the contours of my surroundings. My toes brushed against the kneeler. I discerned the partition that separated penitent from priest, lowered myself to my knees and clasped my hands in front of me. I heard the murmuring of a heavy male voice punctuated by the sounds of a woman who was farther away. A moment later, the priest shifted his weight. The panel slid open. I saw the profile of a well-fed man, jowls dangling, stubby fingers holding up his chin.

I was supposed to say the words. I opened my mouth. Nothing came out. I croaked and coughed and tried to speak again. A guttural sound came from my throat.

The priest asked what was wrong.

I almost told him that I no longer had faith in these rituals.

I did not believe that saying a few words to a man I could not see clearly would absolve me from the consequences of all the terrible acts I had committed.

I raised myself. I felt for the curtain. Light came into the confessional as I walked out.

McCracken handed me an assignment as soon as I got to work that night. The story concerned a soup kitchen on the Bowery that was on the verge of closing. In the early forties the place had been underwritten by a wealthy young man, but he had died in the war. Nobody stepped forward to take his spot. The kitchen was almost out of money, and the people who ran it were unsure how they'd feed the poor souls who came in during the holidays. Just when it appeared that the place would have to close, a miracle occurred: a check arrived in the mail for ten thousand dollars. The donor was anonymous, but he or she said the money was in memory of the young man who once funded the kitchen.

The story was sob-sister shit. I told McCracken I was surprised he wanted it.

"I don't," McCracken said. "The publisher does. Eleven months out of the year, he's a proper newspaperman, with a healthy respect for blood and sex. But at Christmastime, he wants us to run a heart-warming piece of crap every day."

McCracken stood over me, rocking on his heels. I smelled mouthwash masking bourbon. He put his hand on my shoulder as I typed.

"Get the name of the original benefactor in the lead," he told me. "Names make news, Grimes. I've told you that a thousand times, and one of these days it'll get through that thick Irish skull of yours. Have you checked the clips on this fella?"

I shook my head.

"It rings a bell with me. See if we have anything on him before you send the story to the desk. For all we know, he was a goddamn hero."

The benefactor's name was Donald Wetherby. His file was

placed in front of me a few minutes later. I put my feet up and started to thumb through his life. Since I wasn't sure what I was looking for, I picked out stories at random. Wetherby had been a young man on the make, a goo-goo type, active on the charity circuit, law review at Columbia, fervent internationalist in the days of America First. In his pictures he looked blandly handsome, with slick dark hair and lips perpetually poised in an embryonic smile. Several stories noted that leaders of the Republican Party had sounded him out about entering politics. He said he was honored by the attention, but any such plans would have to wait until after the war.

He became a bomber pilot and flew nineteen missions, winning the Distinguished Flying Cross for leading raids against ball-bearing plants in the Ruhr. His commanders praised him as a fine pilot, and the men in his crew said he was the best Army Air Force officer in England. But in September 1944 his B-17 was lost over the Channel during a storm. The plane was never recovered, his body never found.

That changed my angle. I rolled the copy paper out of my typewriter, crumpled the sheets softly and let them drop into the wastebasket before putting in two blank pieces. When I was almost done, I went back to the clips because I couldn't recall if it was Thomas Dewey or Wendell Willkie who had encouraged Wetherby to go into politics. I pawed through the pieces of yellowing paper strewn across my desk, tossing aside the pictures of Wetherby, but my subconscious must have made a connection, because I picked up one of the photos again. I examined it more carefully. Taken in February 1943, it showed Wetherby, in uniform, shaking hands at a war bond rally. He seemed to be the center of attention; the men and women on the podium all looked at him as if he were their hope for a better tomorrow.

Off to the side stood a thin girl with hair that looked reddish even in the black-and-white of the newspaper page. I would have sworn that he was looking at her, and that the spark in his eyes bespoke a desire greater than love of country. She seemed to be glancing shyly at him, an unaccustomed smile on her face, as if good fortune had finally visited her and she didn't know how to receive it.

At least twenty other people were in the photo, and the caption did not identify her, so there had been no reason to put the picture in her file. But I recognized Amanda Price right away.

It was a coincidence, but in the news business it was far from unusual to find an unexpected connection between one story and another. This discovery gave me a chance to contemplate the timeline of the abbreviated lives of Donald Wetherby and Amanda Price. If my hunch about their relationship was correct, after he went missing in September 1944, all her subsequent troubles had an explanation.

As I leafed through the *Examiner* the next morning, perched on the edge of the Murphy bed in my apartment, I noted a small story about Robert Moses's plans to use the United Nations deal to clear out Blood Alley. He announced he would use eminent domain to level the slaughterhouses, breweries, tenements and flophouses that blighted the area. Nothing could stop him. By the time the architects and builders and workers were done, the East River waterfront would sparkle and glimmer. Turtle Bay would be rejuvenated, just as Midtown had been by Rockefeller Center.

In the article's last paragraph, a lawyer for some people who lived in a tenement on 46th said he was going to seek an injunction to prevent his clients' eviction. The lawyer's name was Howard Munzer.

I had found his name in Amanda Price's purse. Terry had told me to call him. I hadn't because I was afraid he'd give me the brush-off unless I knew exactly why Amanda had held on to his business card. But now, even though I was discovering many things about her, I was having trouble connecting the information. So I decided to force the issue and call him.

He picked up on the third ring. A man who answered his own phone. I identified myself as a reporter for the *Examiner.* Munzer said he was always happy to talk to the boys in the press. "I filed the motion this morning," he told me. "Unlike a lot of people in New York, I'm not afraid of Robert Moses."

"That's not why I'm calling." I sensed a wire fence of caution going up around Howard Munzer. Everyone who talks regularly to newsmen is caught off guard if his dealings don't go exactly as planned. "Actually, I want to ask you a few questions about Amanda Price."

His voice dropped. "Why are you calling me?"

"I found your business card at the scene of her death."

"Oh." It was a simple word, but the way he conveyed it suggested I knew something that he preferred to keep quiet.

"Why did she have it?" I asked.

He sighed. "I dealt with her on a case."

"What was it about?"

"I'm not at liberty to say."

"Was it about the settlement house?"

"I can't tell you." He sounded more nervous with every word.

"There's a gambling joint across the street. Did you know that?"

"There's gambling all over the city, Mr. Grimes."

"Did Amanda know anything about it?"

"I have no idea."

"There's a lot of gambling in Blood Alley, isn't there?"

Howard Munzer sucked in a lungful of air. "That assertion is not incorrect."

He was a man who brushed all his words clean before letting them out. I needed to get past his legalisms. I raised my volume and quickened my pace as I barked into the phone: "You have to help me, Mr. Munzer. A man has been charged with killing her. His life is at stake. I—"

"I read the newspapers, Mr. Grimes. I know what's going on. I'm sorry, but I can't tell you anything more. In fact, I've probably told you too much."

I had never met Howard Munzer, but my anger at him was rising. He knew the truth, or at least part of it, and he was keeping it to himself. "You haven't told me anything. Just cryptic bits of—"

"I've said everything I intend to say, Mr. Grimes." His voice had regained a measure of balance. His tone was steadier than mine. "If you call me again, I'll take some form of action."

"But—"

"I'll file charges. I'll have a judicial order put out directing you to stop. I'll complain to your superiors. You'll wind up out of work, possibly in jail."

He stopped. I had the sense of utter defeat I thought only my mother could inflict upon me.

"Do you understand what I'm saying?" Munzer asked.

At work that night I knocked on the door to McCracken's office just as he reached into his bottom desk drawer. Without looking up he asked, "What is it, Grimes?"

I wondered how he knew it was me. Sometimes I felt he could see 360 degrees.

I told him I wanted to have Monday night off. McCracken lifted a bottle of Jim Beam and placed it with a hard thud right in front of him. Then he reached into the small drawer directly under the desktop and deftly grabbed a shot glass with his thumb and forefinger.

He asked if I wanted any. When I declined, he shook his head and muttered something about me never becoming a proper newspaperman. Then he raised his voice and said, in the casually suspicious tone favored by journalists, "This city is alive with the unlimited potential for fun and mayhem six days a week, my young mick friend, but on Mondays, even the goddamn museums are closed. So I have to ask you, of all the nights in the week, why do you want that one off?"

I thought about telling the truth: I was working on the Amanda Price story. In fact, I shouldn't really have to take any time off at all. What was more, the *Examiner* should pay the expenses I was sure to ring up. But I knew McCracken would never approve. The Amanda Price story was just about over. William Anderson was guilty. McCracken was interested only in covering his trial and execution.

Before I could reply to his question, McCracken chuckled, as if he had figured it out for himself.

"You're chasing some dame, aren't you? And it's the only night she's free."

I was paralyzed for a second. Then I nodded. He knocked back a shot of bourbon.

"Go ahead, Grimes. We'll cover for you."

I thanked him and stepped away. Before I was out of earshot he said, "I hope you get some action."

Chapter nine

I was standing on Park Avenue just before nine at night. The door behind me swung open. Heels struck concrete. A mink coat brushed the ground amid breathless words I could not quite make out.

Sylvia Price's hair was swept back. She had applied small but perfectly placed touches of rouge. For a moment everything inside me got stuck in my throat.

"We have to do something about your coat," she announced with a touch of annoyance.

I said it was the only coat I owned.

"You should have told me. I would have taken one of Father's."

I said he wasn't my size.

She kept eyeing me critically, as if I'd be easy to take in for alterations. "We could have said you shrank during the war."

It was true. I'd lost fifteen pounds that I hadn't regained. I wondered if she knew.

I went to the curb and raised my arm. Sylvia asked what I was doing. I said I was trying to hail a cab. She shook her head and told me I was silly. The car would be around for us in a minute.

Sylvia Price never went to the Stork Club on Mondays, but I told her it was the only night that would work. She asked why. I said it was because Amanda had been killed on a Monday. The same people were likely to be working. I needed to talk to the band members and the help. Sylvia had responded by sighing deeply.

A long black car stopped in front of us. On top of its sleek vertical grille were a winged ornament and a logo with overlapping letters. For the first time in my life, I'd be riding in a Rolls-Royce. I tried to keep my jaw in place as the driver ran around to the passenger door, opened it and held out his arm. Sylvia leaned on him while she climbed onto the running board before getting inside. When I followed, I almost slipped before grazing my head against the top of the doorway.

The backseat was a wide leather sofa that could have accommodated four people. I brushed my fingers against the furnishings; they felt like mahogany. Sylvia reached for a silver case, removed a cigarette and turned to me. I took out a lighter that I'd purchased only hours before because I'd expected something like this.

I asked if I was still her Cousin Matthew from Portland, Oregon. She assured me I was.

"Why Matthew?" I asked.

"I like the name."

"Why Portland, Oregon?"

"Everyone has heard of it, but nobody has actually set foot in the place."

"What happened to San Francisco?"

"Have you ever been there?"

"No."

"A lot of people have. It would be too easy to trip you up."

"But I don't know anything about Portland, Oregon."

She smiled. "Neither does anyone else."

We drove south on Park, past ten-story apartment buildings worth amounts I could not begin to calculate. Sylvia put her hand on my knee, and I felt a surge of everything I had tried to suppress.

"You want to ask me something," she said.

My mouth hung open. No words came out. I must have spoken with my eyes.

"You've been on the verge of exploding with a question since I first saw you tonight. So go ahead and ask. I promise to lie." As she laughed, a mouthful of smoke escaped her mouth.

"Tell me about Donald Wetherby," I said.

Sylvia let her tongue rest under her front teeth for a second. I suspected this was not the topic she'd been expecting.

"He was a good-looking man," she said. "You've seen his pictures?"

I nodded.

"They didn't do him justice. He was one of those attractive men who didn't photograph well. And then there are unattractive people who devour the camera. Isn't that unfair?"

"A lot of things are unfair."

Sylvia wrapped her mink tighter and shook her cigarette over an ashtray to her left. I heard McCracken's voice in my ear as he imparted knowledge one sliver at a time: "Sometimes, my young mick friend, when you want them to talk, you have to pretend you know more than you do."

What I was about to say was wild speculation, but I wanted to make it sound as if I had all the information I needed and just desired one last piece of confirmation.

"So when were Donald and Amanda getting married?"

Sylvia jerked about sharply. I kept my gaze steady. After a moment she tilted her head and closed her eyes, as if a night that had just begun was already an ordeal.

"I'm dying for a drink," she said. "A martini, I suppose. What do you drink, Patrick Grimes?"

"Beer, usually."

She sighed. The car turned right on 53rd, where the apartment buildings gave way to four-story brownstones. Once we passed Madison, we'd be at the club.

"You never answered my question," I said.

Sylvia blew a last trail of smoke and stubbed the cigarette in the ashtray. Her words came quickly, as if she'd been thinking about them while she took the conversation on a tangent.

"They never set a date," she said. "It was always vague—'after the war,' that sort of thing."

"She must have been devastated," I said.

We stopped at the light on Madison. I figured we had less than a minute before we were out of the Rolls and into the club. We'd be surrounded by people and I'd lose my best chance to talk one-on-one.

"I suppose she was."

"What do you mean by that?"

"We never talked about it. We weren't close. I've told you that."

She turned toward me. Her face was inches away. I could smell the scents of wealth and breeding, the sweet odor of a life that would never be spent anyplace dull or ordinary. As I gazed at her, trying to take her all in, I realized that this was what temptation looked like.

The Rolls stopped. Even on a cold Monday night in December, a line a half-block long stretched from the Stork Club's entrance, filled by people with anxious, pleading looks, as if being allowed to enter would validate their lives.

Sylvia held out her arm and led me toward the door without a glance at the unchosen ones. From behind us I heard an outer-borough accent full of anger and resentment: "Lookit those swells jumpin' the line. Who do they think they are?"

Without moving her head in the slightest, Sylvia asked, "Did you hear something, Matthew?"

A doorman in white gloves and a full-length blue uniform regarded me as if I were a piece of flotsam, but when he saw Sylvia he nodded. "A pleasure to see you, Miss Price." I sauntered with her into the foyer. The gold chain that separated the aspiring worshipers from the sanctum was swept aside. When we stopped at the coat check, the girl at the counter smiled at us. Finally Sylvia saw me in the tuxedo I had rented earlier in the day. Raising her eyebrows, she leaned toward me and said in a voice so low I found it thrilling, "I guess we'll have to tell everyone that's top of the line in Portland, Oregon."

I wanted to keep her near me. I wanted to put my hand on

her knee and run it up her thigh. Sylvia snapped her purse shut and led me on.

Gold-framed mirrors lined the walls from top to bottom. They sparkled and made the place seem both bigger and more crowded. I glanced at myself as I went past the bar. I thought I looked okay. From the main room off to my left I heard rumba music reaching out, trying to drag anyone who walked by onto the dance floor. I drifted toward it, but felt a tug on my arm. Sylvia motioned toward the right with a slight nod. I held my breath as I realized we were heading toward the Cub Room, a quiet cul-de-sac that provided safe harbor for the elite of what Walter Winchell liked to call Café Society.

At the door the maitre d' told Sylvia it was good to see her. He asked whether she was still expecting a party of five.

Sylvia said she was.

The maitre d' picked up gilt-edged menus and escorted us to a table at the far end of the narrow room. The walls were lined with satin-draped banquettes and still more mirrors, which allowed me to watch people without gawking. I'd heard that Winchell always sat at Table 50, just inside the door to the left, but when I glanced that way I saw a middle-aged woman wearing a pillbox hat and a long-sleeved black dress. I bit my lip and hoped Gracie Paquette didn't recognize me.

Winchell was in Miami. He went there every winter, returning north about the same time the robins did.

Gracie was talking on a black desktop phone. I could hear her saying that she certainly did want to talk to Lana Turner when the girl was in town, but she wasn't going to do it if Lana insisted on giving Ed Sullivan an interview first. Gracie thanked the person she was talking to, put the receiver down hard and muttered something that sounded like "bastard" before a waiter whisked the phone away.

The maitre d' asked if Miss Price would like a bottle of champagne.

Sylvia put her finger to her chin in a gesture that indicated this was a matter that deserved the most serious consideration. After a few moments she said she had been thinking about a martini, but a bottle of champagne would be nice. Moët, of course.

The maitre d' said, "very good," and stepped away. He hadn't noticed me at all.

"So you see, Cousin Matthew, this is how the other half lives." She was enjoying herself, as if the daring of the masquerade excited her. A minute later a waiter brought the champagne. When he popped the cork, he asked how Miss Price was this evening. She said she thought her evening was about to get much better.

The waiter filled two ribbed flutes. Sylvia raised hers to mine, and we sipped. I'd had champagne just a few times, on special occasions, and had never liked it much, but this stuff tasted different. I almost told Sylvia how good it was, but I was afraid I really would sound like someone from Portland, Oregon.

The waiter asked if we felt like ordering food now or preferred to wait for the rest of our party.

Sylvia said we would wait.

I drank more champagne. The waiter refilled my flute. I reminded myself that I needed to keep my head clear. I was looking for information. A man's life was at stake.

I sensed something hovering above me. When I looked up I saw a girl with a Speed Graphic. She smiled and hoisted her camera and asked if we minded. Mr. Billingsley had seen us. He owned the club and he wanted a photograph.

Sylvia's eyebrows arched upward. "What do you think, Matthew?"

I shrugged, but I felt nervous. I didn't want to make a scene by refusing, but I didn't want my mug to wind up in a gossip column, either.

"This is my cousin," Sylvia said. "He's here all the way from Portland, Oregon."

The girl asked how I liked New York. I said it was swell. She pointed her camera and asked us to look natural. A flash turned the room spotty. As she thanked us and went off, I tried to imagine Finkel taking pictures in a place like this. Probably he'd want everyone to lie on the floor, and then he'd pour ketchup all around.

"Is something funny, Matthew?"

"Everything is, tonight."

In the mirror I saw the reflection of an approaching couple. The man was tall and slender, in his mid-thirties. His blondish hair was beginning to thin. I thought I recognized him. The girl on his arm looked fifteen years younger, and as wide-eyed as I felt. When they reached the table, I rose and extended my hand to the man while nodding at the girl. Sylvia introduced me to Peter Van Duzer.

His grip was firm. "Always glad to meet a relative of Sylvia's."

I'd never met him before, but I had seen him in photographs. He was the father of three-year-old Lara, the poor girl I had read about who'd been abducted and killed.

Of course I didn't know any of that. I was playing the role of stranger from out of town.

"I'm sorry," Sylvia said to the girl Van Duzer was with. "I didn't catch your name."

"Francine."

"Of course it is."

Van Duzer pulled out a chair for the girl, who wobbled as she sat. The waiter asked if Mr. Van Duzer and the lady would be having champagne.

They would.

I was starting to feel high and giddy. I wondered when we'd order something to eat. It had been a long time since lunch, and I'd always heard good things about the food at the Stork Club.

Van Duzer held his flute in front of his face and turned to me. I thought his eyes flashed with some kind of special knowledge.

"Where did you say you were from again?"

"I didn't. I thought Sylvia told you."

Sylvia leaned forward and spoke softly, as if she were taking everyone at the table into her confidence. "Matthew is from Portland, Oregon, although he doesn't like to admit it." She gave me a wink that seemed a touch too dramatic.

Van Duzer looked perturbed, like a man who couldn't figure out the last clue in a crossword.

"I've never been there," he said. "What's it like?"

I tried to recall if I knew anything about the Northwest. "It rains a lot," I said.

He nodded as if he hadn't been listening and took out a Camel that he lit with one of the pink matchbooks on the table. He leaned back in his chair and then, almost as an afterthought, offered a cigarette to Francine.

"Why are you in town?"

He wasn't facing me, so I hadn't expected him to say anything. I felt exposed, but Sylvia looked at me confidently. She seemed certain I could keep the game going.

"Sylvia didn't tell you?"

"Sylvia never tells me anything. She never tells anyone anything."

Van Duzer smiled at her, but there was no mirth in his eyes.

Sylvia raised her champagne. "You're a big boy, Matthew. Why don't you tell him?"

I looked from her to him and back again. Sylvia and I had not worked out a story that would explain the presence of a cousin, hitherto unmentioned to anyone, visiting all the way from Portland, Oregon.

"I felt bad about Amanda," I said. "We all did, on my side of the family. I wanted Sylvia and her father to know that."

Van Duzer drummed his fingers on the table, then downed the rest of his champagne in a gulp. The waiter refreshed his drink and asked Mr. Van Duzer how everything was.

Fine. Everything was fine.

Francine leaned forward and blurted, in a voice filled with Flatbush: "Amanda? Amanda Price? You talking about that girl who was murdered?"

Van Duzer covered his face with his hands.

"She was my sister," Sylvia said quietly.

It took a second before the shock of comprehension crossed Francine's face. When it did, she closed her eyes and put her hand over her mouth. "Oh Gawd. I didn't know. I'm sorry. I didn't know. I'm so sorry."

Sylvia patted Francine on the wrist. "It's all right," she said in a voice that was, for once, without artifice.

Van Duzer looked across the room. Following his eyes, I recognized George Stavros, Sylvia's fiancé, from his pictures in the *Examiner.* As he approached our table he seemed both smaller and stronger than the photos conveyed.

I had been expecting him. Sylvia would not go to the Stork Club unless her fiancé showed up.

"Thank God he's here," I heard her say. "We can eat now."

As soon as the waiter had cleared our dinner plates—I ordered the steak, medium rare, and made a point of telling everyone that you couldn't get a New York cut in Portland, Oregon—Francine turned to Van Duzer and said: "I wanna go dancing. That's what you told me. You said you'd take me dancing."

Van Duzer closed his eyes before extending his arm. As they left the Cub Room to head for the dance floor, I saw Gracie Paquette gazing after them.

Stavros ripped a Chesterfield out of its pack and asked how long I planned to stay in town. I said I wasn't sure. We sat there a minute, not talking, while Stavros blew out long and heavy clumps of smoke. Finally I glanced at Sylvia and suggested that perhaps she and her fiancé should join Van Duzer and his girl on the dance floor in the main room.

Sylvia patted my hand. An electric shock ran through me as she said, "George is the only Greek in the world who doesn't like dancing."

The champagne made me bold. "Then waddya say, Cousin? Wanna dance?"

Sylvia looked at Stavros with a touch of pleading. He said it was okay. He had seen someone he needed to talk to.

When I stood up I held out my arm in a sweeping gesture that made me feel like Clark Gable. Sylvia wrapped her hands around my bicep. Her touch sent a jolt that went all the way to my toes. I couldn't believe I was walking through the Cub Room of the Stork Club with a girl like her.

"Sylvia, darling, a word with you."

It was Gracie.

We stopped. Sylvia could not ignore her summons, but I

wondered if I could flee. I'd seen Gracie only a few times in the newsroom, and I was sure I had blended into the background like an overstuffed wastebasket. But I had talked to her on the phone, and I was afraid she might pick up my voice, put it together and blow my cover.

As Sylvia slid into the banquette, she introduced me as her cousin, all the way from Portland, Oregon. Gracie nodded distractedly and said she was pleased to meet me in a tone that indicated she wouldn't care if the floor opened up and swallowed me whole.

"Likewise," I said as I avoided making eye contact.

"That girl Peter is with," Gracie said to Sylvia.

"Her name is Francine. Beyond that, you know as much as I do."

"I doubt they're longtime acquaintances."

"These days, Peter regards a longtime acquaintance as someone he's met at lunch."

"He's playing the field like a bookie at Saratoga."

"He's allowed. He's divorced."

"I keep thinking he'll make a suitable choice. But perhaps it's hopeless."

"Perhaps it is." Sylvia half rose from the banquette. I could tell she wanted to get out of there, so I began standing, too, but Gracie kept talking. Almost imperceptibly, we lowered ourselves back down.

"He and Elizabeth made a handsome couple," Gracie said in her plummy voice. I made a note to tell McCracken that he should find a way to get her a radio show. "I knew it would never last, but when they walked into a room together, all eyes turned to them. She was regal, and it lent him the same kind of air."

"Elizabeth wanted to go back to making movies," Sylvia said.

"That's what she said. And if it's the truth, he should have gone to Hollywood with her. I never had any doubt that he adored her."

"You don't think it's the truth?" Sylvia asked. Now she was the one who sounded intrigued.

"What happened to their daughter," Gracie said. "That poor girl. It was an awful strain."

I was tempted to chime in about the death of Lara Van Duzer, but then I remembered that I was Cousin Matthew from Portland, Oregon, and hence unfamiliar with New York stories.

"Of course, Elizabeth is a Manley," Gracie continued, enjoying the sound of her own voice, "and that family has always stressed the importance of elegance and propriety. The Van Duzer men, on the other hand…" Her voice trailed off. She shrugged in the classic manner of a woman who has given up trying to figure out life's ironies.

I had to know what Gracie thought, so I flattened my voice and asked, "What about the Van Duzer men?"

"They're scamps," Gracie said as she lit a cigarette that was attached to the longest holder I'd ever seen. "Charming in a way, but scamps nonetheless."

Sylvia said Van Duzer had his good qualities. Gracie challenged her to name one. Sylvia leaned close to Gracie's ear and whispered something. Gracie's cheeks flushed. A huge laugh, coupled with smoke, escaped her mouth. Then she put her hand over her lips and said, in so low a voice I was sure I wasn't supposed to hear, "I can't print *that*."

Sylvia twisted out of the banquette. With a smaller flourish, I extended my arm again. As we left the Cub Room, finally on our way to the dance floor in the main part of the club, I glanced at the table where Sylvia and I had first been seated. What I saw made me stop.

Stavros was deep in conversation with a middle-aged man whose back was to me. He wore a double-breasted suit. His hair was slicked back. I could tell from the mirror that he had deep lines on his face.

Sylvia Price's fiancé was talking to Frank Costello.

When Sylvia and I reached the floor, the rumba band was swinging full blast. She brushed against me at our first pass. I wanted to bring her closer. I wanted to tell her I'd never been with a girl who turned me upside down the way she did.

"Gracie is little more than a grifter," Sylvia said in a voice that managed to slide under the music.

"Then why were you so cordial?"

"I don't have a choice. None of us do. About anything."

"What did you tell her about Van Duzer?"

"Nothing I'm going to repeat to you," she said. "Even I have some shame."

The music was urgent, insistent, percussive. I had trouble thinking, but Sylvia kept me focused by asking, "What's your next move, shamus?"

She'd seen the same movies I had: tough but noble guys like Bogart and Cagney busting through walls of indifference and hostility until they finally discovered the truth. Hollywood teaches us that everything works out in the end.

I motioned toward the band members, who were dressed in white tuxedos. "Are they going on break soon?"

"I think so."

"Where do they go?"

"One of the rooms upstairs. I'm not sure which."

"I'll follow them."

"I doubt they would have noticed her. Amanda wasn't the dancing type."

"I have to start somewhere."

I pressed Sylvia against me, spun her out, grabbed her hand with mine before letting go. Her hair seemed to glow, as if she were backlit by one of the cameramen at MGM. I wanted to twirl her around by the waist, pretend we were dancers in a musical as the crowd around us eddied to the sides to watch, men in tails and women in gowns clapping and swaying, while I wooed the girl through the graceful movement of our bodies. At the end she'd throw her arms around me.

The music stopped. The musicians gathered their sheets and instruments while a second band composed of men in black tuxedos came onto the stage. The other dancers drifted toward the tables, but Sylvia stayed where she was. She looked into my eyes. She ran her fingers across my palm. It seemed to take hours for her arm to fall to her side.

"I better go," I said.

The musicians' backs were sweaty and stooped. As I climbed the stairs after them I heard a foxtrot start up in the room I'd just left. I wondered if Sylvia was dancing again.

The band entered a part of the club that I assumed was a lounge. When I peered in, I found most of the men slouched in chairs, making no moves except for the mechanical lifting of cigarettes to mouths.

As I walked in I expected all eyes to turn toward me, the intruder, but the musicians seemed fixed on their own space. I wasn't sure who I should talk to first. Then I heard McCracken, always the teacher, even when he was trying to draw to a full house: "First thing a reporter's gotta learn is this—when you're sizing up a situation, and you know less than nothing, look for the man in charge."

The bandleader, a dark-skinned man, sat by himself at a table in the corner. He loosened his tie and unbuttoned his collar before running his hand through sopping wet hair. His eyes had the unfocused gaze of a guy who hadn't gotten a good night's sleep in months. As I trudged through the room I expected somebody to say something, but no one noticed me.

I stopped in front of the bandleader and wondered how I should start. The first words to a stranger are always the hardest.

"Flatter them." McCracken's voice again, talking as he dealt and drank. "When you want somebody to open up and you don't know how to start, shower them with kindness, even if you don't mean it." He paused to knock back his bourbon. The cards kept flying. "Especially if you don't mean it."

"Excuse me, sir."

"What do you want?"

The voice had an accent from somewhere exotic: Cuba or Mexico or one of those little Latin countries.

"I just wanted to tell you how much I enjoyed your music."

The bandleader drew deeply on his cigarette before letting the smoke escape through his nose.

"What do you really want?"

His careworn face spoke of years spent in half-filled firetraps. I pictured him hiring and firing musicians until he finally had an ensemble he liked, gradually moving to better clubs and more money. Of course the pace would have been killing, on the road every year for forty weeks or more. But then one magic day, at a club on the Jersey Shore or in the Catskills, a man approached with no warning, extended a card and asked if he was interested in playing the Stork Club.

"I was wondering if you could help me."

"I'm not hiring anyone," he said as he flicked his cigarette.

"That's not it. That's not it at all. I couldn't play a note to save my life."

I laughed, then launched into my story: I was from out of town—Portland, Oregon, in fact—and I was here to help comfort my relatives who had suffered a tragedy a couple of weeks ago when my Cousin Amanda had been found dead. Murdered, to be honest.

The bandleader looked at me as if I were one of those unshaven bums on the Bowery who mumbled to himself all day.

I said I was sorry to bother him about this, but I had reason to believe my cousin had met a man at the Stork Club the night she was killed. The police, for whatever reason, had never followed this lead. Amanda's family really wanted to find out who this fellow was. He may have heard the girl's last words.

The bandleader dragged on his cigarette. His eyes registered something between suspicion and interest.

I took out a picture of Amanda that had run with one of my stories. After a second the bandleader picked it up and looked at it from several different angles.

"I've seen this picture," he said.

"It's been in the newspapers."

"They arrested a colored fellow. I heard he was set up."

I wouldn't have been more astonished if the bandleader had admitted committing the crime himself. Almost everyone I had spoken to regarded the case as closed. William Anderson had confessed. Even if he hadn't, he was guilty. We all know what the colored are like. Now here was a man I'd never met agreeing with me before I'd even started, going along in tones as casual as the ones he would use if we were discussing LaMotta's next fight at the Garden. And I realized that, unlike whites, dark-skinned people knew what happened when one of their own ran afoul of the police.

"Where did you hear that?" I asked. I tried to keep my voice as casual as his. I wanted to sound like a concerned relative, not a newspaper reporter.

He shrugged. "Around."

I pointed to Amanda's picture. "Did you see her here that night?"

He shook his head and pushed the picture back toward me. He said he rarely took notice of the customers. He had to concentrate on the band. I asked if any of the musicians might have seen her. He said I could ask all of them if I wanted, but the nights were a blur, one running into another until it seemed like one long mass of dancing and drinking, except for the two or three times a year a fight broke out.

I was on the verge of thanking him and leaving. I was already wondering how I would approach the waiters and busboys. The simplest way would be to tell my story to the maitre d', but it was easy to imagine him relaying what I'd asked to Mr. Billingsley, who wouldn't like some hick from the Coast going around his club asking questions about a dead girl.

I had half risen, nodding my thanks to the bandleader.

"Ask Ricardo," he said.

I stopped short. I felt awkward in my crouch, but I wanted to make sure I'd heard him correctly.

"What was that?"

"Ricardo. On clarinet. He sits in front. He sees everything."

Before I could respond, the bandleader made a small motion. Within seconds a small, slight man with a mustache appeared beside him. The two conferred in Spanish.

Finally, the man I assumed to be Ricardo nodded. The bandleader told me I should show him the picture. I pushed it his way. He held it close to his eyes before turning it sideways and upside down. He finally turned to the bandleader and spoke Spanish again.

"Ricardo says she was here a few weeks ago. He saw her picture in the paper. He wondered if it was the same girl."

Ricardo kept talking.

"He says he remembers her because she was the skinniest girl he ever saw. Also the saddest."

"Who was she with?"

The bandleader turned to Ricardo and asked my question. The musician shrugged and said a few words.

"He says he isn't sure. A fellow with dark hair, about thirty or thirty-five years of age. He didn't get a good look at him."

I shook my head. Ricardo's description reminded me of the details cops handed out about suspects in open cases. The profiles were so vague they fit half a million people.

"What did my cousin do that night?"

The bandleader translated. Ricardo shrugged again and said a few more words.

"She danced once."

"With the dark-haired fellow?"

A short translation and reply. The bandleader shook his head. "Not with him. He looked like he wanted to be someplace else."

"Can he describe the man she danced with?"

I waited for the reply, which came in seconds. "A tall fellow, skinny, with curly hair. When the song ended he walked away quickly, like he was in a hurry to leave."

"What did she do when he left?"

This time my wait took a while, until the bandleader said: "She stood a little straighter, as if she was determined to do something. Then she went back to a table by the wall, and the first man rejoined her. They talked very deeply, but Ricardo doesn't have the feeling they were lovers. He thinks something was troubling her. Perhaps the man was trying to comfort her. Perhaps he was the source of the troubles. Ricardo isn't sure."

I faced the musician directly. Even if he couldn't understand me, I wanted him to realize I was about to ask an important question.

"Why does he say she was the saddest girl he ever saw?"

Ricardo paused. Then the words poured out of him so quickly the bandleader had difficulty keeping up. After what seemed like five minutes Ricardo fell quiet. The bandleader looked up at the ceiling, as if seeking forgiveness.

"I will summarize. He is telling you this because you are blood; these are things strangers would have no right to hear.

"The girl, Amanda, seemed flat, almost lifeless, as if there were nothing in the world that could give her joy. Ricardo says—and he begs your pardon, he does not mean to upset you—but he says he has the impression that she was already dead, or somehow knew she was about to die. And that perhaps it was almost a relief for her."

I waited a few seconds before asking, "Did Ricardo see her leave the club?"

A quick translation, followed by a shake of the head.

I had one question left, but again I heard McCracken's voice: "Here's a trick, Grimes. A trick all reporters have to learn. When you're almost done, thank them. They'll be disarmed. And then lay that one last question on them, that one thing you've gotta know."

I told the bandleader I was grateful and said "Gracias" to Ricardo. I stood up before smacking my head in a gesture I immediately regarded as too theatrical.

"I forgot one thing," I said.

"Please," said the bandleader.

"Do you remember who their waiter was, or who cleared their table?"

The question was posed to Ricardo, who said a few words.

"Their waiter was Dmitri. He's in the main room tonight. He's very busy, of course."

Minutes later I was hanging back in a doorway, watching the swirl of evening clothes on the dance floor. When the song ended the crowd applauded lightly, as if everyone expected a new number almost immediately. But the band didn't start up again. Instead a tall man in his mid-forties walked onto the bandstand. I felt that I should recognize him. His dark, thinning hair was combed over, but if not exactly handsome anymore, he was still good-looking, and it was easy to picture him with movie-star looks when he was younger. He smiled diffidently and kept his head down, as if he were afraid of making eye contact. A cigarette was wedged between his fingers. He said he hoped everyone was having a good time.

This prompted cries of "Yes!" and "Swell!"

He said it was December sixteenth, which meant Christmas

was coming soon. He realized everyone had lots of presents to buy, especially with all the boys finally home from the war.

His voice had an oddly flat sound, a gentler version of McCracken's Texas twang.

He said he knew everybody could use a little help at Christmastime and the Stork Club wanted to do its share, and so, without any more folderol, he was going to shower everyone in the room with gifts of his own. As he walked off the stage I realized it was Sherman Billingsley himself, addressing his patrons as if he were a tuxedo-clad version of Santa Claus.

His exit prompted a primal cry, high-pitched squeals of delight mixing with the deeper roar many of these people would emit during a touchdown run in the Harvard-Yale game. Everyone looked upward, so I did too, as dozens of balloons floated down from the ceiling.

The people on the floor strained and grasped and clawed. Desperate smiles disfigured their faces.

At the first *Pop!* I cringed. That sound was followed by another, and another, until they came in a staccato rhythm. I covered my ears, but I still heard the *Pop! Pop! Pop!* as the squeals and the roar filled my head. I was back in Tuscany, dug into the brown earth, waiting for the artillery to stop and wondering if the shells were being fired by their side or ours.

I wanted the music to begin again. A feather brushed my cheek. I tried to wipe it away, but it rubbed against my hands and clung to my body. Finally, when I looked, I saw a twenty-dollar bill perched on my wrist.

Other bills floated in the air, riding invisible currents, slipping past dozens of clutching hands. Occasionally someone snatched a bill and moaned ecstatically. One piece of paper managed to drift to the floor. Two men dove after it. The bigger guy threw an elbow against the smaller one's forehead, then snatched the prize.

I stuffed the twenty in my pocket and walked into the heart of the room. A few bills were still fluttering about, but the frenzy had subsided. The musicians took up their instruments.

I saw Sylvia standing near the bandstand. I almost called out, but then watched instead as she jumped, trying to catch one of the few remaining bills. She laughed and reached for it again before a big hand, heavy and masculine, grabbed the money out of the air.

The hand was Van Duzer's. He lowered his fist until it was just under her chin. Then he opened it, revealing a crumpled piece of green paper. She snatched it and slid it down the front of her dress, then threw back her head and laughed. Van Duzer put his arms around her. They began to dance. I watched them move around the floor, wanting her to turn to me, but her smile was only for her partner.

The world felt wobbly. I bumped into a table. Some unseen guy told me to watch where I was going. I stumbled off the dance floor and into the Cub Room. Stavros was still at the table. I plopped down and reached for a napkin to wipe the sweat from my face.

"Shame what happened to Chick," I heard Stavros say.

"They're sending a message," a raspy voice replied.

I lowered the napkin. I hadn't noticed that Stavros was still in conversation. Now I was seated only a few feet from Frank Costello.

I told myself not to stare. I reminded myself that I was from Portland, Oregon, and didn't know who Costello was.

Despite my haze of alcohol and disappointment, the name Chick stirred a memory. I remembered the stiff Finkel had photographed in front of the Turtle Bay Settlement House: Irving Horwitz, nicknamed Chick, a dead gangster McCracken had used in his ferocious attempts to close some of the distance between the *Examiner* and the *Daily News*.

"A message to Ben?" Stavros asked.

"I think so," Costello said.

"How's he doing?" Stavros asked.

"Bad," Costello said. "That hotel he's building. Everything costs a fortune and there's no end in sight."

"That's too bad. I like Ben."

"I do, too. But I don't think anyone can help him."

I felt sorry for Ben, whoever he was. Suddenly another piece of memory crashed through: Chick Horwitz had made his bones with

Dutch Schultz while also running with Bugsy Siegel, who preferred to be called Ben.

I again raised the napkin to my face, this time to hide. From the corner of my eye I saw Stavros and Costello shake hands. Then Costello headed out of the room with a woman roughly his age. For a moment I found myself admiring the man: he'd brought his wife to the Stork Club.

Of course, LaGuardia had insisted for years that the true owner of the Stork Club, and indeed many of the city's other swank spots, was none other than Frank Costello, and every time New Yorkers went to these places they put money into the hands of the rackets.

Stavros asked if I was all right. I said I was swell. He asked where Sylvia was. I thought for a second. Since Sylvia and I had left the Cub Room together, she should have returned with me. I said she was in the ladies' room.

Stavros took out a cigarette that he lit with the deliberation of a man deciding how to spend his last nickel. He asked if I was staying with Sylvia. I said I was at a hotel. I wouldn't dream of imposing.

I was afraid he was going to ask what hotel, and I'd have to tell him the Plaza because I couldn't think of any others, but he just gazed at the line of smoke curling up from his cigarette. My tongue felt thick and stupid. I was afraid I might blurt out something true. When our waiter appeared and asked if I'd like another cocktail, I almost prostrated myself in gratitude and ordered a martini.

Very good, sir.

The waiter glanced at Stavros, who shook his head.

I put my hands on the table and tried to adopt a rube voice: "Sylvia was afraid you'd be bored here sitting by yourself. But now you can tell her you were talking to someone."

Stavros raised his cigarette and held it in his mouth a long time. Finally he blew out so much smoke I thought he was trying to hide his face.

"A business associate," he said.

"Really? What kind of business are you in?"

"My business."

The waiter put the drink in front of me. I raised it to my mouth and sipped. It tasted like nothing.

"Poor Amanda," I said. "We're all still upset."

"Is that right?" Stavros said. If he had raised his brows any higher, they would have merged with his hairline.

I drank some more. The martini made my tongue roll.

"I'll be honest with you," I said. "I'm not sure what everybody in the family really thinks. But I'm upset."

"Somebody should be," he said.

I tried to make myself sound drunker than I was. "What do you mean?"

Stavros waved his arm around. "This." I must have looked confused. "Her sister's dead, but Sylvia still goes out all the time. It isn't right."

I drank more of my martini. The glass was almost empty.

"Life goes on," I said.

"Sometimes it should stop for a while."

I saw Sylvia in the mirror, walking quickly, her face flushed. Stavros pulled out her chair when she reached the table. She gave him a perfunctory smile that grew into a genuine one when she saw a pink, gift-wrapped box of cosmetics and perfume at her setting. Mr. Billingsley often gave favors to his most treasured guests.

Sylvia pushed the box toward Stavros and asked if he could take care of it. Stavros nodded stiffly at us as he left the room. Sylvia's eyes sparkled with the mischief of a girl who was confident she would always get whatever she wanted. She leaned toward me and asked, "What's the scoop?"

"Amanda was here that night. One of the guys in the band saw her. She was with a man, but she had one dance with someone else."

"Is that a fact?" Sylvia removed a cigarette from her purse and waited for me to take out my lighter. I was reluctant to obey, but I did it anyway. Sitting so close to her, I could fully comprehend the power she wielded over men.

I lowered my voice to a confidential register I didn't even know I possessed. "And your fiancé does business with Frank Costello."

Sylvia inhaled, then dropped her voice to match mine. "Don't be naïve, Cousin Matthew. Everybody in this city does business with him."

I thought of the roulette wheel I'd seen in the place across the street from the settlement house. I almost asked what she knew about it. Then I reminded myself to focus. I was still working on Amanda's movements the last night of her life.

"Your sister and the man she was with were served by a waiter named Dmitri."

"That's interesting," Sylvia said in a tone that suggested ennui.

"Which one's Dmitri?" I asked.

"The one with the Russian accent."

"You're not as clever as you think."

Sylvia faked a pout. "What's the matter, Matthew? Boys in Portland, Oregon, don't like it when girls tease them?"

The waiter placed another martini in front of me even though I hadn't asked for one. Sylvia said it looked divine. She'd like her own, please. With a twist.

Very good, Miss Price.

"Let's get back to Dmitri," I said.

"I saw him in the main room tonight. He's six foot three, with sandy hair and a mole on his right cheek."

"A Russian with sandy hair?"

"I think his family were aristocrats. Back in the old days."

I should have accepted the information with the grateful nod she was expecting. Instead I took a long sip of my martini and asked, "Ever afraid that'll happen to you?"

She looked at me sharply. "I beg your pardon?"

"That you'll wind up waiting on tables? After the revolution?"

Sylvia tapped her cigarette on the edge of the ashtray. Her eyes narrowed. She looked like she wanted to slap me, if I'd been worth the trouble.

"There's never going to be a revolution here, Cousin Matthew. People like Father would never allow it."

I stood a few feet inside the door of the main room, hoping I looked like a man who was wondering where his date had gone.

I searched along the walls and around the stage. And then I saw a tall man—sandy-haired, mole on his right cheek—hurrying up from the kitchen with a tray over his shoulder. He went to a booth along the far wall, put down the food and exchanged a few words with the customers. Then he hoisted the empty tray and headed back toward the stairs.

I picked my way around chairs to intercept him, stopping by an empty table as he was about to walk past.

"Are you Dmitri?"

He eyed me guardedly. "Yes?"

"My name is Price," I said. "Matthew Price. You waited on my Cousin Amanda here a couple of weeks ago."

He said he had many customers. How could he possibly remember them all?

His accent was Russian. It was hard to pick up his words through the noise.

"She was the girl who was killed." I tried not to shout. "It's been in the papers. I'd like to ask you some questions."

He said he could not help me. He took a step away. I put a hand on his shoulder.

"Please," I said. "It's important to the family."

I have often pondered the mysterious process that causes people to change their minds. It is always easier to choose a certain course and stick with it no matter what. Dmitri could have walked away. But there is always that other part of the human equation—the one that wants to show off what we know.

He made a motion to follow him as he headed toward the kitchen stairs. He said he'd meet me outside, in back, in five minutes. I asked how I'd get there. He said there was an emergency door to the right of the bandstand. He would open it himself from the outside, but I had to make sure I was there on time.

I drifted into the shadows and watched the couples dancing across the floor. After a minute I slid along the wall until I saw a red sign marked EXIT. Pasted on the door was a smaller sign that said "Emergency Use Only."

The band hit a high note as the drummer struck the down-beat.

The door rattled open. I felt a rush of cold, bracing air, and stepped into it.

Dmitri lit a cigarette. The ember went up and down like a piston as he waited for my questions.

"Amanda was with a man that night. Do you know who he was?"

Dmitri said it was funny. He realized she must have been somebody because Mr. Billingsley stopped at her table. So Dmitri kept expecting the police to come by to ask questions. But so far they hadn't. He couldn't understand. He realized things were done differently in the United States, but checking her movements before she died struck him as a routine assignment.

"The man she was with, Dmitri. Who was he?"

Dmitri said the gentleman was here tonight.

"Could you point him out to me?"

Dmitri said he didn't think that would be necessary. He had passed by the Cub Room a short while ago and saw the gentleman there.

"Where is he sitting? Who is he with?"

He said the man was with Miss Price's sister, as was I. He had noticed me sitting there, too.

I tried to keep my voice from rising as I asked if Amanda had been with Van Duzer.

Dmitri shook his head. He said she had been sitting with the other gentleman at the table: Mr. Stavros, Sylvia's fiancé.

The air was as dry as windblown sand, but I took out a handkerchief and wiped my forehead and mouth. I wondered if Sylvia knew that Stavros had been with her sister that night. I assumed she didn't, but it was possible she was playing a game. Perhaps she knew everything, but wanted me to find out on my own.

"What did they talk about?" I asked. My voice sounded faint and far away.

Dmitri said he was sorry. He did not listen. He always tried to avoid eavesdropping on the customers.

I said I knew a suspect had been arrested, but our family had doubts. We were afraid the wrong man was being punished while Amanda's killer went free.

Dmitri said he had heard rumors as well. An innocent man was likely to die. He shrugged, as if the matter was of no consequence.

"What time did Amanda leave that night?" I asked.

About nine-thirty or ten.

"By herself or with him?"

By herself. Mr. Stavros went to the bar and made several phone calls.

"Was either one of them drunk?"

They each had only one glass of champagne. Mr. Stavros ordered fish while the lady had chicken. She barely ate her food. Dmitri asked if she wanted to take the rest home and she shook her head. He said he'd tell the chef to recook it if she wasn't satisfied. She said the meal was fine. She just wasn't hungry.

"How did they seem?"

Dmitri said he didn't understand the question.

"How did they act? What was your impression of them? I want to know. This could be important."

Dmitri took a long drag on his cigarette, as if the smoke would help him remember. He tilted his head back to look at the sliver of sky we could see over the tops of the darkened Midtown buildings. He started to speak but the words came slowly, as if he were thinking in his native language before translating.

He said he was Russian so he knew about sadness, the fine gradations that ran from vague feelings of unpleasantness to a profound loathing of life itself. He said he sensed in Amanda a deep and lasting sense of disappointment in humanity.

"You sensed that by serving her food?"

Dmitri shrugged. He told me not to believe him if I didn't want to. I had asked for his impression and he had given it.

When I returned to the Cub Room, the table I'd been sitting at with Sylvia and Stavros was empty. It had been bussed. A pristine white cloth was draped over the top. New place settings were arranged perfectly, down to the spotless silverware.

I backed out of the room. Our waiter squeezed past and murmured, "Excuse me," as he brought a large round of drinks to one of the tables.

I thought my companions might have relocated to the bar, but there was no sign of them. Our waiter walked toward me. This time his eyes locked on my face.

"Can I help you, sir?"

I gulped and pointed at the table. "I was with a group of people. They were sitting right there."

"They left, sir."

"Left?" I was having trouble comprehending the notion.

"Could you wait at the bar, sir? Just for a minute."

I took a seat. The percussion from the bandstand pounded against the inside of my skull. Somebody asked if I was all right. I was inclined to tell the questioner to mind his own business, but the inquiry had been made by Mr. Billingsley himself.

"I'm swell. Thank you."

"You're Sylvia's cousin, aren't you?"

"That's right."

"They had to leave suddenly. They send their regrets. Something about Sylvia's father."

A range of terrible occurrences ran through my mind. I saw Harrington Price stiff on the floor, his hand clutching his chest. Perhaps he was writhing in the back of a private ambulance, his brain in the grip of a violent seizure.

"Uncle Harrington. Is he all right?"

"I'm not sure. I'm sorry."

I reached into my pocket and ran my handkerchief over my face. I wondered how long I had been sweating so badly. I nodded weakly at Billingsley and said I supposed it was time to get my coat.

"There is one thing," he said.

"What is it?"

"I'm almost afraid to bring this up at a time like this, but Sylvia said you could take care of the bill."

I looked at him stupidly for a few seconds before saying, "The bill?"

"It was an emergency. They had to leave right away and didn't know where you were. They said you'd understand."

It was easy to see Sylvia leaning forward while I was away from the table and bringing everyone else into a conspiracy, saying in a voice that was lighter than air, wouldn't it be grand if they pretended something had happened and they had to run out this instant, but it was all right because Cousin Matthew from Portland, Oregon, was a sport, and he'd be more than happy to settle their account.

Billingsley reached into his jacket and pulled out the check. When I looked at the amount I told myself there must be a mistake, it was all a horrible mistake, but when I went down the list I remembered the things we had ordered and they were all there, the champagne and the martinis and every bit of food. It totaled almost two hundred dollars, and I made forty-one fifty a week.

"I'm not in the habit of carrying around a lot of cash," I said.

"Who is?" Billingsley flashed a crooked smile. "Are you staying with Sylvia?"

I shook my head. "I'm at the Plaza." Suddenly I saw a way to escape the predicament Sylvia and her companions had created for me. "Why don't you send the bill to my hotel in the morning? The front desk will get my safe-deposit box and we'll settle the whole thing."

"Why don't we do that now? The Plaza isn't far. I'll send Gregory with you."

I stood unsteadily. At the coat check I handed my claim to a brunette. The space was filled with minks and vicuñas and calf-length wraps made of finely crushed serge. My battered cloth rag made me as obvious as a hobo at a coming-out party. The girl said she hoped I'd had a good time. I said it was swell. She smiled at me as I opened my wallet and, trance-like, placed a five-dollar bill in the tip jar.

Billingsley helped with my coat. As we stepped into the freezing Manhattan night, he motioned toward the doorman and told him that I needed to stop at the Plaza so I could pay the bill. Gregory nodded and said it was a pleasure. He'd be happy to accompany me.

Fifty-third Street was three deep with limos and taxis. The line straining at the club stretched almost to Park. I wondered how Gregory could leave his post, but another man stepped right in. Gregory said we'd better get going.

We'd head toward Fifth, less than a hundred feet away, then turn north. I wondered if I could dash down one of the side streets before Gregory could recover, but that was too risky. A better solution was to walk up Fifth with Gregory, chatting about our families and the holidays. Once we reached the Plaza, I'd bolt for the shelter of darkness the park provided.

We had taken a couple of steps when I heard a woman's laugh. It was high-pitched and loud, as if it were mocking every mistake I'd ever made. I knew the laugh was directed at me, probably because of my coat, so I turned sharply and was about to tell off whoever it was. Then I noticed the blond hair falling nearly to shoulder length and the two men beside her, the fair one joining her laughter while the swarthy one smiled as if he sympathized with my humiliation.

"Matthew," she said. "Oh Matthew, Matthew, Matthew."

I looked at Billingsley. He was smiling, too.

I forced myself to grin at Sylvia. "You had me worried. I thought your father had taken ill."

"Father never takes ill. It's against his principles."

"That's funny. I didn't know he had any."

Even under the pallid glow of the streetlights, I could see her face darkening.

"That wasn't nice," she said in a tone as cold as the air.

"I wasn't trying to be nice."

Van Duzer hit me on the shoulder with a bit too much force. "We were just playing a little joke, friend. Don't take it the wrong way."

"What happened to Francine?" I asked.

"I seem to have lost her."

I looked at Stavros, who was hanging back like a man who preferred working in the shadows. I was tempted to ask what he and Amanda had talked about when they together at the club on the final night of her life. I wanted to know who she had danced with, and where she had gone right after she left.

Billingsley stuck out a hand that was surprisingly warm and soft. "No hard feelings," he said. "I'll always go along with a gag."

I looked at the ground to study the polished shoes I'd have to return to the tuxedo shop.

"Here," Billingsley said. "I want you to have this."

He extended a glossy print. It was the picture his photographer had taken of Sylvia and me sitting by ourselves in the Cub Room. The photo was from earlier, much earlier in the night, when the world had held so many more possibilities.

Chapter ten

I slept badly, my head a swirl of alcohol, noise and cigarette smoke. As I ran through the fragments of my night at the Stork Club, one image kept repeating: George Stavros and Frank Costello talking together for a long time, like two old friends catching up on things.

Stavros had been with Amanda at the club the night she was killed. And Stavros had become acquainted with Sylvia while she was gambling one night. Since Stavros did business with Costello, it seemed reasonable to assume he was in the racket himself. What was more, there was a gambling joint across the street from the settlement house. I wondered if Amanda knew about it; if she had threatened to expose it; if that was why her body had ended up in an alley beside a warehouse a short distance away.

I nodded off around dawn and stayed in bed until the phone rang at three in the afternoon. I didn't want to talk to anyone. Then I thought it might be Sylvia, offering an apology and suggesting that if it wasn't too much trouble—she knew what it was like to cancel plans and she realized how last-minute this was—perhaps we could get together for coffee or tea.

Of course. I'd like that. I won't stand on propriety. Not for you.

"I was about to give up, Pat."

"Hi, Kathleen." I did not try to disguise how tired I felt.

My sister asked how I was. Waves of awkwardness and resentment came at me over the line.

I said I was swell.

I heard her pause, then gulp, always Kathleen's prelude to bad news.

"There's no good way to tell you this," she said.

I waited.

"Dan's mother is having Christmas this year. At her place in Sunnyside. It's just Dan's family and there's no room for anybody else. I feel awful about it—"

"It's okay, Kathleen."

"—but he's my husband and I don't know what else to do."

"It's all right."

"I argued and pleaded, but he wouldn't listen—"

"I'll be fine."

"He's so stubborn sometimes."

I waited a few seconds. My sister sounded as if she was breathing through a mask. She always let things upset her.

"Don't worry about me," I said at last. "I'll probably wind up working on Christmas anyway."

"How can they make you work on Christmas?" Kathleen sounded horrified.

"The paper comes out three hundred and sixty-five days a year," I said. "Somebody has to be there."

At work that night Higgins called just before eight. He said he had a good one.

"Body found way out on Staten Island. Annadale section. Guy had been there a week, maybe two."

I told myself it was important to act professionally, distance myself, maintain the proper objectivity and above all pretend I knew nothing about what Higgins was going to tell me. I started typing.

"Discovery made in some tall grass a couple of hundred yards from a colony of summer bungalows. Place is deserted. Nobody heard or saw anything. Might as well have happened on the moon."

"How'd he die?" I asked.

"Shot in the face. At close range. With a police revolver."

"So a cop shot him."

"Maybe yes, maybe no. If he was shot by a cop, it didn't happen in the line of duty, you know what I mean?"

"Maybe an off-duty cop got into a dispute with the dead man."

"Whoever got into a dispute with the dead man was really pissed off. Victim was also hit over the head with the butt of the revolver. Half his skull smashed in. Medical examiner can't figure out which injury killed him. Now lemme give you an ID. That's why this is a good one."

I told him to go ahead.

"Peter Cangelosi. Lemme spell that last name for you."

After he did that, he gave me Cangelosi's background, which I already knew. I told Higgins nothing. Instead I asked, "When was the body found?"

"Two days ago. Some guy brings his dog down to the beach to let it run around. Dog runs into the grass. Guy gets all nervous and runs after it. Gets even more nervous when he sees what the dog's found."

Cangelosi's partner hadn't found him. I tried to figure if that was a good thing.

"More details," I said to Higgins. "You're right, this is good. I'm sure McCracken'll eat it up."

"Whatever happened, it happened there. They think Cangelosi was killed near the road, then dragged farther into the grass. Why they were in that godforsaken spot is anybody's guess."

"Why'd it take so long to get an ID?"

"His wallet was taken."

"Maybe it was a robbery."

"Then why was he shot with a police revolver?"

"Maybe it was his own."

"No way, Grimes. He had to give it up when he got kicked off the force."

I wanted to contradict him.

"Anything else?" I asked.

"Yeah. Cangelosi was forty-one. He lived in Brooklyn and had a wife and two boys." Higgins gave me the names, which I tried to forget. Two more kids growing up without a father. I cleared my throat and asked, in what I hoped was a matter-of-fact voice, "What's he been doing?"

"Waddaya mean?"

"Cangelosi. Since he got bounced from the force. He's got a wife and two kids. How's he been putting food on the table?"

I wondered why I kept using the present tense.

After the first edition, McCracken slid a chair out from the next desk, wheeled it over and kicked up his feet, which landed on a stack of copy paper inches away from my Royal.

"So why was Peter Cangelosi—heroic cop turned rogue, a dago with a dream—all the way out on a deserted part of Staten Island? What's your theory, Grimes?"

I decided to concoct a story that conformed to the tale Higgins was spinning. "Meeting someone," I said. "Probably a cop. That explains the revolver. But whatever they were doing, they needed an out-of-the-way place."

McCracken nodded. "Plausible. And then they get into an argument, and the guy with the gun wins." He stared at the ceiling. I wondered what he found so interesting up there. "But I disagree with your idea about the meeting, my young mick friend. There are out-of-the-way spots in Brooklyn he could have used if he needed to."

"So what do you think he was doing?" I tried to keep my voice level. This was all professional curiosity, the thinking-out-loud speculation that newspapermen engaged in every day.

"I keep coming back to this notion, Grimes, although it's more a hunch than anything else: I think he was following someone. Or waiting there for somebody else—let's call them parties unknown—to have a meeting. So then the questions become who, and why." He patted me on the knee. "Tell Higgins to follow that up."

I resisted the urge to gulp. I felt I was on the verge of being found out. But above all else I wanted to be a pro in the news business, so when Higgins called just before eleven, I told him that McCracken had a request.

"What are you, his errand boy?"

Higgins's words sounded thick and slurred.

"He thinks Cangelosi was following somebody," I said. "Or waiting for some other people to show up for a meeting. He wants you to check on that. Better do it fast, or we'll miss the second edition."

"I see your game, Grimes. Get ahead by sticking your head up McCracker's ass."

It took no effort to sound impatient. "I bet you have something, Higgins. What is it?"

I heard a choking sound. For a moment I thought Higgins might be gagging on a mouthful of alcohol.

"I hate this," he said. "God, how I hate this." I heard a hard thunk over the phone. I wondered how big a glass he was using.

"You better give me what you have," I said.

"I knew the guy, Grimes. He had his problems, but he gave me good stuff when he was on the force. He doesn't deserve this." Higgins's voice was full of despair. It was one thing for Cangelosi to be dead. Everybody died eventually. But only a few died disgraced.

"Doesn't deserve what?"

Another hard thunk. "He was working for Costello. Sometimes he got loaned out to Albert Anastasia."

I whistled, and felt the twinge of fear that had occasionally encircled my heart during combat. Even by New York's standards, Anastasia was a bad man. In the thirties he ran Murder Incorporated, but all the witnesses against him either clammed up or died. Costello, who considered himself a businessman, then put Anastasia in charge of the rackets in Brooklyn and delegated all the mob's nasty stuff to him.

"What did Cangelosi do for those guys?"

"Enforcer. Bagman. Whatever was necessary. Whatever he was told."

I began typing. "Who are you getting this from?"

"Cangelosi's former friends in the NYPD."

"Is that why he was killed? Gangland stuff?"

"Most likely. They're not a hundred percent sure."

They didn't know. They would never know. I had to keep this knowledge inside, where it would swim around before clotting with all the other horrible things I had done in my life.

I was still concerned about the man Cangelosi had always been with, the short guy in a fedora with a scar on his face. I had not seen him for a while, but I was certain he would show up again.

The discovery of Cangelosi's body was sure to generate a reaction from the people who were determined to keep a lid on Amanda Price's murder, and my questions about her death had yielded tantalizing bits that had yet to cohere. I needed to make something happen, so the next morning, with a renewed sense of urgency, I walked unannounced into Howard Munzer's office in a shabby building that bordered Union Square.

He extended his hand as I entered. When I told him who I was, he began to shake his head—slowly at first, then with increasing force.

"I can't believe you had the nerve to come here," he said. "You must leave, Mr. Grimes. Right now. And if you ever tell anybody you even set foot in this office, I'll sue you for slander."

He pointed toward the door. I looked around, hoping I could learn a few facts from a glance. The place was dimly lit. Chipped wooden bookcases were filled with material that had been piled haphazardly. I couldn't tell if his desk was an antique or merely battered.

A familiar tide of rage began to surge within me. Howard Munzer was not a bad man, or an easily frightened one, but he was scared, and I was gripped with the type of anger you can direct only against somebody on your side.

"Goddammit, Munzer, you knew Amanda Price and you're

not telling anybody what happened between you and her, but an innocent man is going on trial for her murder and you have a duty to say something."

Munzer's reply was steady. "I have no idea what you're talking about. Good day."

I thought the language of the trenches might shake him into talking. "No idea? Your fucking business card must have been in her fucking purse for a fucking reason. Maybe I'll put that in the fucking newspaper."

I yanked open the door and stepped into the hallway. I was flushed. The cold made me shiver.

Then I heard a voice behind me, soft and faint and suddenly drained of its conviction. "I knew you had my card. But I thought they never found her purse."

I turned around. Howard Munzer's pasty complexion was the only bright thing in the room.

"The police didn't find it," I said. "I did."

"And you gave it to them?"

"No. I gave it to her father."

He motioned for me to come in. I closed the door quietly behind me.

"You committed a faux pas, Mr. Grimes. If Harrington Price believes his daughter was in contact with me…"

"Harrington Price told me he'd never heard of you."

Munzer laughed before coughing so badly it sounded as if his lungs were trying to force their way up his windpipe. He ran his hand through his hair, which looked as if it had been cut with hedge clippers.

"I took several depositions from him," Munzer said.

"In connection with what?"

"Those documents are sealed."

"Why?"

"That's what the judge wanted."

"Why did the judge want it?"

"Because Harrington Price is a powerful man."

I was getting tired of people refusing to give direct answers to straightforward questions, but I told myself one explosion of temper per interview was enough.

"What was the case about?" I asked.

"I'm not at liberty to discuss it. In fact, if the judge discovers I've ever talked about it outside court, I could be held in contempt and disbarred."

Munzer shook a cigarette into his hand. He wasn't going to volunteer any information, but I sensed he might guide me if I could parse out what he knew.

"Amanda was a volunteer at the Turtle Bay Settlement House," I said.

Munzer blew a plume of smoke toward the ceiling. Small red dots glowed on each of his cheeks, finally giving his skin a bit of color.

"Is that how you met her?" I asked.

"I can't tell you that."

"Who owns the settlement house?"

"I can't tell you that, either."

"But it's had a number of owners, hasn't it?"

Munzer nodded. "It's passed through various hands. Originally it belonged to a church. I forget which one. But Christian charity gets to be awfully expensive, Mr. Grimes."

I scratched my head. "What do you mean by that?"

"Running the settlement house costs a lot of money. And it's located in a part of town where there are now possibilities to make it."

I thought for a second before deciding to ask the question I considered most important. Alone among the people who knew something about the case, Howard Munzer might have the answer.

"Why was Amanda in Blood Alley that night?"

Munzer took another drag on his cigarette, then shrugged elaborately.

"I think she was going to meet someone," I said. I was guessing, but I needed him to respond. "I think she found out about the gambling that goes on in that area, and she was going to expose it."

His eyes narrowed. "Then why did you ask me why she was there?"

"Because I think she was going to meet you."

"Do you have any evidence?"

"Nothing besides the business card."

Munzer leaned back in his chair. I had a vision of him finding a sinecure as a professor, lecturing his students about the wrongheadedness of *Plessy v. Ferguson.*

"The great benefit of the legal system, Mr. Grimes, is that your case gets thrown out unless you have facts to support it."

I reached for the door. I was hungry. Lüchow's was down the street. During the holidays it had a Christmas tree that rose through a hole in the second floor. I was turning the knob when I noticed a picture on the wall. It showed Munzer with a girl I did not recognize. He was wearing a tux. She was dressed to the nines. It reminded me of the photo that had been taken of Sylvia and myself at the Stork Club.

I still had that snap in my overcoat. I kept it there all the time.

I licked my lips and turned to Munzer. "William Anderson's trial starts the second week of January. Unless somebody does something soon, he's going to die."

Munzer inhaled deeply on the last bit of ash in his cigarette. "You asked me before about the case where I deposed Harrington Price. I'm going to tell you more than I should." He blew smoke in my direction. "The case was about the matter that has been the most important in Manhattan since the Dutch arrived: where people live, and where they work. The limited amount of space on a small but extremely important island."

"That doesn't help me much."

"You're a newspaperman, Mr. Grimes. Do some digging."

"Where?"

"Every real estate transaction in this city is recorded." Munzer arched his eyebrows in a manner that reminded me of Groucho Marx trying to put another one over on Margaret Dumont. "Good luck."

I took the El to City Hall. The municipal buildings around the station were dingy but imposing. The room I wanted was warehouse-sized, filled with rows of metal bookcases stretching over my head. The books that rested on them looked big and heavy, with black covers hiding whatever lay between. No sunshine reached this place, which seemed suspended in perpetual gloom. The only illumination came from a few weak bulbs screwed into the ceiling high above.

Way in back, as far from the elevator as it could possibly be placed, was a small desk that looked one termite away from turning into sawdust. Sitting behind it was a man no more than five foot three, with a bald head fringed by wisps of hair just above the ears. He wore round glasses, a bow tie and a vest, but no jacket.

When I told him what I was looking for, he led me down one of the rows of heavy books, all the while talking about the volumes that lined the room from floor to ceiling as if he were familiar with each one. I noticed a yellowing handkerchief sticking out of a pocket in pants that were two sizes too big. He said few people were aware that Trinity Church continued to be one of the largest landowners in Manhattan. I must have looked skeptical because he continued, musing that it was interesting, wasn't it? We always thought of the past as something dim and distant, but Old New York continued in so many ways.

He stopped and peered up and down one of the stacks before nodding slightly. "This is what you want," he said.

"Which one?" I asked.

"All of them. Every real estate transaction in Turtle Bay since 1940."

"But I'm only interested in one place specifically. The settlement house. On East 47th."

"We don't break it down in that kind of detail. Sorry."

At first the books told me nothing: names and amounts entered in a barely legible bureaucratic scrawl, mind-numbing details about the processes of acquisition and sale. I had to brush away pieces of cobwebs. The pages threw off a musty smell that indicated they had hardly been opened. I saw nothing about the Turtle Bay Settlement House. After a half-hour my back hurt from all the bending and lifting.

I was halfway down another list, still trying to make sense of what I was staring at, when an item I had passed over nudged into my consciousness. I went back to the top and read down slowly before stopping on the fourth line, which revealed the following fact:

In January 1943 a property on East 48th Street, between Second and Third Avenues, had been sold by the 79 Wall Street Corporation to an entity called the Manley Holding Company.

With that single word—Manley—I felt as if I was finally getting a flashlight to work, however dimly, in a long and dark tunnel. It added even more significance to the note I'd found in Amanda's purse, although I was now charged with figuring out exactly what her cryptic scribbles meant.

On the next page, another transaction was recorded (this time on 45th, again between Second and Third) in which the Manley Holding Co. bought another parcel of land from the 79 Wall Street Corp. On the next page I noted another purchase by Manley Holding from the same business. Two pages later, I spotted one more.

A possibility swirled in my head. Perhaps Jeff Manley—long ago mentioned by Sylvia—was involved in the real estate company. Although he'd been in Florida when Amanda was killed, a clever man could have pulled the strings on something like that from out of town.

I no longer felt the pain in my back, although I swore at myself for having more theories than facts. I wrote down all the transactions the Manley Holding Co. had been involved in, the vast majority from the 79 Wall Street Corp., almost filling the pages of my reporter's notepad. Hours later, as I put the last book away, I regarded these once-forbidding volumes as my friends for revealing a previously hidden aspect of the way the city was truly run.

As I walked out into December's early twilight, McCracken's voice tolled in my head, another seminar in the newspaper education of Patrick Grimes, held at Lunney's: "One of the biggest problems with the business, my young mick friend, is this: You'll reap an awful lot of chaff, and you've gotta keep all of it in your head, because you never know when something's gonna come in useful."

As I stepped into the wind-whipped air of Lower Manhattan, with the smell of fish from the Fulton Market wrapping around me, I remembered that Harrington Price worked at 79 Wall Street.

* * *

In the newsroom that night O'Shea tossed a photo in front of me. He said it was running with Gracie's column. The picture showed

Sylvia Price sitting at a banquette in the Cub Room. She was leaning forward and showing a hint of décolletage. Her face was lit up; she was smiling at whomever she was talking to across the table.

The man on her left was cut in half, but what I noticed most was the line of her body. Her left arm stretched straight down until it reached the seat, where her palm rested. The man had his hand clamped over hers, as if he wanted it badly and was afraid to let loose.

I wondered who the guy was. The automatic assumption was Stavros, but this guy's skin tone didn't seem dark enough. I tried to swallow, but my mouth was dry. Finally I croaked a few words in an effort to sound witty: "The very rich are different from you and me."

"Yes," O'Shea said. "They have no morals."

I studied the picture and asked, in what I hoped was the tone of idle curiosity newsmen were supposed to use on the job, "We have any idea who the fella is?"

"I figure it's her current fiancé," O'Shea said. "That hood, whatshisname?"

I said it looked like somebody else. O'Shea leaned back in his chair. He said in that case we might have something that belonged in the newspaper. He suggested I get Gracie Paquette on the horn.

I called the Stork Club and asked to be put through to Table 50 in the Cub Room. When Gracie came on the line I told her about the picture and asked if she'd seen it. She said she hadn't. One of the club's photographers must have sent it over. I asked Gracie if she'd seen Sylvia at the club earlier. She said she hadn't. Sometimes the girl made only a token appearance before heading over to Swing Street.

I asked if there was any sign of trouble between Sylvia and Stavros. Gracie said she had asked her about that very topic a few nights earlier. Although the girl had said everything was fine, with Sylvia it was almost impossible to keep up with the rumors.

Gracie said she'd love an item if I could find one. Sylvia Price was the It Girl of 1946, and probably of 1947, too.

I asked my next question in as casual a tone as I could muster. "If this came out, Stavros would dump her, right?"

"I suppose he would."

We all have fantasies and now this one crowded my mind: a swank apartment on Fifth Avenue; coming home after a stint in the newsroom, finally on dayside at a respectable paper; Sylvia greeting me at the door with a smile, a kiss and a drink; the two of us sitting in a nook watching the sun set over Central Park while we listened to the children play.

"It might be difficult for her, though."

Gracie's voice had tones of concern I had never heard before.

"What do you mean? She's had a bunch of fiancés."

"Never one like him."

I wanted her to tell me more, so I encouraged one of the most notable traits of newspaper people: more than anything else, they like showing off how much they know, especially if they can't get it into print.

I said I'd heard that they met while she was gambling.

Gracie dropped her voice. "Stavros runs some of Costello's joints in the East Forties," she said. I had a silent feeling of vindication. "Sylvia got in over her head one night. She lost a lot of money and couldn't cover it. He helped her out of the jam and she was, well, grateful. I didn't run anything about it because Sylvia has given me a lot of goodies over the past few years, and I want her to keep talking to me."

"She thinks everything's a game, doesn't she?"

"And she believes that if she falls behind, she can change the rules. Don't get me wrong. I'm fond of Sylvia. She's fun and vivacious. But she's also careless, especially with people."

Gracie said she had to go, but if I could find proof that Sylvia was seeing somebody other than her fiancé, she was definitely interested in running it. If an item from a staffer panned out, Gracie believed in paying a reward. She'd even go as high as ten dollars.

When my shift was over I knocked hard on the door to the photo lab.

"Waddya want, Grimes?"

"Good guess, Finkel. How'd you know it was me?"

"I never guess. Everybody has a different knock."

He opened the door a crack and poked out his head, reminding me of a subway rat making sure the express had passed. His eyes were barely open. He needed a shave. I realized I had just woken him up.

"This is something different, Finkel. It might be amusing."

"I don't like amusing. I like dead."

"Society stuff. For Gracie's column."

"I hate that shit."

He started to close the door, but I wedged in my foot before he could shut it.

"We think some dame's two-timing her fiancé. If we can prove it, we'll get ten bucks."

Finkel looked at the floor.

"I could buy something with that," he said. "Something nice for my ma, like a handbag. She keeps saying she needs a new one, but they're too expensive."

"The dame is Sylvia Price," I said. My voice sounded a thousand miles away. Somebody else was doing this.

"The dead girl's sister," Finkel said. "That stiff we saw in Blood Alley."

"It's Monday night," I said. "Most likely she's at a jazz club on 52nd. The Downbeat."

Finkel scurried away. I heard the frantic clutching of small hands grabbing things. A minute later I was jogging after him as he rushed for the elevator. Once we got outside Finkel barreled north in his Packard. The glow from Times Square only an avenue away created a surreal halo around his head. We sped up Sixth and never came close to stopping, even when Finkel cut off a Studebaker as he made a hard, sharp right onto 52nd. For a moment I was afraid the car was going to topple over, but then Finkel stopped short in a no-standing zone in front of the club.

Swing Street was lined with brownstones that had been speakeasies during Prohibition before making a smooth transition to jazz clubs after Repeal. In the thirties even the Midtown swells needed money so they didn't mind the clientele, but now that the war was over, the same people were feeling flush and complaining that these dives lured the coloreds to their part of town.

I told Finkel I was going to walk inside to see if Sylvia and the guy were there. If they weren't, I'd come out right away. But if they were, I'd stay until they looked like they were getting ready to leave. Then I'd rush out and tell Finkel to start shooting.

Inside, smoke filled the club. I smelled tobacco, of course, but also something pungent that I assumed was marijuana. As my eyes adjusted, I could see that the stage was dimly lit. Standing on it were four dark-skinned men, three in the background riffing off the sax player out front. His eyes were closed and his body was bent, but his head appeared to be somewhere high above the city. He blew into the mouthpiece and fingered the keys as if he were engaging in foreplay, snatching notes from the air because this tune had been around since the beginning of time, waiting only for the right man to deliver it.

Heads swayed around the room. I sat by myself in a small booth against a far wall. I kept looking around until finally, at a table right in front of the stage, I saw a head turn sideways.

It was her, the nose small and buttonlike, the chin smooth and straight, the hair perfectly in place despite the hour. She leaned close to the man she was with and put her elbow next to her martini glass. He reached into his jacket, took out a cigarette and slipped it into her mouth. She smiled. He put his hand on the table. She ran her fingers over his. He brought his other hand close to her mouth. I saw a flame burning low as she inhaled. The ash glowed red.

Sylvia was with Peter Van Duzer.

The sax player hit a note that was both high and soft, a sound plucked from a smoky eddy. Then he stopped. The crowd cheered and whistled. He bowed a bit, took a handkerchief from his breast pocket and wiped his face. The musicians said nothing as they left the stage.

Sylvia stretched her arms. Van Duzer began to help her into a mink. He glanced my way, but I covered my face with my hat as I headed for the door.

Outside, the cold rushed into me. My eyes watered. I wondered if it was from the air or from disappointment. Sylvia could choose any man in the world, and she had ended up with him.

Finkel leaned out a window on the passenger side. The camera dangled from his hand.

I told him we didn't have much time, opened the door on the driver's side and got behind the wheel. Finkel twisted around and asked what I was doing. I said we'd have to pull away as soon as he got the shot. The front seat was pulled up so far my knees banged against the steering column. I turned the ignition, letting the engine run, before pulling the knob that poured heat into the cold and drafty car.

"Ain't that the dame?"

I tried to look, but not too hard. I didn't want Sylvia's sixth sense to kick in. She was wrapped in the mink. Van Duzer's arms were around her. She looked up at him and smiled. I wondered why she couldn't look at me that way. Suddenly something registered; her face clouded as she glared at the car we were in. I slouched down, pulled my hat as far over my face as I could and yelled, "It's her!"

The night lit up. Sylvia screamed. Van Duzer shouted, "What the—?" in a tone that mixed anger with befuddlement. Finkel pulled his head and camera back into the car. He told me to go go go goddammit go. From the corner of my eye I saw Van Duzer rushing toward the passenger door as Sylvia shrieked, in a tone of hate and command I didn't know she possessed, "Get him!" Then Finkel was shouting what the hell was wrong, I had to get going now. Van Duzer was almost at the door. Finally it clicked—the synapse for survival that always worked in Tuscany whenever the fighting got too bad. I floored the accelerator and pulled into the street even as I heard cars screeching to a stop behind us. Finkel laughed.

Chapter eleven

"Merry Christmas, my young mick friend," McCracken said as I walked into the newsroom. He poured a long finger of bourbon into a glass and knocked it back, then asked if I wanted any. I declined. McCracken said I should have some. It was the best stuff, sent over straight from Bill-O and his boys at City Hall.

He hovered over me. "You know what I love most about Christmas, Grimes?"

I asked if it was the peace on earth or goodwill toward men. McCracken barked out a laugh. He said I was funnier than I looked.

"What I love most about Christmas is listening to the stories as they come in at night."

"Stories?" I asked.

He said nothing, just rubbed his hand over my back as he left.

Because of the holiday, we were using a lot of stringers, most of them Jewish kids from City College who had more enthusiasm than sense. A guy named Applebaum phoned in from Hell's Kitchen. He said two cops were walking their beat on West 45th when they heard a commotion inside a tenement. When they entered the building they knew right away which apartment they needed because the noise was so loud. They knocked but got no answer. So they broke down the door and saw an overweight man in his forties holding a knife to a woman's throat. She was screaming in terror, but he was yelling even louder. It took the cops a few minutes to figure out his problem: he wanted chocolate pie for dessert, but the woman had baked a fruitcake.

"That's good," I said to Applebaum while I turned his facts into a story. "Where'd you get the information?"

"Whaddya mean?"

I didn't think the question was difficult, but I rephrased it anyway. "Who told you what happened?"

"Some guy."

"Try being more specific."

"He was wearing a cop's uniform. He was sitting at the front desk at the station house."

"I need a name."

"Oh."

The calls kept coming. McCracken had been right about the stories, holiday cheer turning to nightmares all over New York. When he stopped by to look over what I'd written, he asked if I was absolutely sure about my refusal to partake in some of the comfort and joy offered on this, the holiest day of the year, by his good friend in the bottle.

I said I was sure.

"I like the one about the fruitcake," McCracken said. "We'll break that out as a separate, maybe even turn it into the wood."

"I have the headline."

"What is it, Grimes?"

"'Fruitcake Drove Him Nuts.'"

I tried not to think about Sylvia, but I could see her on Christmas morning looking over gift-wrapped boxes from Saks and Tiffany's before tossing items she regarded as trinkets into the bottom of a little-used drawer. The butler would ask what she wanted for breakfast.

She'd say toast please, with a mimosa. She had a bit of a hangover. She needed to take the edge off.

The copyboy bellowed that I had a call. I wondered if by wishing I had made it happen.

"Is this Mr. Grimes?"

It was William Anderson. I wished him a Merry Christmas, then winced at my words. The man was in jail. In two weeks he'd be on trial for his life. If he was having any thoughts about Jesus, they must have concerned Calvary.

"We haven't talked for a while, Mr. Grimes."

"I'm surprised to hear from you."

"They said I was allowed one call on Christmas."

"How have you been?"

"That's a difficult question to answer these days."

He sounded weary and defeated. For a second I grew afraid. In Tuscany we always knew who was going to die.

"Try for me, Mr. Anderson."

"My days are long, Mr. Grimes. Long and boring. They're broken up when the guards come in and beat me."

"I'm sorry, Mr. Anderson. I'm awfully sorry. I'm trying my best, but..."

My voice cracked. I didn't know what to tell him.

"What is it, Mr. Grimes?"

"I feel like I'm running in place. I've learned things—bits of information from all over—but I don't know what they mean, or how they fit together. Or if they fit together at all."

I heard a long, low whistle, as if he were close to taking his last breath.

"Have you talked to my lawyer?" he asked at last.

"You finally have one?" I asked.

He said he'd met the man just once. He gave me his attorney's name and suggested I meet him.

It was close to midnight. I smelled McCracken before I saw or heard him. The booze from Bill-O and the boys was having its effect.

"Let's have a little fun with this, Grimes."

He dropped a piece of copy paper on my desk. Heavy dark letters indicated the words had just come over the teletype.

"Get the clips and punch it up. I wanna run it up front for the final."

McCracken weaved slightly from side to side before walking away. The article, out of Los Angeles, concerned a bad storm that had swept in from the Pacific and closed down the airport, stranding dozens of Hollywood celebrities who'd been planning to fly to a dusty town in Nevada to celebrate the opening of a hotel named the Flamingo. The story noted that Elizabeth Manley, now back at MGM and starring in the new musical *Martinis for Lunch*, fell asleep on a couch using her full-length mink as a blanket.

The article pointed out that the Flamingo was the brainchild of Bugsy Siegel, real name Benjamin, protégé of Dutch Schultz and colleague of Frank Costello. When I read that the hotel had wound up costing far more than its backers originally expected, I recalled the Cub Room conversation between Stavros and Costello:

"That's too bad. I like Ben."

"I do, too. But I don't think anyone can help him."

McCracken read over my story and said he liked the way I'd handled it. Although Siegel was Jewish, I had played up the holiday angle: "Bugsy Siegel's Christmas stocking wound up filled with coal as a winter storm washed out the opening of his brand-new hotel in the desert town of Las Vegas."

"What made you think of the coal angle?" McCracken asked.

Mother always told us never to look at our presents before Christmas morning. That made Christmas Eve the longest, most awful night of the year. One time I heard the door to Kathleen's room creak open, followed by the tiptoeing of small feet into the living room. Then I heard a squeal, almost like a mouse, that ended with a running sound and the slam of a door. I wanted to look as well, but my fear was more powerful. I stayed in bed. In the morning, Mother came out of her room looking grimmer than usual. She held out her hand to my sister. They marched to the living room. Mother pointed to the girl's stocking. Kathleen looked in and saw lumps of black sooty stuff. She plunged her hand in deep, then her arm, too. Her nightgown and half her body turned black as she asked in a panic where were they, where were her presents? Mother laughed, almost a cackle. She said Kathleen must have been a very bad girl indeed, because this was what happened to children who looked in their stocking before Christmas morning.

"Something my mother did," I said. My voice was low, almost inaudible. "All I ever wanted was a normal, happy family. I guess that was too much to ask."

McCracken tried to laugh, but the booze made him cough. "All that nonsense you hear about happy families is a myth," he said between hacks. "It's a good thing, too. Otherwise, the world would be a cheerful place with no problems, and there'd be no need for newspapers."

The phone rang the next morning while I was reading *The Trib*—my favorite paper, the place I aspired to work, serious about the news but much livelier than *The Times*. One of the sports stories reported that the Dodgers who hailed from the South did not like the idea of playing with a Negro. While they had no personal beef with this Robinson boy, baseball was a white man's game, and they were making their views known in no uncertain terms to Mr. Rickey.

The call was from Kathleen. I asked how her Christmas had been. She said it was fine, but her voice sounded as if it were twisting around a cord.

"I hope it wasn't too bad for you yesterday," she said.

"It was swell."

"I felt bad, but..." She stopped. I wondered what she was going to ask of me. Then she started, her words rushing together: "We were talking yesterday. About that nigger. The one you saw in the alley. And we all agreed how horrible they are and how awful it's getting and, oh God Pat, everybody's moving but we're stuck, we're just stuck, and I think it's gonna kill me."

"Do you need money?" I asked. "I'll give you what I can. It's not much, but—"

"We don't need your money," she said as she cried. "We need your help."

I was tempted to hang up, but I didn't want the conversation to end this way. Kathleen was the only family I had left.

"I thought about you yesterday," I said. "About you and Mother and the holidays."

"I'm not surprised. She was always at her worst at Christmastime. I think it's because we had no money."

"I think it's because she liked being cruel."

"That's unfair." Kathleen's voice got stronger. She had kept something inside for a long time that she now decided to let out. "You resented Mother, and blamed her for everything that was wrong in your life. And you always sympathized with Dad. I suppose that's natural, you guys sticking together. But do you know something, Pat?"

I now regretted not hanging up when I had the chance. I hoped I sounded weary as I said, "What is it, Kathleen?"

"At least Mother stayed."

I took the El downtown, got off at City Hall and walked south toward Beekman, just past the bridge. In the nineteenth century all the newspapers were housed in the gargoyle-happy buildings along Park Row. But when the business of the city moved uptown, the press followed, leaving the municipal government behind to operate undisturbed.

I climbed narrow stairs to a second-floor landing, where I rapped on a door with a smudged nameplate. A male voice told me to come in. He said the door wasn't locked. He kept it closed because of the draft.

The office belonged to Joshua Zwelnick, William Anderson's court-appointed lawyer. The space was slightly bigger than my bathroom, and it was so stuffed with papers and books there was no place to sit. Near the back wall was a desk that Zwelnick was standing over. Behind him was a framed diploma from Brooklyn Law School. He was tall and thin, with bushy hair and oversized glasses. His overcoat was draped over his shoulders. I doubted he was much older than I was. Three legal pads were arranged in front of him on his desk. Beside them was a bulging folder.

I told him I wanted to talk about William Anderson. He asked why.

"He's innocent."

Zwelnick ran a hand over the yellow paper on his desk. His fingers were long and tapered, almost like a violinist's. I'd never seen a man with such delicate hands.

He said nothing at first, so I told him what I saw that night in Blood Alley right after Amanda Price's body was found. As I gathered my breath to talk about all the real estate transactions in Turtle Bay, he asked how I felt about Chinese food. It was time for lunch and Chinatown was close.

We passed by City Hall and the Tweed Courthouse, the Boss's triumphant monument to corruption. Tammany Hall kept resisting all efforts to kill it, and now its survival instincts were being rewarded. LaGuardia was out, O'Dwyer was in, and Costello controlled everything.

"The city is for sale, Mr. Grimes."

"That's what I hear."

"What disappoints me most is how cheaply the politicians are letting it go."

Zwelnick stooped to tie his shoe. Winter-wrapped people brushed by. The pedestrian bustle was commonplace, so what I noticed was a point of stillness—a figure about thirty feet behind us that had crammed itself into a doorway. The stocky man looked familiar but he also seemed to be missing something. After a moment I realized what it was: his large companion, the one who always looked more menacing—Peter Cangelosi.

Zwelnick and I resumed walking, but I kept turning around.

"Have you seen a ghost, Mr. Grimes?"

"In a manner of speaking."

The stocky man had disappeared. I wondered where he'd gone, and considered the possibility that he wanted to be spotted so I'd know the surveillance on me had resumed.

The sidewalks stayed packed, but the nature of the crowd changed. Soon we were surrounded by Chinese women lurching from one fishmonger to the next, always arguing in singsong cadences. Pungent odors of garlic and cabbage cut through the cold. Storefront signs advertised chop suey, which I'd heard of, but never eaten.

Zwelnick stopped before a narrow window. He announced that this place had the best wonton soup in the city. Just the thing for a cold winter's day.

We sat at a rickety table. The ceilings and chairs were painted red. Calendars adorned with dragons lined the walls. I heard sizzling sounds coming from the back, where I assumed the kitchen was. I smelled onions. Zwelnick ordered a few items that sounded strange. When I asked about chop suey, he shook his head in a manner that indicated he was deeply disappointed in me. Within a minute two bowls of clear soup that each contained an enormous dumpling were placed on the table in front of us. I sipped some soup and cut through the dumpling with my spoon. When little bits of what I assumed were pork floated to the top, I wondered what kind of a Jew Zwelnick was.

"Have you ever heard of the Manley Holding Company?" I asked.

Zwelnick shook his head and asked what it was.

"Most likely a front."

"For whom?"

"I'm not sure."

"I'm an attorney, Mr. Grimes. I need facts. What does this company do?"

"It buys property." I described what I'd found while I looked through the real estate records at the Municipal Building.

"Buying property is perfectly legal, Mr. Grimes."

"Even if it's done through a shell corporation?"

"If a well-known individual were involved, he wouldn't want anyone to know he was behind the purchases. It would drive up the cost of the land in that area astronomically. That's just smart business, Mr. Grimes."

I had a thought I was afraid I'd forget, so I took out a pen and scrawled on one of the paper napkins, "Harrington Price = Manley Holding?" As I wrote the note I said: "You like facts, Mr. Zwelnick. Here are two interesting ones: The Manley Holding Company bought a lot of property from an entity called the 79 Wall Street Corporation. And Harrington Price's office is at 79 Wall Street."

Zwelnick sat back sharply, as if I'd just thrown a tall glass of ice water in his face.

"It is very interesting, Mr. Grimes. But probably not for the reasons you think."

"What do you mean?"

"Harrington Price may work at that address, but he doesn't own the 79 Wall Street Corporation."

"Who does?"

Zwelnick wiped the corner of his mouth. He seemed to be considering just how much to tell me.

"The 79 Wall Street Corporation truly is a shell company. It's owned by Frank Costello."

Something tight squeezed my spine. I lowered my voice but hoped it carried to Zwelnick as I asked, "Why does Frank Costello need a shell company?"

"He has to do something to make all that gambling money legitimate or the I.R.S. will be all over him. Look how the government finally got Al Capone."

Tax evasion. It was like nailing Hitler for double parking, but Capone had gone away for a long time.

"Why is Costello selling all that property?" I asked.

"Maybe he needs the money."

"I'll ask the same question: Why?"

Zwelnick shrugged. "He's a gangster, but he's also a businessman. And every businessman has cash-flow problems once in a while."

I told Zwelnick about the note I'd found in Amanda Price's pocketbook. He said it was interesting, but it didn't prove anything. I said I thought she might have uncovered a gambling ring and was threatening to expose it. He said I could be correct, but right now I had lots of theories but few facts. So I told him about what I'd discovered at the Stork Club. I said I failed to understand why the police hadn't gone there. I couldn't decide if they were cooperating with the people who had killed Amanda, or were just willfully ignorant. Zwelnick said it was most likely the latter. The police had obtained a confession. They had closed the file. They would not change their view of the case, no matter how much new evidence came to light.

I asked Zwelnick if he knew Howard Munzer. The briefest flash of recognition came into his eyes before he shook his head and said no. I told him that I thought Amanda had been trying to make contact with him shortly before her death.

When our main courses arrived, Zwelnick heaped his plate with rice and beef, so I did the same. He used chopsticks. I had to resist the urge to stare. I had no idea how the food stayed on the ends of those things.

"If you don't mind me saying, Mr. Zwelnick…"

He waved his chopsticks in a manner that indicated I should go ahead.

"I've given you good information here. Solid. But you've shot a lot of it down, and don't seem much interested in the rest."

Zwelnick brought a broccoli spear to his mouth. "I may sound like a smart aleck Mr. Grimes, and if so I apologize. But I have to ask you a question."

"Go ahead."

"If your information is so good, why haven't you put it in your newspaper?"

I rode the El uptown. I had no plan but I knew what I needed: some dope I could give to Zwelnick. If he made a stink, I could get a story in the paper. From there, the plot to frame William Anderson would unravel.

I puzzled over the facts I knew. It made sense that one of Costello's companies owned a lot of land in Blood Alley. That gave his operators plenty of options to locate their gambling joints; if the heat got bad at one spot, it was easy enough to fold everything and move it to another.

What didn't make sense was Costello selling all these places to something called the Manley Holding Company. It was possible that the company was just another of Costello's fronts. In that case, he would merely be selling properties back and forth to himself in a game only accountants understood.

I kept doodling on my notepad. I had to look into the Manley Holding Company—I should start by finding out who its officers were—but I had no idea of how to begin.

It was mid-afternoon. The ride was dragging, but I had an inchoate knowledge of where I was going: to Blood Alley, this time during the day, when the light offered at least a modicum of protection. I'd start at the warehouse that housed the gambling joint across the street from the settlement house. There had to be a way in. There had to be something inside that would let me know what was going on.

I got off at 47th and walked east. I finally felt the wind at my back. In the distance I heard pigs squealing their last. Canvas-covered barges packed the river. I glanced around to see if Cangelosi's sidekick had followed me, but the only thing I noticed was a truck rumbling from the abattoirs, kicking up gravel and cold winter dust.

As I made my way along the north side of the block, I took note of the settlement house. In the fading sunshine it looked bleak and gray, exactly the kind of place desperate men would flop in after exhausting all other chances. I wondered if my father had ever wound up there, on his way to whatever fate he had decided was better than spending the rest of his life with Mother and his children.

I stopped in front of the warehouse. For a second I thought about just walking up the stairs and peering in. Then I became concerned I might attract unseen eyes from across the street. So I kept walking until I reached the alleyway separating the warehouse from the building next to it. I turned down the narrow path—it still had cobblestones—and picked up my stride.

I was in the back a few seconds later. The only thing of interest was the warehouse's loading dock, which fronted a large cargo door. A few feet to the right of the dock, a short series of steps led to a metal door wedged between two barred windows.

I climbed the steps and tried the door, which was locked. I gazed up and to the right. A fire escape ladder ran to the roof. A plan finally formed in my head: I'd climb to the top, and from there figure out a way to drop into the warehouse. By now I was confident I was alone and had a couple of hours to poke around.

I jumped and grabbed the bottom rung of the ladder. I was ready to haul myself up, in a manner I hadn't tried since basic training, when the cargo door rattled. The noise startled me so strongly my grip loosened. Before I could recover the door was pulled up. I reached for the next rung, but it was too high. In an instant I was on the ground, on my back, telling myself I'd have to move quickly despite the pain running up my spine.

I raised myself until I was crouching like a sprinter. I was ready to bolt as I looked into the opening where the door had been. I expected to see Cangelosi's sidekick, and in a setting like this he'd probably be accompanied by a squad of goons.

A solitary man stepped onto the loading dock. He was about my size and age. He seemed as perplexed by my presence as I was by his.

One of us had to say something, but I couldn't find any words, so he went first: "What's your angle, pallie?"

I shook my head. "No angle." And then McCracken crashed into my head, his advice flowing freely: "We're in the business of printing the truth, my young mick friend. But that doesn't mean you always have to tell the truth."

This mug didn't seem like a trigger man. I didn't think anybody else was around. All I had to do was come up with something plausible.

"I was supposed to meet some guy," I said. "Looks like he didn't show."

"Name?"

I decided to play a big card. I wanted to see what kind of a reaction I'd get.

"Cangelosi," I said. "Peter Cangelosi."

I thought this might produce a gleam of recognition, followed by an order to scram. But all I got was a look that grew more puzzled with each second.

"Never heard of him."

There was no menace in his voice, just an honest expression of ignorance. I walked toward him slowly. I blew on my hands and made sure to keep them out of my pockets. I needed to get a better look inside the warehouse, and I didn't want this guy to think he had any reason to be concerned about me.

I had killed only men who deserved it. That was what I kept telling myself. Even in Italy, I had done what was right and necessary. We were at war, after all.

I knew I had to say something, so I started spewing guff: "He said he was gonna talk to me about a job. Something about working on the loading dock."

The guy shook his head. "You sure you got the right place?"

Maybe *he* had an angle. Maybe I'd stumbled into a trap, or maybe he was the only palooka they felt they needed to watch the place in daylight.

"Pretty sure," I said.

"'Cause we got nuttin' here."

"Nothing?" I asked in as arch a tone as I'd ever mustered.

He shrugged. "Take a look for yourself."

He stepped away. For a moment I was afraid it was a set-up, but my desire to see was too strong. I climbed up to the dock and listened hard for footsteps, or the telltale pop-pop-pop of a pistol. I was ready to drop and roll.

There was nothing inside the warehouse except air. The place had the cleanly swept look of a joint that had been scrubbed by an army of maids, and was now being showcased.

I almost said, "It can't be." Instead I jerked my thumb and asked, "What gives?"

The guy shrugged again. "They're selling it, I guess. They told me to keep an eye on it and make sure it stayed nice."

I feigned nonchalance. "Who's they?"

Another shrug. "Some gink with dough. I think he owns it. But they're all selling out."

Then he waved his arms around, as if he was trying to embrace all the scummy buildings that occupied the blocks between Tudor City and Beekman Place.

"Everything's changing in this part of town," he said. "Don'tcha read the papers?"

Chapter twelve

The year 1947 was ten days old when I walked into the courthouse lobby. I heard echoing footsteps, mine mixed with dozens of others, as well as voices rising to the dome. Statues of John Jay and Alexander Hamilton overlooked the swirling mass of justice.

"Whadda you doin' here?"

I knew the voice, but the context was wrong. I told myself it couldn't be him. He was never out this early.

"Curiosity," I said to Finkel. "What about you?"

"I'm s'posed to take pitchers, but they won't lemme bring my camera into the courthouse. Weasels. What am I s'posed to do?"

Without his Speed Graphic, Finkel seemed even smaller. His hands kept caressing an imaginary box. I told him that Latimer would be covering the story. He was our main reporter out of the courthouse, so he handled the big cases.

Finkel asked if I knew what Latimer looked like. I said I'd met him once. He struck me as competent and tweedy. There were rumors *The Times* wanted him.

"I ain't never done a trial," Finkel said. "I thought it'd be somethin' different, but this is bullshit."

Soft footsteps stopped beside us. Finkel and I turned in time to see Latimer adjusting his bow tie.

"How'm I s'posed to take pitchers when they won't lemme bring my camera in here?"

Latimer pursed his lips and reached into his jacket. He took out a pipe and a pouch of tobacco.

"You must be Finkel," he said.

"How'dja know?"

Latimer turned to me, shook the tobacco into his pipe and said, "What brings you here, Grimes?"

"We were the first ones at the scene. I wanna see how it plays out."

Latimer struck a match, feeding the flame until the tobacco glowed red. He let a mouthful of smoke escape and told Finkel to get his camera and meet us at the Worth Street entrance.

"That's a side door. Why do I wanna—"

"That's where they always bring in the defendants."

"Why didn't somebody tell me?"

"I just did."

Finkel hurried away. Latimer led me through a series of corridors and stairwells with the confidence of a man who had mastered a labyrinth. He asked if I had a pass for the trial. I said I didn't. I thought I'd just join the line. Latimer shook his head. Pipe smoke trailed behind us. He said the courtroom would be full. This was the case all the regulars wanted to see.

When we stepped onto Worth Street, Finkel was waiting.

"Christ, what were you guys doin' in there? Givin' each other hand jobs? I been standin' here ten minutes. I seen a hunnerd lawyers walk by and I dunno which ones to shoot 'cause you're not here. I swear to God, I ain't never gonna do this again."

Latimer glanced at his watch. He said the prosecutor had told him he'd arrive at ten after nine. Zwelnick had said he'd be there at nine-thirty. Court convened at ten and the guards at the House of Detention never brought a defendant over until a few minutes before that.

Finkel toyed with his camera. I turned my back to the stiff wind. Latimer said he should have brought a flask of brandy.

"That's the prosecutor."

Latimer pointed to a short, barrel-chested man with dark, slick hair, coal-gray eyes and a clipped mustache that aged his face by ten years. Latimer leaned toward me and said, "You know that line about Dewey: 'He's the only man who can strut sitting down.'"

I nodded.

"It's wrong. This guy can do it, too."

"What's his name?"

"Hammond. George Hammond."

The prosecutor slowed when he saw us. He greeted Latimer by name. Finkel said he wanted to take his pitcher. Hammond said he was happy to oblige. Anything for the boys in the press. Finkel took a couple of shots head-on, then sank to his knees and pointed his camera straight up.

"Are you confident, Mr. Hammond?"

"I'm always confident, Latimer, but I never take anything for granted."

"The confession's the best thing you've got, and Anderson says the cops beat it out of him."

"That's what they all say."

Hammond went inside. Latimer wrapped himself more tightly in his overcoat.

"It's too damn cold out here," he said. "We're the only ones nuts enough to be standing outside trying to talk to these guys. Everybody else will get them in the courthouse during a recess."

"So why are we standing outside?"

"McCracken wanted pictures of the lawyers and defendant entering the courthouse. I asked him why and he said—" Here Latimer launched a pitch-perfect rendering of the night editor's sagebrush twang "—'You wanna work for a paper that don't believe in pictures, you Ivy League cocksucker, talk to your pals at *The Times*. Our readers need help.'"

"You know what he told me?" Finkel said. "D'ya wanna know?"

I asked Latimer if he really was an Ivy Leaguer. He shook his head. "Fordham," he said. "But in McCracken's part of the country, anybody who went to school past second grade is considered an Ivy Leaguer."

Finkel was talking. I doubted he had stopped. "So anyway McCracken sez he wanted me to shoot this thing and I sez, 'Why don'tcha use Dietrich?' and he sez, "'Cause he thinks he's a fucking artist and I want a straight-ahead snap,' so I sez, 'Waddya want me to do?' and he sez, 'Make the *schvartze* look guilty.' 'Cept he didn't say *schvartze*."

We all looked down Worth Street. As if by wishing it, a tall man appeared at the corner. He was hatless. His overcoat looked even thinner and more ragged than he was. His cheeks had turned a deep shade of red.

Zwelnick slowed when he saw me, as if he thought his mind was playing a trick. He stopped at the door just as Finkel began wielding his Speed Graphic.

"You must be Mr. Latimer," Zwelnick said. "I've met Grimes."

"How confident are you, Mr. Zwelnick?" Latimer asked.

"I'm always confident that justice will be done."

"Everybody expects the trial to be over in a day. What do you say to that?"

"Everybody can be wrong."

"Are you gonna make a deal? Plead for mercy?"

Zwelnick waited a few seconds, considering several possibilities before finally saying: "My client is adamant. He insists he's innocent. He wants the truth to come out."

Zwelnick looked down into the Speed Graphic, which was ready to take a shot that would reveal every hair in his nostrils. "Are you Mr. Finkel?"

"Call me Finkel. Everyone else does."

Finkel snapped a picture. Zwelnick looked like a man who had absorbed a hard punch.

"You were with Grimes when they took my client in."

Finkel nodded. "They beat up your guy. Smacked Grimes around, too. But I seen 'em do worse.

"I've been trying to get a hold of you for a number of days," Zwelnick said. "You haven't returned my calls."

"I don't like to talk on the phone. 'Cept with my ma."

"Then I'd like to talk to you later. In person. Will you be around?"

"I guess," Finkel said. "But I gotta take pitchers."

Zwelnick entered the building. Latimer said he had to bring me inside so I could get a pass. He told Finkel to get a shot of Anderson when the bailiffs brought him over. Finkel said he knew what to do.

The courtroom stirred just before ten. I glimpsed William Anderson for the first time in weeks. The swelling had disappeared and his cuts had healed, but he'd lost weight. His face bore lines I hadn't seen before. Tufts of his hair had turned gray. His shoulders drooped. He walked with a prisoner's shuffle.

Two guards led him to the defense table, unlocked his handcuffs and shoved him into the chair next to Zwelnick, whose attention never left the sheets in front of him. Anderson shook his wrists.

Everyone stood when Judge Otto Schmidt entered. He was short and plump, a loyal Tammany man who'd gotten his start years before as a precinct captain under Silent Charlie Murphy. Schmidt banged his gavel and said something, but the words blended into the pounding.

Twelve jurors and two alternates were chosen by eleven-thirty. Schmidt ordered the court adjourned until two. Latimer asked if I wanted to have lunch. I said it was a swell idea. Latimer had some calls to make, so he told me to meet him at Moran's on Pearl Street at twelve-thirty.

I walked into the lobby. Finkel was leaning against a marble pillar. His hands were thrust in his pockets. He scanned the faces passing by. Finally a man stopped, and the two of them headed for the door that led out to Foley Square. As they walked into the dull winter daylight, I realized that the man talking to Finkel was Zwelnick.

I began to walk after them, but then I saw someone familiar slouched in a corner. His eyes were focused on the door. I had no doubt he'd observed Finkel and Zwelnick walking out. He pulled himself away from the wall, brushed off his coat and adjusted his fedora.

"What do you want?"

My voice sounded too loud in my ears. People turned to look.

"Tell me! What is it?"

The man in the fedora glanced over his shoulder.

"I know you're following me."

He pushed through the revolving door. I ran after him. On the courthouse steps, a blast of wind almost knocked me back into the lobby. The man in the fedora was walking quickly, almost running, going as fast as he could without drawing attention to himself. I took the steps two at a time. My coat almost flew off. I kept shouting, "Stop!"

He didn't, but I caught up with him. He was a few inches shorter than me, with a scar on his cheek. I put his age at forty or so. He looked Italian. I wondered if he'd been on the force with Cangelosi or if he'd done the honorable thing and joined the mob from the get-go.

"Don't make assumptions." McCracken's voice was in my ear. My newspaper lessons were never-ending. "Assumptions are the midwives of all mistakes."

"You all right, pallie?"

The guy's voice had the rasp that comes from too many cigarettes and not enough sleep.

"Stop following me," I said.

He stood his ground. "What the fuck are you talking about?"

"Do you work for Costello or Anastasia?"

"You're nuts."

"Whoever your boss is, tell him it's not gonna work."

A few people had gathered around us. Others slowed and looked, then continued wherever they were going.

He leaned close. His face brightened a bit. He reminded me of a tough little kid who's happy only when he's stuffing firecrackers into a frog.

"I got news for ya, pal. It always works. And someday we're gonna talk to ya about what happened to Cangelosi."

I froze. He turned quickly. Before I could say or do anything, he blended into the lunchtime crowd.

Moran's was a dark place where deals floated through air heavy with smoke and booze. The tables had the slightly chipped quality that comes from too many mugs of beer crashing down for emphasis. Felt-lined booths were occupied by men in cashmere suits.

I asked Latimer if he'd ever heard of a business called the Manley Holding Company. He shook his head. I said I wanted to find its address and a list of its officers, but the incorporation papers had been filed in Albany. Even if I went all the way up there, I wouldn't know where to look.

"This company isn't in the phone book?" Latimer asked.

"No. I can't find out a damn thing about it."

Latimer wrote something on a piece of note paper that he folded into thirds and handed over. Whatever he was telling me, he didn't want to take a chance of anyone overhearing.

"What's this?" I asked.

"A name."

I must have looked quizzical, because he continued.

"A fellow I know in Albany. Give him a call. He might be able to help you."

I put the paper in my jacket and glanced around. I was ninety-five percent certain no one was watching us.

"I'm glad you're here, Grimes. I'm glad we're getting a chance to talk."

I nodded. Latimer seemed like a good egg.

"I'm at the courthouse most of the time. I don't get into the office much. But I hear things, and I wonder how many of them are true."

I told him I didn't hear much at all.

"One of the things I heard was about you."

My eyes must have gone wide with surprise.

"I hear you're McCracken's boy. The fair-haired wonder."

I said I wasn't aware McCracken had any special regard for me. In fact, I thought he was pretty tough sometimes, but then he was tough on everyone.

"Maybe you're right," Latimer said. "Maybe there's nothing going on. But I'll tell you what the dope is."

I leaned closer to Latimer. He spoke in calm and measured tones.

"I hear you're up for Higgins's job."

The prosecution's first witness was Joey Valentine, my boyhood acquaintance, now a member of the police force enjoying a few moments of fame as one of the officers who'd arrested William Anderson.

Hammond asked him to describe what happened the night Amanda Price was murdered. Valentine said he and his partner had received a call about a girl's body lying near a warehouse in Blood Alley. The caller had told them to look for a colored fella. The night watchman was a Negro and he acted queer, so they brought him in for questioning by Detective Koenig.

"Is the man you brought in for questioning present today?"

"He is."

"Could you point him out for the jury?"

Valentine pointed to William Anderson. Hammond said he had no further questions.

Zwelnick walked toward Valentine with the deliberate pace I associated with gunfighters in John Ford westerns. As Valentine curled back in the witness chair as far as he could go, I remembered that he had always been vocal about his hatred of Jews.

"What was my client doing that seemed 'queer'?"

Valentine picked at one of the buttons on his uniform.

"Did you hear my question, Officer Valentine?"

Valentine turned to the judge, who told him to answer.

"He, uh, he wouldn't respond to our questions."

"What questions were those?"

"Where he'd been all night. What he was doing in an alley with a body. Things like that."

"He was the night watchman at the warehouse. Didn't that seem like a reasonable explanation?"

This prompted some chuckles, an objection from Hammond and an admonition from Judge Schmidt reminding everyone of the seriousness of the proceedings. Zwelnick withdrew the question.

"When you and Officer McMahon arrived on the scene, was anyone there besides my client?"

Valentine shifted in the witness chair. "I believe so."

"Who was there, Officer Valentine?"

He waited a few seconds. "A coupla guys."

"They were two newspapermen, weren't they?"

Valentine nodded.

"Please say something, Officer Valentine. We're making a record."

"You're right."

"A reporter and a photographer?"

"I guess."

"You guess? The photographer took your picture, didn't he? He took a picture of you and Officer McMahon while you stood over the girl's body. It ran in the *Examiner*."

Hammond objected. Schmidt asked Zwelnick to get to the point.

"Did the newspapermen alter the scene in any way?"

"Huh?"

"Had they moved things around? Put items around the body that weren't hers?"

"How should I know?"

"Did you ask them?"

"No."

"Did you or Officer McMahon use physical force against my client or one of the newspapermen?"

"I didn't."

"How about your partner?"

Valentine said he couldn't recall what his partner had done.

McMahon was the next witness. Hammond walked him through his testimony, then glanced at Zwelnick and asked, "Was anybody else at the scene when you and your partner arrived?"

"A couple of men from a newspaper."

"Did they alter the scene in any way?"

"Not that I could tell."

"Did you use physical force against either of them?"

"No."

"Did you use physical force against the defendant?"

"No."

Hammond said he had no further questions. McMahon reached for the water jar beside the witness stand, but before his hand had grasped the handle Zwelnick said, "Exactly what was it about my client's behavior that aroused your suspicions?"

Zwelnick was still seated. McMahon glared at him.

"He was acting like a boy who had something to hide."

"Be specific, Officer McMahon."

Zwelnick stood up, but did not move from the defense table. His voice had strengthened; he sounded like a man who was gaining confidence in what he was doing.

"He was, you know, evasive."

"No, Officer McMahon, I do not know what you mean. Perhaps you can explain it to me."

"He wouldn't answer a simple question. He wouldn't tell us what he'd been doing all night."

"He told me he was making his rounds."

"That's not what he told us."

"Did you give him a chance to talk?"

Hammond objected. Zwelnick turned to Schmidt and said, "Your Honor, I have a witness who will testify that Officer McMahon began beating my client at the scene before any meaningful information had been ascertained."

A wave of murmurs rolled through court. Latimer and I turned to each other and said nothing, but my colleague's amazed look must have mirrored my own: Zwelnick intended to put Finkel on the stand.

"I'm going to sustain the objection," Schmidt said. "You can bring this out when your witness testifies, Counselor. Right now you're badgering Sergeant McMahon. He is an officer of the law, after all."

Finkel materialized as soon as we reached the hallway after court had adjourned for the weekend. The trial would last longer than one day, after all.

"Where they comin' out?" Finkel asked. "Ya gotta tell me where they're comin' out. I gotta get some pitchers."

Latimer said it would take a few minutes. The lawyers had to wrap things up first.

"They goin' out the same way they went in? I can get my stuff and meet you there."

Latimer said they'd probably leave through the front.

"Christ, everybody'll be there. How'm I gonna get some good pitchers?"

Latimer assured Finkel that he would walk out of the building with at least one of the lawyers. "I'll steer him toward you."

"I'm glad somebody's using his noodle around here."

I told Finkel that I'd seen him talking to Zwelnick during the lunch break. "What was that about?"

"Some pitchers I took a while ago. He wants to look at them."

"Couldn't he just buy the paper?"

"They never ran in the paper. But I keep everything. A lotta my best stuff's at home. The ones he wants, I already called my ma. She put 'em in a special place."

Latimer drew out his pipe and begun to suck on it. He asked Finkel if Zwelnick was going to call him to testify.

"He wants to," Finkel said. "How hard can it be?"

"McCracken's not gonna like it," I said.

"I ain't worried about him," Finkel said. "Where's he gonna get someone who can take pitchers like me?" Then he poked me hard in the ribs. "It's gonna be a zoo outside, Grimes. Make yourself useful for once and knock some people outta the way so I can get some pitchers. Ya help me out, I'll give ya a ride back to the office."

I remembered what riding with Finkel was like, so I turned to Latimer and said, "I should call that guy in Albany. The one you told me about."

Latimer told me to use his phone in the pressroom.

The guy in Albany was civil service, so he left at five on the dot. Looking at my watch, I saw that I had three minutes. I found the phone and told the operator to put me through. On the sixth ring, just as I was losing hope, a voice answered.

I identified myself and said I'd gotten this number from Latimer. I said I was looking for information.

"That's what I figured."

He had the long, flat accent of upstate New York, so unlike the hard, fast tones of the city. I said I was looking into a business called the Manley Holding Company. I believed it was based in Manhattan, but it wasn't listed in the phone book. I wanted to know its address and the names of its officers and when it was formed.

The voice sighed. It said it was tired of doing favors for people, but Latimer was on the up and up.

I said I understood how draining it could be, trying to please people all the time.

"When do you need this?" the voice asked.

"As soon as possible."

"Call me on Monday."

I reached the newsroom just before six. As soon as I sat at my desk, the large bony hand I'd grown so familiar with began crawling down my back.

"Latimer said you were at the nigger's trial."

I nodded.

"I have no control over what you do on your own time, Grimes. But I can't pay you for those hours you spent in the courtroom."

"That's okay. I had nothing better to do."

"You have strange ways of spending your leisure time, my young mick friend. On the other hand, you are up to speed on the story that'll lead the paper."

I stood up and began walking across the newsroom. McCracken fell in beside me. He said Latimer was reporting the main. Higgins was working a sidebar about the cops. Both of them would be feeding in to me if I thought I could handle it. I said it wasn't a problem. We stopped at the large metal urn just outside McCracken's office. The coffee oozed out in gloppy black dregs. The night editor glanced at the newsroom clock and frowned.

"Our favorite photographer's gonna be here any minute," he said. "So I'll be spending a lot of time in Finkelville. I can't hover over you like a mother hen, Grimes."

"I'll give you what you want," I said.

I knew the number from memory. When the butler answered, I said I wanted to talk to Sylvia. He asked who was calling. There was no sense of recognition in his voice. I had made no impression on him whatsoever.

"Tell her it's Matthew from Portland, Oregon."

I heard the receiver being placed beside the phone. I wondered if she would realize who it was.

"I have something to say to you, Patrick Grimes."

I waited. I had tried to keep my face hidden when Finkel took her photo as she came out of the jazz club, but it was possible she had seen me anyway.

"I could not believe that picture your newspaper ran of Peter and me. And the way that hideous little man ambushed us. I looked so startled—like some kind of animal. Tell Gracie I'm not speaking to her until you run a picture that shows me at my best."

"Gracie thinks I'm your Cousin Matthew from Portland, Oregon."

Sylvia laughed. I could breathe again. She hadn't seen me after all.

"I was in court today," I told her. "At William Anderson's trial. I was wondering why you weren't there."

"Is this going into the newspaper?"

I had thought of the possibility. The story would have to mention the absence of any member of the Price family. There might be a reason.

"I'd like to put it in," I said.

"I don't think anyone would understand," she said.

I waited a minute. I wanted to write up what she said, but I sensed she was adamant and I didn't want to lose her.

"Okay," I said at last. "I won't use it. But I want to know. Why weren't you there?"

Sylvia sighed. "I'm not sure they have the right man. In fact, I'm certain they don't. But if I show up, they'll all assume I'm on the prosecution's side. And then I'd have to say things like, 'I'm here to see justice done,' and I just can't force myself to lie like that." She paused. She sounded as though she wanted to stop being serious, but the weight of what had occurred was dragging her into a part of life she had tried mightily to avoid. "You should be proud of yourself, Patrick Grimes. You've made a convert."

When we hung up, I put my head in my hands. The thought of Sylvia being forever unattainable was hurting me. I'd always have the picture of us together at the Stork Club. I always kept it close. But I wanted her in the flesh.

My phone rang a minute later. I answered absentmindedly. It was McCracken, his voice full of concerned urgency, asking if I had any idea where Finkel was.

I told him that I'd last seen Finkel at the courthouse.

"Call Latimer in the pressroom at court. See if he knows. Then get back to me. I'm still in the photo lab."

I phoned Latimer, who said he saw Finkel hustling toward his car, lugging his Speed Graphic and muttering about what great pitchers he had.

I told Latimer that Finkel hadn't shown up yet. Latimer said he should have reached the office a long time ago. A familiar sense of dread crawled over me, the same awful feeling I'd had in the war whenever the Germans started shooting at us and I knew they had the range and the mark.

I called McCracken in the photo lab. A few seconds later he was in the newsroom.

"What do we do?" I asked.

"In the short run, Brother Grimes, we think about running some wire photos that'll look like crap. In the long run…" His voice trailed off. He put his arm around my shoulder. His breath reeked of Jim Beam. "I want you to call around to every hospital in Manhattan. Especially the emergency rooms. See if Finkel's been admitted. If he's not in a hospital in Manhattan, try the ones in Brooklyn, and Queens, and the Bronx, and even goddamn Staten Island."

I made the calls, but Finkel was nowhere. Midway through them the clerk shouted that Higgins was on the line. I was tempted to tell the clerk to blow Higgins off, but we were still working on the trial story and it was still the wood.

Higgins said he'd been talking to the cops at headquarters. They all thought Valentine and McMahon had been treated unfairly, but what did you expect from some shyster Jew? Higgins had also talked to McMahon, who said it took all his self-restraint not to go over the railing and punch the fucking kike right in his Hebe nose.

"I'll leave out the obscenities," I said. "And the Jew stuff. People will get the point: Cops hate it when somebody forces them to tell the truth."

"You've got a big mouth for a rookie. But you know what your biggest problem is, Grimes? You've got more ambition than brains."

I was tempted to hang up. I'd gotten all the useful stuff I could. There was no reason to stay on the line.

"I know what you're up to. I know you want my job, and I know exactly what you're like. In this town, punk assholes are a dime a dozen. McCracken goes through them like cheap handkerchiefs."

I told myself to slam the phone down.

"But I've got bad news for you. He's already got his favorite sissy, and it ain't you. It's some nancy boy at *The New Yorker.* I hear he writes like a fucking angel."

A noise erupted in my head that sounded like a pile driver breaking through bedrock. In one of those weird convergences that occur at times of too much stress and too little sleep, Higgins's voice merged with Mother's. All I could hear was that I had turned into a great disappointment, despite all the efforts everyone had put into me. I'd never amount to anything.

It was close to midnight. There had been no word from or about Finkel. O'Shea waved me over and slapped a picture on the copy desk. He said it might take my mind off things. In any case it was interesting.

Sylvia Price was wrapped in a mink. She was accompanied by her father, who wore a cashmere overcoat. They were walking into the Opera House on Broadway and 39th. A poster announced that tonight's performance of *Faust* was for a policemen's charity and would be conducted by Bruno Walter.

"They didn't bother going to court," O'Shea said, "but they showed up at the opera."

I asked what he planned to do with the picture. He said McCracken wanted to run it in the final edition beside the story about the trial. It was more interesting than the static shots we'd used from the wires.

"Grimes!"

McCracken's face was mottled. I wasn't sure if it was from rage or alcohol.

"Grab your coat. Take a shooter."

I must not have moved quickly enough because he said, "Now, Grimes!"

I asked what was up. He said Higgins had just called. A body was hanging from a meathook at a slaughterhouse in Blood Alley. The cops were rushing to the scene. I had to get to First and 46th right away.

The watchman opened the steel door. A blast of refrigeration assaulted me and Dietrich, who was working overtime because of Finkel's absence.

Dietrich kept saying he couldn't do it. I stepped behind and shoved him forward.

Thousands of slabs of frozen meat hung from hooks that ran on conveyor belts just below the ceiling. Raw red carcasses stretched as far as I could see.

"He's over here," the watchman said.

We walked between two rows of dead slabs. Dietrich and I looked at each other but said nothing until we saw the back of a short, squat body from about thirty feet away. Dietrich's voice cracked. He said he couldn't look. The watchman said we were acting as if we knew who it was. I said it was a strong possibility.

Something had been placed in the body's right hand. As I approached, I realized it was a Speed Graphic.

Dietrich said he couldn't go any farther.

I walked around and looked up. Finkel's body was encrusted in frozen blood. His eyes had been ripped out. His nose was smashed flat against his face. One of his flashbulbs had been shoved into his mouth. I bent my head and tried to say a prayer, but the words sounded meaningless. So I sent out an angry question instead: Why do You always allow the strong and ruthless to prevail?

The floor was hard cement, the color of a dirty beach. I noticed something dark sticking out of a crack, so I bent down and picked it up.

It was a matchbook from the Stork Club. I put it in my pocket. Behind me I heard the soft moan of a man trying not to cry. I looked back at Dietrich, who was hunched over like the wailing women I remembered from the war.

"Take his picture," I said.

Dietrich tried to walk away. I grabbed him by the arm and pulled him back.

"Take his goddamn picture," I said. "It's what he would have wanted."

Chapter thirteen

The phone rang me awake at two in the afternoon. I was still drunk. It was Saturday. There was no reason to sober up.

"That you, Grimes?" It was McCracken.

I must have grunted.

"When was the last time you were at The Garden?"

I conjured up a day when I was a boy. Father had the bounce in his step that he affected whenever he wanted to persuade us that things were going better than they actually were. I could hear him saying it was grand, just grand, and we kids were going to have a grand old time. This was something we would cherish all our lives. It was our first visit to the circus. And in my other ear was Mother, trying to make it sound as if she was talking under her breath but conscious that her words were just loud enough for all of us to hear, saying she couldn't believe we were wasting so much of our hard-earned money on frivolities.

"It's been years," I said.

It was just before eight. The cold strengthened the odor of cigar smoke. My stomach churned faster. I passed by a phalanx of round guys in fedoras asking if anyone needed anything down by ringside, up in the rafters, first-row balcony, anywhere at all. LaMotta was on the card. He was always a tough ticket.

McCracken stood outside Schraft's. He looked even grimmer than usual, as if his typical dark humor had left him and all that remained was the bile it masked.

"I was beginning to wonder about you," he said.

"It was hard getting out the door."

"After you've been in the news racket a few years, you'll know how to handle a hangover."

"It's not a hangover. I'm still drunk."

"You're gonna be a great newspaperman, Grimes."

The Garden smelled of beer and sweat. Klieg lights shone down on the ring, which was set up six feet above the floor. McCracken said he loved the fights. It showed a man what was really important.

"And what's that?" I asked.

"That you've gotta beat the crap out of people who get in your way."

I followed McCracken as he picked his way down a narrow aisle that barely separated rows of padded folding chairs. Our seats were just off LaMotta's corner, about ten yards back. McCracken asked if I wanted a beer, then motioned to a passing vendor before I could say anything. Two Rheingolds, fifty cents.

"I thought you didn't drink beer," I said.

"If it comes down to a choice between piss water and nothing, I will always do the honorable thing."

The undercards blurred by, fighters who looked scrawny or desperate clawing at each other before heading out to the hard dark edges of Manhattan's West Side. I had a few more beers. The pain began to subside. Instead my head felt dull and thick. I told myself perhaps it was better this way. If I went through life in a happy haze of drink, I would stop caring so much about everything that was wrong in the world.

Just before the main bout the fight fans began to sway like tall strands of grass catching the beginnings of a breeze. As the men emitted full-throated cheers, I thought a movie star was approaching.

But when I caught sight of who it was, I spun around in my chair and tried to sink as deeply into my coat as I could.

Costello.

His double-breasted suit was spotless. A dark serge overcoat was slung over his arm. He nodded in every direction and shook a few hands. He walked with his head tilted up, acting like the man who owned the joint, and for all I knew he did.

"Hey, Frank."

McCracken called out as casually to the man who ran the rackets as he did to O'Shea when he wanted to change a headline.

"Hey, how ya doin'? Who's gettin' the paper out?"

It sounded as if Costello ran the words over sandpaper before letting them escape. I glanced sideways. McCracken and Costello had their hands clasped together.

"That's the weekend crew's problem," McCracken said. "I just wanna enjoy the fight."

"You will. Jake's a little wild, but he's learning to be a good boy. He'll get a title shot one of these days."

As Costello headed to his seat, I tried to resist the urge to stare at McCracken with slack-jawed astonishment. I must have failed because he said, "For God's sakes, Grimes, you look like a man who's just lost Lana Turner's phone number."

"You never told me you knew Costello."

McCracken poked a bony finger into my chest.

"That fella runs this city," he said. "What kind of newspaperman would I be if I didn't know him?"

After the fight McCracken asked if I'd ever been to Toots Shor's. When I told him I hadn't, he threw his arm around my shoulder and led me down 51st, past rows of cheap walkups. I must have been drunker than I thought because I kept stumbling into garbage cans.

Toots Shor's was smoky, loud, dense with people. On our way to the bar we passed by Shor, a big man with a red face who nodded at McCracken and asked in a booming voice who was editing the worst goddamn rag in the city tonight. McCracken laughed.

They were three-deep at the bar. McCracken and I were both

sweating by the time we reached it. A shot of Jim Beam appeared in front of my boss. The barkeep pointed to me. I said I'd have a Rheingold. McCracken said I was hopeless. He clutched his tumbler and raised it to his lips.

"I haven't felt this bad since my dog died," McCracken said. He finished his shot and slammed the tumbler down. The barkeep was quick with a refill. "Back in Texas. Mangy thing. Bad temper. Couldn't hunt worth a damn. My pa and me, my ma and my sisters, we spent all our days and half our nights talking about how we'd been saddled with the most worthless specimen of the animal kingdom. But then one night he lay down, and he never got up again. For weeks after that we were beside ourselves, crying and feeling sorry for that flea-ridden mutt, and wondering if our curses had somehow contributed to his demise."

"What was his name?"

"I forget."

I drank some Rheingold. It had stopped tasting like anything long ago.

"Who in the world would wanna kill that little Jew bastard?" McCracken asked.

I almost blurted out my suspicions: whoever had killed Amanda Price. I imagined McCracken's voice rising as he said he didn't want to hear any theories, we all knew who killed that girl and it was that nigger. He was gonna be convicted after a fair trial and then the state of New York would do everyone a favor by frying his black ass an even deeper shade of charcoal in the chair at Sing Sing. I heard all that in my head even as I reached for the Stork Club matchbook I'd been carrying in my pocket since I saw Finkel's body. I was about to ask McCracken to explain it away.

I stopped. I drank more beer. They say alcohol loosens the tongue, but it usually deepens my silence.

McCracken regarded his tumbler as if he were mentally undressing a lover. "I wonder what it's like," he said.

"What what's like?" I asked.

"To kill somebody."

I drained my beer. The barkeep refilled it right away.

"I've killed people," I said.

McCracken shook his head. "That's not what I mean. You were in the war."

For a second I considered telling McCracken about Cangelosi. And then I'd pose the question that had been bugging me for what seemed like years: "He mentioned your name. He knew who you were. Why was that?"

I kept that thought inside. Instead I said, "It doesn't matter what the circumstances are."

My tongue was thick and dry. I felt like I was atop a steep slope that led directly into the worst part of myself.

"Then tell me about killing, my young mick friend. The straight dope. I'm a big boy. I can take it."

I remembered Mother lecturing me about how important it was to confess all the sins on my soul. Even one blot against me when I died would condemn me to hell for eternity. Eventually I realized she was feeding me nonsense. Confessing your sins was like admitting weakness; instead of giving you a new beginning, it just invited attacks, condemnation and ridicule. It was better to keep everything inside, never tell anyone anything.

But McCracken's smug certitude offended me. He believed he knew more than anybody else in the room, although in the end he had only observed life, not experienced it.

"It was in Italy," I said, "just north of the Arno River."

McCracken sighed. "I cannot believe I'm gonna listen to a goddamn war story."

I ignored him. "We'd been in a bad fight. Some krauts ambushed us. They'd been hiding in a church and they opened fire after we passed by. Bastards killed some of my buddies—Henderson, O'Connell, a guy from California named Escobar I'd been with since basic training."

"You're getting weepy because of a wetback?" McCracken asked.

I smacked my open palm down so loudly several of the men around us turned to look. "He was the best G.I. in Italy, you fucking cracker."

McCracken leaned close to me. He stabbed a bony finger into my chest. "You better calm down, Grimes."

I pushed his hand away. "Stop touching me." My breath was short. Now my words escaped in staccato bursts. "We surrounded the church. Fired everything we had into it. You can imagine how I felt, a good Catholic boy like me, shooting up the sanctuary of Our Lord." I laughed at myself, grabbed more beer and gulped it down. "After a while we saw a white flag waving from a window. Five of them came out. Their hands were raised. About twenty of us gathered around them."

"So you shot the fuckers. Good. I don't blame you."

I shook my head. "None of us could do anything. It was like we were paralyzed. Finally our lieutenant told me to take charge of the prisoners. I felt like telling him I didn't want to, but it was an order."

McCracken drummed his fingers on the bar top. "You ever gonna get to the point?"

"My unit was moving out. We had to take a new position. But now we'd lost all these men, and I had to bring the krauts to a holding place behind the lines. It would've taken me all day. So, just as I was about to leave, another officer came up. It was a captain this time. And he said two words that changed everything."

I reached for my beer again. I've never liked talking on and on, but now that the story was finally coming out, I felt I could keep going the rest of the night.

"What were the two words, Grimes?"

"'Hurry back.'"

McCracken raised his tumbler to eye level. "So what happened next?"

"I led those men down the road. They were walking ahead of me, sharing cigarettes and laughing. Why shouldn't they? They'd lucked out. American prisoners. They didn't have a care in the world." My lips were cracked. I licked them and went on. "I was carrying a submachine gun. We walked for about fifteen minutes. It was awfully still around us. They were about twenty feet ahead of me, all five of them, side by side and walking together, stretching about halfway across the road."

McCracken pulled away a bit. "I don't think I like where this is going, Grimes."

"You said you wanted to know. So I'm telling you." I drained my beer. I'd lost count of how many this was. "The gun was at my hip. I raised it up. I wanted to make sure of what I was doing, so I stopped walking."

I motioned to the barkeep. Another Rheingold appeared.

"It's incredible what men can sense," I said, "because I didn't say anything. I thought I was being absolutely quiet. But when you're constantly on edge, when your life is always in danger, a lot of times a sixth or seventh sense kicks in, and you know something bad's about to happen."

I smiled and drank.

"That's when they slowed down," I said. "Those fuckers slowed down. One of them even turned around to look at me."

I remembered it clearly, of course: all the details had imprinted themselves in a part of my brain that was immune to forgetting. The prisoner who'd turned raised his hands and looked ready to shout, so I squeezed the trigger. A burst of bullets struck him in the chest. He staggered back and tried to say something, but the only things that came out of his mouth were gurgling sounds followed by spurts of blood. He fell to his knees before his already dead body sprawled on the ground.

My other prisoners stared at him, then twisted to look at me. For a second, even though they were anticipating what I was about to do, they were overcome by the same paralysis that had gripped me and my buddies not even an hour before.

I squeezed the trigger again, working from right to left. Three of them went down right away, but the guy on the end broke toward the field at the side of the road before I was finished. I only winged him before my gun jammed.

He started swaying, hunched over, his arm grasping his side. I ran toward him as I put in a fresh clip. The gun still wouldn't work.

I reached him as he stumbled into the ditch that separated the road from the field. Rows of olive trees stretched for miles.

The German tried to wriggle up the side of the ditch. The blood oozing out of him covered his hand and stained his gray uniform down to his knees. His face was ashen. His teeth were clenched. I was gazing at a man who was desperate to preserve his life.

His free hand grasped for something that could pull him up. I slid down into the ditch but remained upright. I towered over him. I had never felt so tall. I had never felt this kind of power.

"Nein."

The word was a grunt. Although I didn't understand his language, I knew exactly what he meant.

I lifted the barrel of my gun over my head. The German removed his blood-covered hand from his side and tried to lunge at me. I swung the gun down and hit him in the throat. He collapsed back into the dirt. Then I was above him, my arms like pistons as I raised my gun and struck him in the head with all the force I could muster, over and over again, his "nein"s growing softer with each blow. After a while he became quiet and still, but I kept going until I heard his skull crack open and saw his brains trickling from his ears.

I climbed up to the road. My uniform was covered with mud, dirt, blood and goo. I walked a long time and tried to keep my mind empty. When I rejoined my unit, the captain asked what had happened. I said I'd killed the prisoners as they tried to escape. He said my information would be reflected in his report. He was going to put me in for a medal.

For the first time in what seemed like hours, I glanced at McCracken. He was as far away from me as the crush of the crowd would allow. His eyes had gone wide, as if all the alcohol had had no effect whatsoever. Here was a newspaperman staring not at a disembodied piece of copy describing the darkness of the human spirit, but at the real thing, and it had been working side by side with him for months.

"You wanted to know what it's like," I said. I tried to keep my voice quiet, sliding it in under the drunken din of a Saturday night.

McCracken recoiled a bit more.

"I thought it would feel great. I was the righteous avenger. Even more than that. When I stood over that German as he thrashed for his life in the ditch, I felt I had the power of God."

"You're a cold-blooded killer," McCracken said from a thousand miles away.

I ignored him again. "But that feeling lasts only a short while. It didn't even survive until the next day. And I started thinking about it, and I keep thinking about it, because after a few days I realized that when you kill somebody, part of you dies, too.

"And that's what I've been trying to do. Ever since then. I've been trying to get that part of me back."

I don't think McCracken heard me. Instead he slinked farther away and muttered: "A killer. In cold blood."

He eased himself off his barstool and threw his coat over his shoulders.

"What's the matter?" I asked. "Don't like the truth?"

He was hurrying the buttons, again reminding me of a lover, but this time one trying to escape an ill-advised liaison. "I've decided I don't much like you, Grimes," he said. "In fact, I've decided your probation at the *New York Examiner* is over, and you've flunked it." He paused. He kept looking down. "Savvy?"

And then he was gone. I asked the barkeep for a shot of Jameson's. As I stared at it I shook my head and chuckled, because I had kept the worst thing of all hidden from McCracken.

After I climbed out of the ditch, I walked back to look at the other Germans I'd shot. I wanted to make sure they were dead.

Their bodies were already stiff, arms and legs stuck in grotesque angles. And then I looked at their eyes, which I thought would be blank or at least vacant. But they all looked terrified, and I was seized with an awful knowledge. With their last breaths, they had peered over the boundary between life and death, and they were silently telling me what was on the other side: absolute dark, an infinite void, nothingness for eternity.

Chapter fourteen

I tried to look confident as I walked into the courthouse on Monday. I told myself to stand straight, throw my shoulders back, stride like a forceful man who knew the answers to everything. Although I no longer worked for the *Examiner,* I could not let go of the story. If I could unravel it, I was sure I could sell it somewhere.

I stopped in the lobby and stared at a statue of Justice, her eyes covered, the scales unbalanced in her hands. Latimer slipped in beside me.

"I used to think it meant Justice is blind," he said. "Now I think it means Justice can't see a goddamn thing."

We walked toward the courtroom. Latimer said the cops had asked him about Finkel. He had told them everything he knew, which wasn't much.

"They think it was a professional job," Latimer said. "So do I. Which raises the question: why would professionals want to kill Finkel, of all people?"

I had my suspicions, of course, but now that I was totally on my own I felt even more strongly that I had to keep my thoughts and knowledge to myself. I didn't know how to respond to Latimer's question, but I was saved when a whooshing sound swept through the lobby. Bodies surged toward the courthouse steps. I joined them in pushing outside. A regiment of newsmen engulfed a man and a woman making their way toward the door one slow step at a time. The shouts of the photographers sounded like the explosions of small shells: "Here!"

"Over here!"

"Look this way!"

"This way, Miss Price!"

Sylvia wore a calf-length wool coat, as well as a hat with a veil that would have looked appropriate at a wake. Her eyes were fixed on the ground.

"Why are you here, Miss Price?"

"What made you come today?"

"Why weren't you here on Friday?"

Rising over the shouts was a man's voice, smooth but hard, a voice I kept trying to place: "Gentlemen. Please. Gentlemen. Give Miss Price some room."

"Who are you?" It sounded like the guy from *The News*.

"Peter Van Duzer."

"Why are you here, Mr. Van Duzer?"

"As a friend of Sylvia's."

"What about you, Miss Price? Can't you give us something?"

Sylvia lifted her head a bit. Her eyes were watering. As I looked into them, I realized she was engaging in an action somebody had forced her into.

"I want to see that justice is done," she said.

Detective Walter Koenig had an enormous bald head and deep-set, coal-colored eyes. His shoulders were yards wide. His chest seemed ready to burst through his shirt. As he described how he obtained William Anderson's confession, his voice was deep and rumbling, a bass with no modulation. Throughout his testimony, Koenig insisted that Anderson had never asked for a lawyer.

On cross-examination, Hammond objected to all Zwelnick's

questions. Judge Schmidt sustained the prosecutor on every point. Zwelnick closed his eyes and lowered his head. His voice dropped to a mumble as he said that the judge was making things quite hard on his client, whose case had already been greatly damaged by the murder of a potential witness late Friday. The judge slammed his gavel and instructed the jury to disregard Zwelnick's remarks. He told the lawyer he was courting a citation for contempt.

I jotted some notes in the pad I'd brought with me. They helped me to think. Finkel was dead, but the evidence he had intended to give Zwelnick might still be in the apartment he had shared with his mother. I also needed to check back with the source in Albany that Latimer had given me. Then I'd have to take the El to the end of the line in the Bronx.

I wondered why Zwelnick hadn't asked me to take the stand. I assumed there was something in my demeanor he didn't trust. He had always kept me at more than arm's length. I thought of approaching him during a recess, but decided against it. I'd have to wait until I had something tangible to show him.

Schmidt adjourned the proceedings at ten minutes to five. I planned to call Albany after I rushed up to the pressroom. The door there was always unlocked, and all the reporters would be chasing comments from the lawyers.

But even then, with a man's life at stake, I had to glimpse her one more time.

Mother was astute: I could not resist temptation.

Van Duzer patted Sylvia's shoulder as he helped her into her coat. She rubbed her hand on top of his. It took all my self-control to refrain from shouting, "No!"

I must have gazed a second too long. Sylvia turned her head and looked right at me with the dismissive look of a Park Avenue lady walking past a beggar.

I sprinted out of there. As I had suspected, the pressroom was empty. I pushed open the door, picked up the phone on Latimer's desk and barked that I needed an operator.

After what seemed like days, I got through to Albany.

"I called the other day." I tried not to sound as desperate as I felt. "About the Manley Holding Company."

"I've been waiting for you. I found that information."

I uncapped my pen. Ink spilled onto Latimer's blotter.

"Incorporated on November 2, 1942," he said.

"I need its address."

"Post Office Box 697, Church Street Station."

The next words barely escaped: "I need the officers."

"Current, or when it was incorporated?"

"Both."

A long sigh. The obligations of the phone call were growing with every word.

"When the company was incorporated, the chairman was Donald Wetherby."

The pen squirted out of my hand, drenching the manila folders on Latimer's desk with ink. Amanda Price's fiancé, a man with a sterling reputation, was the original head of a company that struck me as a flimflam outfit.

"Hello? Are you still there?"

"I'm sorry," I said. "I dropped something."

"There's a note that says the presidency of the company changed hands in December 1944."

"So who replaced Wetherby?"

"A man named Vincent Fiore."

The name meant nothing. I'd have to dig to find its significance. But there was still some information this fellow could give me.

"Does the name Harrington Price appear on any of the incorporation papers?"

The source laughed. "Even I've heard of Harrington Price, all the way up here in Albany. No, he's not listed."

Sometimes in a fight, a boxer who was way behind in the late rounds would start swinging wildly, hoping he'd land the great knockout punch. The tactic was rarely successful, but when it worked the guys in the upper deck went berserk, raining hot dog wrappers and beer cups down on the ring. The fans who had bet on the favorite would start chanting, "Fix! Fix! Fix!" Once in a while the cops had to climb through the ropes to escort everyone out. Sitting in his usual spot, Frank Costello would try not to smile.

"Is anybody else named Price listed?" I asked.

This question produced a long, low hiss. Seconds later, the voice said, "In the fall of 1943, the name of Amanda Price was added to the board."

The earth opened up beneath me. It took all my strength to ask the next question: "Does the name Sylvia Price appear anywhere?"

"Why, yes," he said. "Early last year, Amanda Price's name was removed, and Sylvia Price's was added."

My body became unmoored. My half-formed suspicions began to cohere: the Price sisters were far from being insulated from the shady dealings in Blood Alley. I floated above myself, looking down at the desks and chairs and papers before being pushed along by a draft and getting sucked through a window. For a moment I hovered over the city, looking down at City Hall and the Woolworth Building and all the freighters and passenger ships plying the Hudson. I thought of how soothing it would be to drift down to one of the boats heading into the Narrows. I'd land gently on its deck. When the captain asked where I was going, I'd say anywhere, just take me out of my life.

As I rode the El uptown I slouched back and watched the skyscrapers get smaller. The train passed by Colonel Ruppert's brewery in the nineties. The area always smelled bad, but he'd used his beer fortune to buy the Yankees. In East Harlem the buildings were low and dim, the passengers black and brown. They looked at me furtively, as if they were afraid I was a cop.

The train rolled up the east side of the Bronx until its last stop at Tremont Avenue. I walked a few blocks past rows of drab apartment buildings, most of them filled with railroad flats. When I found the number I wanted, I hiked up four flights and stopped at the door on the landing. From inside I heard the solitary sound of an old woman crying.

I knocked, then called out: "Mrs. Finkel? My name is Grimes. I worked with your son. I just wanted to tell you how sorry I was."

I wanted her to open the door. I needed to get inside.

"Arthur?" the voice said. "You know my Arthur?"

The knowledge that Finkel had a given name came close to astounding me.

"Yes, ma'am. We worked together." I tried to think of something nice to say. "He was a wonderful photographer."

"Stay. Please. You come all this way."

A chain was pulled loose. The door opened. Finkel's mother was about four foot six, round as a bowling ball and dressed entirely in black.

The room was furnished with Salvation Army castoffs. Mrs. Finkel motioned toward the sofa. I tried to sit between two uneven lumps, but one of them kept pushing against the back of my thigh. Mrs. Finkel took a chair catty-corner to the sofa. Her feet dangled an inch above the floor. She asked if I wanted something to eat. I said I wasn't hungry.

"You know my Arthur well?"

I told her I felt awful about what had happened.

"Many times these last few days I ask—" here Mrs. Finkel lifted her eyes skyward, "—why He allows this. But He doesn't seem to be home."

On the table between us stood a framed photo of two small people staring straight into the camera. I pointed at the picture and asked if that was Mr. Finkel. She nodded and said: "Arthur took it. Many years ago. We were on Essex Street and he was small boy. He loves his camera always, so he took our picture. Good, you think?"

I nodded, then asked if Mr. Finkel had passed away. She said he had. I squirmed on the sofa. A new lump pressed into my buttock.

"Such a good son," she said. "Two, three times a day he calls from work to ask how I am. How many boys do that?"

"Not many."

"You're not Jewish."

"No, ma'am. Irish Catholic."

She shrugged. "They're nice people."

On the table next to her I saw a black handbag with the stiffly shiny look of something that had just been bought.

"Why?"

Mrs. Finkel pitched forward and dropped her head into her hands. Her tiny shoulders heaved.

"Why they do this? Why they do this to my boy?"

Thoughts I could not express ran through my head: We were up against an evil force that was almost impossible to stop. Perhaps I should have walked away. But I couldn't. Now Finkel was dead; it was my fault; I had yet one more thing to atone for.

"You know." Her words were hissed more than spoken. "You know why they kill my boy."

"Not entirely," I said. "But I'm pretty sure he knew something. He knew something I didn't or else they would have killed me. But what was it? What could he have known that I don't?"

Mrs. Finkel sat back in her chair as far as she could go. "You talk crazy."

"I'm just trying to find out the truth. Maybe that makes you crazy."

I was finally turning to my real reason for coming here. It had nothing to do with comforting an old woman whose son had been murdered. "He was supposed to give something to a lawyer," I said. "Some pictures he took that never ran in the newspaper. He said he told you about them, and you put them in a special place."

She shook her head.

"You don't have to hand them to me, Mrs. Finkel. Just show me where they are."

"No."

The word echoed like cracking chalk. I stood up and looked around. The apartment had much the same layout as the place I'd grown up in, which meant the boy's room would be just past the kitchen.

I headed for the back as quickly as I could. Two long strides through the living room and then another three through the kitchen put me at the door, which was open a crack. From behind I heard a squawk of surprise, followed by a shriek of disapproval.

When I pushed open the door, I saw a room filled with stacks of prints that stretched almost to the ceiling. There was barely enough room for a man to make his way to the bed. I began to wonder again if the rumors were true, and Finkel actually slept in the photo lab.

I heard feet brushing against the floor. A voice mixed with anger and despair said, "Why you do this?"

I had only a few minutes. The old woman was likely to start yelling at me, and those sounds could attract the attention of her neighbors. I grabbed a few pictures off the top of the stack nearest me. Most were of crime scenes and had never appeared in the paper. I guessed that Finkel couldn't bear to get rid of them, so he brought the prints home, piling them up until they became an archive of mayhem.

The backs of the pictures were all marked with a date written neatly in red ink. The photos in my hand had been taken in January 1947 and December '46. Even if the stacks went in a chronological procession, with the most recent near the door and the ones from his days as a cub photographer somewhere by the closet, it would still take me days to sort through them—and what was I looking for, anyway? Would it be obvious, or was it a subtle detail in a years-old picture that only Finkel would notice?

"You get out."

The old woman stood in the doorway. She looked at me as if I were desecrating a shrine.

"Where are they, Mrs. Finkel?"

"Get out now."

"I need the pictures. A man's life is at stake."

"This room is Arthur's. You no belong here."

Since the prints in my hand didn't help me at all, I put them back and left the room. As I walked through the apartment, defeat once again filling me, my eyes settled on the new handbag, which I assumed Finkel had purchased for his mother with the ten dollars he received for taking the photo of Sylvia Price and Peter Van Duzer leaving the Downbeat.

Someplace special.

I walked over to the bag. The clasps were metal and hard to manipulate, but eventually I pried them open and looked in. By now, of course, she was yelling:

"Get away!"

Inside the bag was a small manila envelope with a single word in red ink: "ZWELNICK." It felt as if some pictures were inside. I shook them into my hand.

"I call right now!"

The pictures came out with their backs toward me. In the same neat handwriting I had seen on all the photos in Finkel's room was a date: April 28, 1944. The day Anthony Mancini was executed.

I flipped over the first picture. It was a shot of Van Duzer. The caption under the photo said it had been snapped outside his townhouse near Gramercy Park. From the angles of the shadows, it looked as if dusk was moments away.

In the picture Van Duzer was walking down Irving Place with two men who were described as being unidentified. But I had no doubt who they were. On the day his daughter's convicted killer was executed, Van Duzer had met with Peter Cangelosi.

Trailing behind them was a smaller man with a scar on his face, the guy who had melted into the lunchtime crowd outside the courthouse after telling me that his side always won. I was willing to bet all my meager possessions that his name was Vincent Fiore.

I put the photos back in the envelope. "I'm going to take this, Mrs. Finkel."

"You put it back."

"He told you to take these photos out because he was gonna give them to a lawyer. Since he can't do it, I will."

"Nothing leaves that is Arthur's."

She stood inches in front of me, blocking my way. I thought of just shoving her aside. I raised my hand. But then I couldn't move it anymore. Instead I said: "A man is on trial for his life, Mrs. Finkel. For a crime he didn't commit. These pictures might help acquit him."

She wobbled a bit. I decided to press on, as if I were the lawyer making the final plea to William Anderson's jury: "Your son, Arthur, was going to give these photos to the man's lawyer. So he could help. Fink—Arthur isn't here anymore. But he can still do some good."

Her shoulders sagged. Her mouth began to open and close rapidly, small bursts of air entering and leaving her body. She was on the verge of losing it, and I felt like crying, too.

"Please, Mrs. Finkel. Haven't enough people been killed for no good reason?"

She walked to the door and jerked it open. I thanked her as I passed. My eyes were wet. As I stepped into the hallway, I heard a sob bursting out behind me.

The air was stifling. I had to get outside, so I ran down the stairs. Seconds later, out on the street, the cold snapped me alert. The El was just a few blocks away. Soon I'd be back in my apartment. In the morning I'd go downtown and hand the pictures to Zwelnick. If he was going to present them as evidence, I would have to testify, and I knew I had a good story to tell. All I had to do was create reasonable doubt in the minds of the jurors, and William Anderson would be acquitted.

"Did you find it?"

The voice came from the shadows. I kept walking as a pair of footsteps fell in behind me.

"I'm talking to you."

The envelope was in my hand. Anyone could see it.

"You better slow down. Before I do something."

I crossed a side street quickly, just in front of a DeSoto with high beams as intense as searchlights. Its horn blared. I looked ahead. No one else was on the street.

Heavy feet came up behind me before slowing about a step away. Hot breath blew against the back of my neck.

"What kind of stunt was that?"

I told myself to ignore the words.

"Say something, you fruit."

The Tremont station was getting closer with every step. All I had to do was get there and climb the stairs.

Then he moved in front of me, standing right on the curb, a short and stocky man in a fedora blocking my way. He pointed a gun at my stomach. The scar on his face seemed to twitch.

"What's in your hand?" he asked.

"Some pictures of you."

He reached for the envelope. I raised it over my head.

"C'mon," he said. "I hafta see if they got my good side."

"I'll tell you about them. They were taken on April 28, 1944. Do you remember what happened that day?"

"I got an egg cream at Schraft's."

"Anthony Mancini was executed. The pictures were taken later that day. They show you and your friend Cangelosi with Peter Van Duzer. What were you talking about?"

"He didn't want an egg cream. But I insisted." He waved the gun a bit. "C'mon. Hand it over."

I extended the envelope a bit.

"Your name's Fiore, isn't it?"

"And yours is nigger lover. Gimme the envelope."

"Have you been waiting for me here?"

"Yeah. We knew you'd show up for the stuff Finkel was gonna give to the nigger's lawyer. You're pretty fucking predictable, pal."

Behind him, down Tremont Avenue, a solitary Buick was going much faster than the speed limit. The car weaved over the median line and back toward the curb in a manner that indicated the driver had enjoyed a few too many cocktails at the nearest dive.

"Tell me about Cangelosi," I said.

"I knew you killed him. But nobody else believed it. They didn't think you were that kinda guy."

"That's because they don't know me," I said. "Why didn't you look for his body?"

"Woulda caused all kinds of problems if I'd found him. I knew some dumbass upright citizen would do it. Then my guys finally started listening to me about you."

The Buick slowed slightly and swung to the left side of the avenue. I realized the driver meant to turn onto the side street we were facing.

"Where were you that day?" I asked.

"I took care of that broad from the flophouse."

"You killed Terry?"

He shrugged. "Maybe I did. Maybe she just hit the road. That's what you shoulda done." He flashed the type of grin that belonged to a torturer who enjoys his work. "Some things in life are just a fucking mystery, pal."

"Speaking of mysteries, how did you guys find out where I lived?"

"Your boss. McDougal, whatever the fuck his name is."

"McCracken?" I wished I had been surprised. I told myself I'd been right not to trust him.

"Then my guys told me to lay off. Guess your boss had second thoughts." He shook his head, like a disinterested observer wondering how things could have gone so wrong. "We just wanted to scare ya, kid. But you didn't have enough sense to drop it."

I raised the envelope a bit more. The button man reached for it, leaving himself off balance. As the Buick careered toward a right turn, I reached forward and shoved him in the chest as hard as I could. He backpedaled a few steps, into the street, his arms pinwheeling so he wouldn't fall to the cold hard asphalt. He looked surprised and angry. I knew he was going to shoot me as soon as he regained his footing.

The Buick turned. It was doing forty.

The button man must have seen its headlights in his peripheral vision because he twisted his head and screamed, "Oh shit!"

The last sound I heard before averting my eyes was the solid *thunk* of a human body being struck by a moving machine that was large and powerful.

I ran. I ran even before I heard tires screeching too late, followed by the solid crash of metal slamming into metal. I ran before I heard doors opening, with bewildered shouts and curses coming immediately after. I ran without looking back at what I had caused.

Chapter fifteen

As I took the El downtown the next morning I flipped through the *Examiner.* I was looking for one particular story, which I found buried in an ad well. Under a small headline that said "Fatal Accident in the Bronx," I read that a former NYPD patrolman named Vincent Fiore, who had been dismissed from the force in 1943 for reasons the article did not make clear, was killed at an intersection near Tremont Avenue after being struck by a car driven by a guy the cops described as a well-known local lush.

At the courthouse I stopped outside the entrance the lawyers used on Worth Street. I waited alone. All the reporters and photographers were loitering on the front steps, hoping Sylvia Price would appear.

At a quarter to ten I saw a tall, thin, hatless figure trudging up the street. I kept my back to him. I didn't know how he'd react if he saw me. I waited until he was only a few feet away before I turned and said his name.

Zwelnick said he didn't have time to talk. Wordlessly, I extended the envelope I had taken from Finkel's apartment. Zwelnick halted, then shook out the pictures inside. I pointed to the men with

Van Duzer. I was going to identify them. Before I could say anything Zwelnick started in:

"You don't have to tell me anything about them, Grimes. I've done my own digging, and I know all about Cangelosi. Since Fiore had less seniority, he served as the bagman for Cangelosi and everybody else in the Blood Alley precinct. That's the way the pad usually works."

He put the pictures back in the envelope. He had the sad eyes of a man who knew he was right, but was certain he would lose.

"My job is to create a reasonable doubt in the minds of the jurors, and it's curious that Peter Van Duzer, now a regular attendee at the trial, was an associate of crooked cops in the very same precinct where Amanda Price was murdered. I was gonna slide these pictures into evidence after I put Finkel on the stand to testify about what he saw when McMahon and Valentine arrested my client."

He nodded to himself, satisfied with his summation. He'd never have the opportunity to use those words in front of the jury, so I had to do. Then he put his head down and tried to get by me.

"Put me on the stand," I said. "I can tell how I got the pictures. And I saw what the cops did to your client. Then I can talk about the Manley Holding Company. Do you know who its president was?"

Zwelnick shook his head.

"Vincent Fiore. Who died last night. Hit by a car. It was tragic."

Zwelnick licked his lips.

"It gets better," I said. "Sylvia Price is on the board. She replaced Amanda on it about a year ago."

Zwelnick's face registered a glimmer of something a few steps short of hope. Then his all-encompassing sadness returned.

"It's all very interesting, Grimes. But there's no proof that connects the facts you've just raised to this case."

"You've gotta try something."

"I will try something. But I'm not gonna put you on the stand."

"You were gonna have Finkel testify. Why not me?"

Zwelnick looked at the ground, drawing my eyes down as well. His shoes were scuffed and faded.

"You have a history with Officer Valentine, don't you? You two grew up together."

"We lived in the same neighborhood. We weren't close."

"You went to the same school. And there was lots of antagonism there—the Irish kids picking on the Italians."

"What's your point?"

"Maybe you've forgotten what happened, but Valentine hasn't. He thinks you've got it in for him. And if you testify, he'll go right back on the stand to impeach your credibility."

"I'll put my word against his any day."

Zwelnick looked at me with a mixture of disgust and contempt, the way Mother used to glare at my dad whenever he got home from the pub. "It will be the word of a New York City police officer against a newspaper reporter," Zwelnick said. "I don't have to tell you whom the jury will believe."

Zwelnick led Anderson through testimony I expected: he had been badly beaten by the police, had never seen a lawyer until after he had signed his confession, and most definitely had not killed Amanda Price.

When Zwelnick was done, Hammond said the People had one question and one question only. The prosecutor walked toward the witness stand. He held a piece of paper aloft.

"Is this your signature?"

Anderson squinted hard before allowing that it was.

"In this document you admit to killing Amanda Price, a defenseless girl, for money. You admit everything in your own words. I don't see where the People have to prove anything else."

Shouts and cries swept the courtroom. Zwelnick objected. He was overruled.

After the lunch break Zwelnick said he had one last witness. Hammond objected. He said he had been made aware of this man only this morning, and in the necessarily abbreviated checking his office had carried out, it found no relevant link between him and the crime.

"Begging the court's pardon," Zwelnick said. His voice had unexpected tones of respect and deference. Whatever he wanted, it was so important he was willing to grovel.

"Hear this man out," Zwelnick said. "Let him tell what he knows. If you deem it irrelevant, tell the jury to disregard him. But my client is on trial for his life, and he deserves the opportunity to let his counsel present all the evidence that might exonerate him."

Judge Schmidt stroked his two chins. I sensed that he did not want to allow the witness, but Zwelnick had raised some points he could use on appeal. Schmidt glanced at Hammond with a pleading look that asked the prosecutor to provide a way out. Hammond rose.

"Your Honor," he said, "I believe this witness is extraneous and a waste of the court's time. He will discuss issues that should not be made public, and that are covered by a restraining order from a previous case."

My eyes wandered around the courtroom. I had an idea of who the witness was. A sighting would provide confirmation.

Hammond continued: "What I propose is this, Your Honor. Let's hear a summary of what this witness has to say privately. It shouldn't take long. If you decide his testimony is pertinent, the entire court can hear it."

Schmidt nodded. I thought I saw him smile. He said the prosecutor's suggestion was excellent. Court would be recessed for fifteen minutes.

The lawyers followed Schmidt into his chambers. Reporters milled in the courtroom a few seconds. When Sylvia and Van Duzer headed for the lobby, everybody followed but me.

I waited. I knew what was going to happen, but I had to see it myself.

A side door opened. A man emerged. He had a pasty complexion and wild hair that looked as if it had been cut with hedge clippers. A bailiff accompanied him.

Within a second, Howard Munzer disappeared into the room where Schmidt and the lawyers were waiting.

When court resumed, Schmidt said he had heard the testimony and decided it was irrelevant. What was more, he wanted all mention of it stricken from the record. Then he told the attorneys to present their closing arguments.

Hammond went first, followed by Zwelnick. I kept looking at William Anderson, whose breath grew increasingly shallow. By now he was fully comprehending the fate that awaited him.

In the first row of spectators, Sylvia twitched and fidgeted. Van Duzer yawned. Schmidt issued instructions to the jury that somebody near me described as a hanging charge. The jury left the room, as did the judge. A bailiff led Anderson away. The crowd emptied out. I heard reporters in the hallway shouting at Sylvia.

Zwelnick sat slumped in his chair, his head tilted back, his legs sticking far in front of him. He seemed to be trying to sleep, or at least to forget what he had just experienced. I stopped at the rail that separated the spectators from the participants.

"You lied to me," I said.

Zwelnick turned his head. He looked like a man who needed six days of sleep. If he had any energy left, he would have addressed me more forcefully.

"I don't appreciate remarks like that, Grimes."

"I once asked if you knew Howard Munzer, and you denied it. But he was going to be your witness, wasn't he?"

Zwelnick rolled back his head until he was looking straight at the ceiling.

"I did not lie to you, Grimes. I don't know the man. But I had heard of him."

"In connection with what?"

"A couple of years ago he was the talk of the legal profession. He had the nerve to sue Harrington Price. He made the man testify as well."

"The case was about real estate," I said. "But that's all I know."

Zwelnick stood. He thrust his hands deep in his pockets before trudging toward me.

"Somebody should know the rest, Grimes. I guess you'll do."

I returned his sarcasm. "Thanks."

His voice regained its serious but weary quality. "I feel sorry for people in your profession. Journalists have their flaws, but the best ones are deeply concerned with the truth. The problem is, nobody ever wants to hear it."

I waited. He poured himself a glass of water, drank half of it, and began to tell me about a group of men who had lived at the Turtle Bay Settlement House a long time, twenty years or more. The men gave some stability to a transient place. Besides that, they regarded it as their home. One day in 1944, out of the blue, they were all told they'd have to leave. They'd been there too long. It was a new policy.

The men talked among themselves and decided they wouldn't go. One of them knew about an attorney named Howard Munzer who took on a lot of long shots and won a fair number of them. After accepting the case, Munzer got an injunction that stopped the evictions. Then he launched his own investigation to find out exactly who owned the building. It was difficult to discover that the owner was the Manley Holding Company, and next to impossible to find out that Harrington Price was actually pulling the strings, but Munzer did it.

He called on Price to testify. The old man didn't understand why he had to take the stand. If he wanted to get rid of those low-life bums, the city should thank him. The magistrate agreed; the injunction was lifted. What's more, the magistrate ruled that nobody involved in the case could talk about it outside court.

Munzer appealed. In the meantime, the men he represented were evicted. One by one, they were swallowed by the streets.

When Munzer was about to abandon hope, he received a call from a girl who sounded almost otherworldly. She said she knew the real story of the Manley Holding Company. He agreed to meet her at his office.

The girl was Amanda Price. She was a shattered soul who rarely made sense. She kept talking about blood money: she was on Manley's board, and she knew the company had been launched with tainted funds that befouled everything they touched.

Munzer said he was a lawyer. He needed proof. She said he was as bad as they were and fled the room. He assumed that was the last he'd ever see of her, but she called occasionally with cryptic bits of information. She said the scandal involved so many people. Even Frank Costello was in on it.

Finally, one day, she called to say she was ready to prove everything she'd been telling him. Half wondering if he should believe her, he asked where they should meet. She replied by inquiring if he'd ever gone to the Stork Club. He said he had, a couple of times, with friends from out of town. She said she'd be there early that night. She didn't get out much these days, but George Stavros wanted to talk to her. While she was there, she could bump into Munzer accidentally on purpose.

Munzer arrived early and sat at the bar, nursing a martini with a club soda on the side. Amanda got there at seven with Stavros. They were seated in the main room. An hour later, Munzer saw Stavros walk into the Cub Room. Munzer slipped off his stool and walked to Amanda's table. He bowed slightly and asked if she wanted to dance. She smiled. She said she hadn't danced since her fiancé died during the war. Out on the floor, they agreed to meet in front of the settlement house later that night. Amanda knew the woman on duty at the front desk. Her name was Terry. She'd let them into the office, where Munzer could retrieve some documents that would let him reopen the case.

Amanda never arrived, of course. Munzer stayed past midnight, silently cursing himself for listening to a girl who seemed so unreliable. As he began to walk away, two men materialized out of the dark and asked if his name was Munzer. It was a simple question, but there was no mistaking the menace in their voices. Munzer tried to say that he was, but he only emitted a gurgle. The men said they knew why he was there and if he had any sense at all, he'd forget everything he'd ever heard from that nutso girl. The next day, Munzer read about what had happened to Amanda Price.

Zwelnick stopped talking and shook his head. He struck me as a man who wanted to remain quiet for the rest of the day, but I still had questions.

"How did you get Munzer to talk?" I asked.

"I went up to his office on the lunch break and showed him the pictures Finkel had taken."

"The ones I took from his mother?"

Zwelnick nodded. "I asked if he recognized the men. Munzer said the two fellas with Peter Van Duzer were the ones who had threatened him."

"I'm surprised he talked to you," I said.

"Believe it or not, Grimes, there are men in the world who have not surrendered their consciences."

"Yeah. And if he reads the papers, he knows they're both dead."

"That helped."

I asked Zwelnick what he was going to do now.

"I told the judge I'd be certain to raise this issue on appeal. And he replied that if I did, he'd make sure I was disbarred."

The jury returned a few minutes later. The guilty verdict was so unsurprising it produced only a murmur. Schmidt thanked the jurors, twelve men good and true, for dispensing justice so swiftly. Three bailiffs took Anderson away. As he was led toward the door the prisoners used, he kept looking back at the spectators. Finally, when he was almost through, he saw me, and his eyes opened full in a silent plea for help.

Hammond walked toward Sylvia, leaned against the rail and whispered something. She nodded and turned to Van Duzer. Hammond opened the gate and let them into the area reserved for lawyers. Reporters swarmed forward.

Hammond raised his arms and said: "I'll answer your questions, boys. Let's step outside."

He headed toward the hallway. The reporters shouted that they wanted to talk to Sylvia.

"Please, boys. The girl would like some privacy. She's been through an ordeal."

Van Duzer said a few words to one of the bailiffs, who pointed toward a side door. Van Duzer held out his arm, which Sylvia grabbed. The two of them went where the bailiff had indicated.

The reporters followed Hammond out of the courtroom, looking for an easy quote. I approached the bailiff, who had the air of a man ready to take offense at the slightest challenge to what little authority he possessed.

"Waddya want?"

"The girl who just left. And the guy she was with. Where'd they go?"

"Beats me."

I told him I was with the *Examiner.* My editors really wanted me to interview the dead girl's sister. I'd seen her slip away and figured I had a chance to talk to her exclusively. To be honest about it, my job was on the line.

I could not remember the last time I had strung together so many untruths.

"Sorry, pallie. No can do."

I took out a notepad and said if he gave me a quote about the trial, I'd make sure it got into our story.

"Niggers are ruining the country."

"What should we do?"

"Kill 'em."

I tried to sound sincere as I thanked him for his comments. He whispered that he'd sent the girl to a ladies' room just a few people knew about. I asked where it was. He gave me some convoluted directions I hoped I'd remember.

I walked out of the courtroom, made a couple of rights and went through a pair of swinging doors that said NO ADMITTANCE. I waited for a harsh, stinging voice to ask what I thought I was doing, but the only sounds I heard were my own footsteps. I kept turning down hallways that seemed to lead to the middle of a maze.

Finally I came to a short corridor with a single door on the left. I walked up to it slowly. The words LADIES ROOM were stenciled over smoked glass, although a couple of letters were scratched away. I didn't know if she was still in there, so I pressed my ear against the door. I wondered if Van Duzer was close by.

I closed my eyes and imagined William Anderson being led into the death chamber, guards all around and a minister trailing behind telling him that God would forgive his sins if he repented.

I heard a noise that sounded like running water. I straightened my back, licked my lips and tried to comb my hair with my fingers. When the door creaked open, my heart stopped beating.

The blush she had applied could not hide how pale her cheeks were. Her eyes were haunted and red. She wore a wool coat that she hadn't buttoned. A tiny hat covered wisps of her hair. She clasped her small purse in her right hand.

"I still have it," I said.

"Have what?"

"A picture of us from the Stork Club. I carry it with me all the time."

Sylvia looked at her shoes, which had heels three inches high. Even though she had walked through the salt and slush of a Manhattan winter, her footwear was polished to a deep, glossy black. Then she raised her head. The faintest trace of a smile appeared on her face, as if I were a doll she could play with whenever she felt like. She reached down and began to fasten her coat.

"I can't believe how cold it is in here," she said. "You'd think the state of New York could afford to heat its courthouses."

I asked where Van Duzer was.

"He had to make a call. God only knows where the nearest phone is. Probably in Brooklyn." She made a face.

"Who's he calling?"

"I have no idea."

"I think you do."

Her finger slipped. She began fiddling with the buttons all over again.

"Is he calling your father?"

"What on earth are you talking about?"

"Van Duzer has to tell him that everything's worked out. Anderson's guilty. You're all off the hook."

"Has anybody ever told you that you can sound like a lunatic?"

She was just a few feet away, but she was so intent on those buttons she didn't see me take the two steps across the hall that separated us. I grabbed her wrist with one hand and put the other under her chin to force her to look at me.

"I know you're on the board of the Manley Holding Company."

"I've never heard of it," she said.

"This company you never heard of started buying property early in 1943 near Blood Alley. Right around the spot where your sister wound up dead."

"You're paranoid."

"Here's something that added to my paranoia: the company bought a lot of property from the 79 Wall Street Corporation. Does that address ring a bell?"

"Father works there."

"And the corporation is owned by Frank Costello."

She shook her head, which broke free of my hand, then glanced down. I wasn't sure if she was trying to think of a lie, or if she was just tired of looking up at me.

"I'll tell you something else," I said. "The company's original president was Donald Wetherby."

"I felt bad when he died," she said. "He was the first, you know. I suppose you always have a special place for the first."

"First what?"

She smiled, but there was no mirth behind it. "You don't know? You poor, silly boy, you really don't know?"

I couldn't say anything. I couldn't even shake my head. Sylvia took what seemed like hours before she said, "We were lovers."

She tried to step away. I put my hand on her shoulder.

"Are you getting rough with me, Patrick Grimes?"

"I'm thinking about it."

"I like you like this."

For a second I thought about smacking her. Force used for a righteous cause always worked in the movies.

"God," she said, drawing out the word so it stretched to four syllables, "I could use a cigarette."

I reminded her that I didn't smoke.

"But I do."

I let her reach down to her purse. She took out a gold-plated case that she opened with a flick of her manicured thumb.

"I suppose you don't have a light."

"Not this time."

"Good for you," she said. "If I didn't have bad habits, I'd have no habits at all."

She reached into one of the deep pockets in her coat and took out a lighter that worked on the first attempt. Then she inhaled and blew a wisp of smoke toward my face.

"This is ridiculous," she said.

"What is?"

"You pinning me against the door like a cop trying to browbeat a punk. I'm not running away from you, Patrick Grimes. Not in these heels."

I didn't want to lower my hand, but I did. Sylvia and I walked down the hallway together. I wished there was a way to muffle the sound of her heels striking the tile floor.

"What did Amanda do when she found out about you and Wetherby?"

"She had a breakdown."

"Was that her first?"

Sylvia blew some smoke. "Yes. Although she'd always been high-strung."

"How many breakdowns did she have?"

"I lost count. She was forever running in and out of asylums."

We turned into a narrow corridor. I had no idea where I was going.

"Do I shock you, Patrick Grimes?"

"Not anymore."

"The funny thing is, I didn't even like Donald that much. He always struck me as a bit on the dull side. But he looked so handsome in his uniform, and it's hard to say no to a man who might die for his country."

"He seduced you?"

"It wasn't his fault. I was flattered and willing. But I was also sixteen, so it was scandalous."

"Did he love Amanda?"

"I never asked him. But I suspected he didn't."

"Then why did he want to marry her?"

We rounded a corner. I wondered if she was leading me into a trap.

"Amanda worshipped him, and Donald liked to be worshipped."

She put her hand over her mouth in an unsuccessful attempt to cover a laugh. I asked what was so funny and she said: "Can you imagine? Can you just imagine Amanda as a political wife?"

Her laughter echoed around the narrow but empty space. She sounded especially cold and heartless, as if she were mocking all the frailty in the world. For the first time since I'd met her, I was furious at Sylvia Price.

"You should have given her the chance."

"Are you angry at me? Father certainly was."

"So he found out?"

"He finds out everything."

"Was he mad at Wetherby?"

"I'm not sure. I have no idea how Father's mind works. Most likely he realized he had something on Donald that he could use whenever it became necessary."

She looked at the floor and bit her lip in a schoolgirlish way. She was trying to flirt her way out of trouble. As we turned another corner, she took a final drag on her cigarette and threw it to the floor.

I asked if she knew who her sister was with at the Stork Club the night she was killed. Sylvia said she didn't. She asked why she should care.

"She was with Stavros." I made sure I enunciated every word clearly. "Remember him? Your latest former fiancé?"

Sylvia fumbled the cigarette she was trying to light. "George always liked Amanda," she said. "Or at least felt sorry for her."

"Is that why he met her that night?"

"I have no idea."

"She was supposed to see a man named Howard Munzer later on."

"That name means nothing to me."

"He once sued your dad."

"Father doesn't like that."

We turned another corner. I half expected to see the ghosts of Cangelosi and Fiore waiting to get their final revenge, but all I saw was another hallway. This one was long and seemed to lead nowhere. Sylvia asked if I had any idea how to get out. I shook my head and said I thought she did. She said she didn't. She was just walking.

We stopped and looked at each other. No one was around and it was easy to imagine we were the only people in the world. For a moment I wished we were, so we could confess all our secrets to each other and start over.

"How do you know I didn't kill Amanda?" Sylvia said. "Let's see...I found out that Amanda and George had dinner together, so I flew into a jealous rage, choked her, then shot her dead. My own sister. I could weep."

"For openers, you're not the type."

"To shoot?"

"To weep."

She pouted. "That's not fair."

"The only reason you took up with Stavros was because he bailed you out on some gambling debts. You never felt anything for him. I doubt you've ever felt anything for anybody."

She raised her free hand and started swinging it toward my face. I caught her wrist just as her open palm was about to strike me.

"I don't know why I ever talked to you," she said. "I should have sent you back to whatever dirt-poor Irish hellhole you crawled out of."

I was conscious of looking down at her. I'd never realized it before, but I was a good eight inches taller than Sylvia Price.

"You talked to me because, despite everything you've done, you don't like what's happening to William Anderson. You know he isn't guilty, and deep down, on some level you're probably not even aware of, it bothers you."

She started moving quickly down the hall, but she had been right before—it was impossible to run in those heels. It took me a few seconds to catch up. Sylvia was breathing hard. I grabbed her by the upper arm and made her turn toward me.

"The nuns used to tell us something—'confession is good for the soul.'"

"That's the silliest thing I ever heard."

"Tell me why you're here. You'll feel better."

"No, I won't. I'd just be telling you what you want to know."

"Okay. Let's play it your way. I'm working on a story. It's the biggest story of my life. And what I wanna know most is this—who killed Amanda?"

"I can't help you with that."

"Because you don't know, or because you don't want to?"

"Both."

"I bet your father does."

"Then ask him."

"I want to. But first you have to tell me what you know."

She sighed so loudly I was sure everyone in the courthouse could hear.

"Amanda was crazy, you know," she said.

"She was crazy because she cared."

"And because she was hurt, and couldn't get over it. I played a part in that. I suppose I should be sorry."

"I realize your sister was crazy." My words had become soft and slow. I needed to coax what Sylvia knew out of her. "But was she wrong?"

Sylvia shook her head. "She was right. The whole thing is rotten."

"The nuns also used to tell us that there are dark blots on your soul that'll eat away at you, and until you get rid of them, you'll never know any peace."

"You're talking about confession again."

"I suppose I am."

"Father says that's why Catholics never amount to anything. Jews, too. They're shackled by their consciences. They always feel guilty about everything."

"At least I have a conscience."

She looked at me with eyes that were clear but wounded.

"You think pretty highly of yourself, Patrick Grimes. And you have your good qualities. But you're unfair. You're very unfair."

"Then tell me something useful. At least tell me why you're here. When you talked to me on the phone the day the trial started, you said you wanted no part of it."

She closed her eyes and exhaled deeply. I realized she was about to give me at least part of the truth.

"It began last week. Father made me attend the opera with him. He was raising money for something. He *is* a philanthropist, you know."

"It was a policemen's charity. What happened?"

"I wanted to go out after. But he made me go home. That was when he ordered me to attend the trial."

"You don't strike me as the type of girl who follows orders."

"You've met Father," Sylvia said. "Do you believe he's the type of man you can deny when he really wants something?"

Her eyes were moist but she wasn't crying. She wasn't asking for forgiveness, but she did want a bit of sympathy.

"If the colored man is convicted," Sylvia told me, "Amanda's murder is solved. If he's acquitted, the questions will persist and grow. That would be bad for Father and the people he knows. It could even be bad for me."

"Why you?"

"If the authorities start looking into that silly company…" Her voice trailed off.

"So you do know about it. That's better. A lot better. What does it do?"

"It buys things."

"Come on, Sylvia."

"Father says it's in real estate in Turtle Bay. First they'll clear out the slaughterhouses and the tenements and the breweries to build the United Nations. Then they're gonna tear down that wretched El and make things that are nice and modern all along Third Avenue. And everyone who gets in on the ground floor will make quite a bit of money."

"How much does your father stand to gain?"

"More than ten million, I think."

"How much did he put up?"

"Very little. He always says that the key is to use other people's money to buy things you can control."

"So whose money did he use?"

"A lot of it came from Peter."

"Peter?"

"Van Duzer. My new beau."

"Great," I said. I made no effort to keep the contempt out of my voice. "You can keep it all in the family."

"I wish I swore like a sailor. I'd tell you exactly what I think of you."

"And I'd return the favor. Christ Almighty, how much do you people need?"

She shook her head slowly. "Peter's strapped. He has been for a long time."

I was tempted to break out an imaginary violin to play a few phantom notes in sympathy with poor Peter Van Duzer, but I recalled a detail from the accounts of his daughter's kidnapping and murder: despite their seeming wealth, Van Duzer and his wife had trouble raising the ransom.

"So where did he get the money?" I asked in a tone of genuine curiosity.

"When his daughter died," Sylvia said. "That horrible kidnapping. He and Elizabeth had an insurance policy for her. It was more than a million."

"Why didn't his wife's family help out?"

She shook her head. "They disowned Elizabeth when she went into acting. You can't imagine how scandalous show people are." For once in her life, Sylvia looked like she truly felt sorry about something. "After Lara died, their marriage couldn't stand the strain. So Elizabeth left Peter and returned to Hollywood. Perhaps that's better. It's the only place she's happy."

I looked past Sylvia. I needed to concentrate, and her presence was suddenly distracting. "That was an awful lot of money to have on a kid," I said, more to myself than to her.

"A lot of people did similar things," Sylvia said. "After the Lindbergh kidnapping. Just in case." She paused. "Father did."

"Nice piece of work, putting a price tag on your kids' lives."

I thought, perhaps cruelly, of Mother. If she'd had the money and the wit, she would have taken out policies on me and Kathleen.

"Father puts a price tag on everything," Sylvia said. "That's why Turtle Bay is so important to him."

"But it all has to be done quietly."

Sylvia nodded. "Some of the methods the company has used would look bad if they were scrutinized. Sweetheart deals, mass evictions, things like that."

"And you were all afraid that Amanda's murder might lead to exposure of the company."

Sylvia nodded.

"But now you have Anderson's conviction. And your father sent you here to help sway the jury. Sweet."

Sylvia raised her hand to her face. I'd always thought of her as a girl too conscious of her own mannerisms, but at that moment her pain seemed real.

"I told you it was rotten," she said. "We're supposed to have everything. Why are we so miserable?"

I lowered her hands and brushed away the tears that finally threatened to drop from her eyes, then held her face in my palms. She seemed more than lonely—she was alone, no matter what happened.

Her eyelashes fluttered. Her lips parted slightly.

I bent down slowly. I told myself I'd stop if she told me to.

My mouth brushed against hers and the surge that ran through me was both electric and primal. My arms wrapped around her. After a moment she returned the embrace. Her tongue danced against mine, and suddenly my fiercest desire was to revel in all the shameful parts of life I'd always been warned about. I wanted to do everything with her. Forever.

When we broke apart, Sylvia opened her eyes.

"Don't fall in love with me," she said.

The next sound we heard was a too loud cough that caused us to look to the far end of the hall.

It was Van Duzer.

As he walked toward us, he said I looked familiar.

I had never sized him up before. Now that I looked at him closely, I could tell he was about my height and weight. He was older than me, although his face was soft and unlined.

He'd avoided the service. He hadn't seen the things I had.

"We met at the Stork Club," I said.

He nodded. "I never bought that line about you two being cousins," he said. "It's your accent. You don't sound like a butter and egg man."

He stopped inches from me. He was trying to intimidate me, but seeing him this way was like confronting my worst fears and realizing they were not as terrifying as I'd imagined.

"Sylvia likes to play games, Mr.—I'm sorry, what is your name?"

"Grimes."

"She likes to play games, Mr. Grimes. And she likes to make people play them with her. Sometimes, when I'm in the mood, I'm indulgent. But at other times it's tiresome."

"I have some questions for you."

"And I have some for you, Mr. Grimes: Who are you? Why are you here? Why were you and Sylvia pressing your faces against each other?"

I tried to locate a spark in his eyes, but I found nothing. His skin was a shell with no life behind it.

"You strike me as a workingman, Mr. Grimes—a reporter perhaps, or a scribbler of some sort. So write this down. Make a note."

He leaned toward me in a manner of mock confidentiality. His voice became a stage whisper. "You can't leave Sylvia alone for a second. I blame myself, actually. At times I think she's the most wonderful girl in the world, but I'm fully aware of the consequences of screwing a chippy."

From behind me I heard a sharp word from Sylvia: "Peter!"

Without even turning to look at her he said: "Don't tell me you're offended, Sylvia. You're called names worse than that every day in the newspapers. Deservedly, I might add."

What I saw before me was a man with the smug satisfaction that comes from getting away with whatever he liked, a man who considered himself tough and shrewd, but who also believed that a life of ease was his birthright. He did not think about what he said, or cared about the effect his actions and words had on others. As I considered all this, the rage that was always churning inside me began to bubble up, and this time I could not contain it. I clenched my fist and swung my arm. When my hand struck Peter Van Duzer's chin, the sound of his shattering teeth was the most satisfying noise I ever heard.

He reeled backward. I grabbed him, but his cashmere coat began to slide out of my hands, so I pushed him hard. The back of his head smashed against the wall. I raised my foot. He reflexively covered his groin. I cracked the heel of my shoe against his kneecap. He howled and bent over. I stood over him and started punching his face—one, two, three, four—the way I'd seen LaMotta do it. As Van Duzer's blood ran over my hands, waves of peace swept over me. I believed I was finally righting a few of the many wrongs in the world.

Somewhere far behind me, Sylvia screamed.

I walked behind Van Duzer, put my arm around his neck and snapped his head back. A gurgle came from his throat.

"What?" he said. The word took all the energy he had. I pressed my arm tighter against him. He wriggled a bit. With my free hand I reached around his head and smacked him in the face again.

"What...do you want?"

"Cangelosi and Fiore," I said.

"What…are you talking about?"

I hit him a few more times. Sylvia screamed again.

"Finkel took some pictures," I said.

"Who…the hell is Finkel?"

"A photographer. I worked with him. Somebody had him killed."

"What in God's name are you talking about?"

"The pictures were taken the day Mancini was executed. You remember him, don't you?"

"He killed my daughter."

"The pictures showed you, Cangelosi and Fiore outside your home."

"You're…insane. Just like Amanda."

I tried to squeeze all the air from his windpipe.

"I've got bad news for you. The photos are in a safe place. And Fiore's dead. I pushed him in front of a car. I croaked Cangelosi, too."

Suddenly I felt Sylvia's hands pulling at me as she called out, "For God's sake, Patrick, you're killing him."

My grip on Van Duzer must have loosened because he pushed my arms away, knocking me backward. He started to run, so I lunged forward and grabbed him by the ankle. He hit the floor with his face. I felt him trying to squirm away, but I rose to my feet and stumbled forward until I reached his head. I grabbed him by the hair and pulled him up. Our noses almost touched.

"I've killed better men than you," I said.

Blood trickled from his mouth.

"So you better tell me the truth. Starting now. Or I'm gonna smash your head against the floor until your brains come out."

A sound escaped him that reminded me of the last bit of air easing out of a punctured tire. My thoughts were galloping. They began with this fact: Peter Cangelosi had arrested Anthony Mancini on a charge of vagrancy, which was how the authorities eventually determined that he was the man who'd kidnapped Lara Van Duzer.

I figured I had ten minutes at most to work it all out.

"Did Cangelosi frame Mancini?" I asked.

"I don't remember."

"You'll hafta do better than that."

I rammed his head against the floor. Van Duzer moaned. Blood flowed from his nose. Sylvia said she was going to get the police if I didn't stop. I yanked Van Duzer's hair and jerked his head. I wished I had a knife so I could press it against his throat.

"Tell me how it started," I said.

"No."

I punched him in the mouth. My knuckles began to bleed. One of Van Duzer's teeth fell onto his coat. Sylvia screamed. She said she meant it this time. She was going to get somebody.

I leaned close to Van Duzer. I made sure my voice was low. Menacing words spoken softly are always more powerful than shouts.

"I'm five seconds away from killing you."

He must have believed me, because the words started rasping out.

Van Duzer had inherited some money, but it wasn't as much as everybody assumed. Generations of men in his family had bet on the wrong horses, the wrong businesses and the wrong women. He himself had followed that tradition. By the time he was thirty he was married to Elizabeth, a beautiful girl who'd once been a movie star, but he was flat broke and she knew it. So he was open to an opportunity. In fact, he needed one desperately.

One day, over drinks at the Harvard Club, Harrington Price told him: "There's a real estate venture. I need partners. But I also need to keep my name out of it. Are you interested?"

Van Duzer nodded.

"Good," Price said. "You'll need to come up with a million dollars."

Van Duzer looked at him as if Price had just suggested he sprout wings and start flying around the room. When Van Duzer finally cleared his throat, he said he didn't have a million dollars.

Price told him to find it.

I looked closely at Van Duzer. The skin under his left eye was purple and swelling.

"How'd you get the money?"

"I'm not gonna tell you."

I pounded his head against the floor.

"I can't let this go on," Sylvia said.

I heard her heels fading down the hall. I wanted to stop her, but it was more important to get everything out of Van Duzer.

"Do you wanna die?" I asked Van Duzer. "Do you really wanna die?"

And then I stopped. Sylvia had supplied the answer.

"You had an insurance policy," I said. "On your daughter's life. It was worth more than a million dollars."

He nodded. "That's how I got the money," he said. "But I did all the work, too. I set up the company. Of course, the banks wouldn't touch me. And I couldn't tell them Harrington Price was backing me up. That would have given the game away."

He coughed. Another tooth spat out.

"So you made Donald Wetherby your front man," I said.

Van Duzer nodded. "He was golden. We all thought he was gonna be president someday."

"And since Price knew he was having an affair with Sylvia, he blackmailed him into fronting the company."

"Something like that."

I punched Van Duzer again. I stopped telling myself I didn't enjoy it.

"The headmaster told Price that Sylvia was cutting school. So Price had a cop follow her around. Cangelosi. He'd do anything, if you paid him enough."

"So Cangelosi found out about the affair. But Amanda found out about it, too."

"That's when she started turning nutso."

Van Duzer's head lolled. His eyes fluttered halfway shut. I was afraid he was going to pass out.

"And then you got in touch with Cangelosi. You had him frame Mancini for Lara's death."

"Whatever you say."

I started to run through what little knowledge I had. I needed to add to it quickly.

"Amanda was on the board of the holding company," I said.

"That's right."

"What was your role in it?"

"I ran it. I still do. But my name isn't on anything."

"That's clever."

"The deal is sweet."

"How much have you made?"

"Hard to say. But the value doubled when the United Nations thing went through. And it's only gonna go up."

"You bought a lot of land from Costello."

"He's a generous man."

I punched Van Duzer in the face. Blood spurted from his nose.

"He needs the cash," Van Duzer said. "That thing he's bankrolled in Nevada. The Flamenco or whatever it's called. A bottomless pit."

"You put Amanda on the board because you figured she'd be a sap."

Van Duzer nodded.

"But she found out what was going on. And she wasn't the kind of girl who reacted well to working with gangsters."

"A Goody Two-shoes. Just like you."

I hit him again, but my punches were acquiring the numbing effect of habit.

"What happened when she found out?" I asked.

Van Duzer told me about a night when he was in Harrington Price's library. They were discussing how good it was to work with Costello. The fellow was an excellent businessman. But then they heard a full-throated cry followed by thrashing from behind one of the drapes. It crashed onto the rug but seemed to be moving, as if it had trapped a creature in its death throes. Price bolted toward it and pulled up the heavy damask and there she was, a writhing and emaciated figure, her sticklike legs flailing as if she had no control over them. It was Amanda and she was screaming, over and over again, "How could you?"

Van Duzer looked straight at me. His lips were so swollen he could barely talk. "They took her to the bughouse again," he said in a dismissive tone that indicated he thought she was worth as much as a cockroach. "They shoulda kept her there. Woulda been better for everybody."

"Go to hell."

"I'm already there. It's not so bad."

He started to talk again. Despite a face that was bloody and broken, he seemed almost garrulous, as if he had longed to tell someone about his prowess in putting together the scheme and keeping it going. Peter Van Duzer had not succeeded at much in life, except for this.

He said that the last time Amanda was shipped to the nut farm, her brain was zapped and she was doped with lithium before she was let out after a couple of months. Price assured Van Duzer that she was harmless. Van Duzer wasn't so sure. He sent Cangelosi and Fiore to follow her. They discovered she was planning to go back to that flophouse on 47th. Van Duzer realized it was only a matter of time before she started telling people what she knew.

"So you had her killed," I said.

"There's so much at stake. The future of the city."

"Why did Stavros go to the Stork Club with Amanda that night?"

"He told her to stop. In a nice way."

"But she wouldn't agree?"

"He saw her dance with Munzer. Then Cangelosi and Fiore tailed her after she left. She was heading to the flophouse. We figured she was gonna try to get Munzer in there."

"What's there that you don't want him to see?"

"Papers about who we bought the land from."

"We're back to Costello."

"We never left."

Van Duzer said that Amanda was a block away from the flophouse when Cangelosi and Fiore snatched her and stuffed her in the back of their car. They broke her windpipe so she couldn't cry out. Then they shot her and dumped her body beside a warehouse before telling Patrolmen McMahon and Valentine there was a dead girl in an alley. The night watchman at the place was a spook. They should pin the murder on him. Cangelosi and Fiore told the cops they'd steer some dough their way.

"So a girl gets killed," I said. "Just so you can make some money, and a bunch of gangsters can build a hotel in the middle of the desert."

"They'll make it work. Blood Alley's gonna turn around, too. Then all the people on Beekman Place won't have to look at that shithole anymore."

"I'm happy for them. Their lives are so tough."

"Everybody has a stake in this, pal. Everybody wants a piece of it. Except for you. What's your problem?"

I thought for a minute. "It's wrong."

"Now I remember. Grimes. Pain in the ass with the *Examiner.* You shoulda listened to that guy you work for."

"McCracken?"

"He's got a share. If you'd just given him that blowjob he wanted from you, he woulda cut you in."

I hit Van Duzer again, with renewed force. He moaned and sank his face to the floor. Blood seeped from his mouth and stained the white tile.

"What about Finkel?" I was aware I was shouting. I wondered if anyone could hear.

"Fiore grabbed him while he was fiddling with all that crap in the trunk of his car. It was easy."

"One last thing. Then I'm gonna go. And maybe I won't kill you."

"Go ahead. You'll never prove any of this. In fact, I bet you go to prison for this stunt you're pulling. And a guy like you—a fucking crusader—won't come out. Especially after the trouble boys find out what you did to Cangelosi and Fiore."

I licked my lips. All those hours in the city room had trained me to ask questions, but this was the most significant one I'd ever posed. I told myself I was beyond caring about my own fate.

My words came out slowly. I wanted to make sure he heard them all. "If Mancini didn't kill your daughter, who did?"

I had the feeling that Van Duzer wanted to laugh, but I wasn't sure if it was at me or himself or all the absurdities and capriciousness of life itself.

"I loved her mother very much. The only girl I ever felt that way about."

My mind went blank for a second. Finally I blurted, "Her mother killed her?"

He shook his head as vigorously as his condition would allow. "No, no, no. It's just that I wanted to keep Elizabeth. Keep her with me. And she was slipping away."

Then I remembered. She was an actress. Her family was wealthy but had disowned her because of her career choice. She had returned to Hollywood after she divorced Van Duzer and had resumed her career under her maiden name: Elizabeth Manley.

"You named the company after her," I said. My own voice sounded as if it were somewhere on the other side of the Hudson. "Price was behind the company, but you ran it, and you named it after her."

"I thought I could keep her. If I got some money." He shook his head. "But you never know people. You never really know them."

"She left you anyway."

"She wanted to move back to California. She doesn't like the cold. And there was this producer…" His voice trailed off. I could figure out what happened.

"You haven't answered my question. About your daughter."

"We didn't want a kid. It just happened. That's why we had to get married. But I was always crazy about Elizabeth. I don't think she felt the same way about me. She was remote. Maybe that made me want her more. Now I have Sylvia." He shook his head, like a man accustomed to caviar who was now forced to eat scraps.

I asked the question again, this time more directly. "So who killed Lara?"

He said the girl had always been a problem. Both he and his wife resented her and all the opportunities she denied them.

A thought flashed of the way Mother regarded Kathleen and me.

One day in passing, while Van Duzer was silently desperate

about how he'd raise the money to join the real estate scheme, Price mentioned that he'd once insured both his daughters just in case something bad occurred. That was how Van Duzer got the idea that would solve his problems.

My breath became sharp and short. It was so cold in the hallway I saw little puffs in front of my mouth. I was afraid of what he was going to tell me, but I had to keep going.

"There was no kidnapping, was there?" I asked.

Van Duzer shook his head. "I grabbed her one night. Elizabeth was out. I tried to choke Lara, but she ran away. Then she fell down the stairs. Hurt her head real bad. So I finished her off. Drowned her in the bathtub." He shook his head. "You have no idea what a fucking brat she was."

I felt my rage returning. This time, I did not want to control it.

"I think Elizabeth figured it out eventually," he said. "But we never talked about it. Amanda knew, too. I told Price all about it that night when she was listening to us from behind the curtains. It wasn't that stuff about Costello, or even Wetherby—it was learning about Lara that caused her worst breakdown."

I summoned all the strength I had left, then hit him again and again as my consciousness floated out of me. I thought I was bringing a small measure of justice into the world, and finally righting at least some of the wrongs I had committed. Weeks seemed to pass. The feeling that came over me was as close to bliss as I ever experienced.

And then I heard Sylvia cry out, from somewhere a thousand miles away: "Stop him. For God's sake, stop him."

I ran from the courthouse and ducked into the men's room at the City Hall subway stop. Bits of Van Duzer's blood stained my coat. I wiped them off as best I could, washed my face and looked at my hands, which were cracked and swollen. I could feel them stiffening.

I wondered what Sylvia and Van Duzer would do. I assumed they would press charges. If I returned to my apartment, the cops were likely to be waiting. I tried to think of a place to stay. The only person I could think of was my sister, Kathleen.

I took the train to Woodside. It was night. The air was frigid and windy. It occurred to me that I hadn't eaten since breakfast. I stepped into a five-and-dime and headed for the phone booth in back. As I called Kathleen, I wondered what I would do if her husband answered.

But it was my sister's voice that came over the line. I'd never been so glad to hear her.

I told her who it was. I said I needed to talk.

"Are you okay?" she asked. "You sound like you're in trouble."

"That's why I need to talk to you."

There was a long pause. I knew she didn't want to continue, but she finally asked, "What is it, Pat?"

"I need to talk to you. Alone. Is Dan there?"

"What is it, Pat? What have you gotten yourself into?"

"Is there any way we can talk? Just the two of us?"

Her voice dropped. She said there was a luncheonette around the corner from her apartment. It stayed open till eight. "Go there and grab a cup of joe and wait for me."

I told Kathleen everything. She gasped and nodded. I said I was a newsman with a story I could sell somewhere, but I needed time and a place to write. She said she'd do what she could. I told her I thought everything would work out. When it did, I'd let her and Ryan use my name to buy a house in Levittown. Kathleen lowered her head until it reached my hand. Her eyes watered. She said she couldn't thank me enough.

I told her I'd like to get some sleep. She said her husband was still so angry at me she didn't think it was wise to bring me to their apartment. But she did think she could clear out a cubbyhole in the basement of her building, although it wouldn't be comfortable. I said I was so tired it didn't matter. I also told her I'd need a typewriter and some paper. She said she had those things in the apartment.

She left ahead of me. She told me to be outside her building in ten minutes.

The wind blew directly into my face. I felt exposed every second I spent on the street.

When I reached her stoop, the door to her building opened immediately. I rushed up the stairs and into the hallway. Kathleen stood there holding a flashlight. She told me to follow. When we were almost to the back, she pushed open a door that was stuck from years of bad paint jobs. She turned on the flashlight and led me down creaky steps. At the bottom she flicked on a light. A single bulb glowed, dangling on a wire. I saw a discarded mattress surrounded by sheets of cardboard, which made me think of the guys we used to see in the Central Park Hoovervilles during the Depression.

Kathleen said she was sorry. This was the best she could do. I told her it was all right. She said she'd come for me in the morning. Maybe I could write my story then.

I said I hoped I'd still be able to type. My right hand was awfully sore.

We both laughed a little. I lay on the mattress, which was dirty and lumpy. Kathleen spread my coat over me like a blanket.

"There's one thing I've been meaning to ask you," I said.

"Can it wait until morning, Pat?"

I shook my head. "It's about Mother."

"What is it?"

"What did she die of?"

Kathleen pulled the flashlight away until it shone in a narrow beam toward the ceiling. The rest of the room was black.

"She died because she wanted to," my sister said.

When Kathleen came down the next morning, she told me that her husband had gone to work. She said had to leave soon, but she could show me where the typewriter and paper were.

She led me up the stairs and into their apartment. The typewriter was on a stand in the living room. A hard-back chair was set up in front of it. A sheaf of papers was stacked neatly to the side.

Kathleen fidgeted. She said she was gonna be late for work. I said I understood. I wanted to kiss her on the cheek, but she was out the door before I could move.

It was drafty in the living room, so I left my coat on. I sat at the typewriter and rolled in a piece of paper and tried to think of where I should start. There was so much to tell. Then I heard McCracken's voice in my ear, always a man who knew exactly how a story should play:

"There are times when you won't know how to get it going. And when that happens, my young mick friend, this is what you do—take a good deep breath, a long gulp of Brother Jim Beam, and start at the beginning."

I began to type—

The door blew open. Cops filled the room. I tried to break free, but big guys in blue uniforms pinned my arms behind me as Detective Walter Koenig walked into the room.

"I've been looking forward to this, Grimes. We all have."

My head whipsawed from right to left. I was being held by Patrolmen Valentine and McMahon. They looked like they had never enjoyed a collar as much as this one.

"That was quite a number you did on Van Duzer," Koenig said. "He might not pull through. At the best, he'll be jingle-brained. A fucking vegetable for the rest of his life."

"He killed her," I said.

"Who killed who?"

"Van Duzer killed his daughter, and he's responsible for Amanda Price. He also got Fiore to kill Finkel."

Koenig balled up his fist and punched me in the gut. All the air rushed out of me.

"Christ," he said, "you smell as bad as that nigger did."

"What should we do with him?" Valentine's voice was unusually chipper, as if he was hoping for an order to start hitting me.

"Take him to the bathroom. Splash water on him. If I hafta ride with him, I don't wanna hold my nose all the way."

Valentine and McMahon pushed me through the apartment and into the bathroom. They threw me against the sink and ordered me to start washing. I began running the water and told myself I might be able to work it all out anyway. If I went to trial, I'd testify about all the things I knew. Even if I spent time in prison, William Anderson would go free.

Then I heard a rustling noise from the living room, the surging sound that occurs when the guest of honor arrives a few minutes late.

"How'd it go?" Ryan asked. I gasped. My sister's husband. At first I thought he'd protest, but as he talked I realized he had orchestrated the situation.

"Fine," Koenig said.

"He's a menace," Ryan said. "To be honest about it, I think he's a nut job."

"It's interesting you say that," Koenig said. "I talked to his old boss, a guy named McCracken. And the cop reporter at the *Examiner.* Higgins. An up-and-up guy. They both said the same thing."

"What can we do?" Ryan asked. "If he goes on trial, I think my wife'll crack from the strain."

"She could sign papers," Koenig said. "We get a shrink to say he's nutso, she commits him to a bughouse, and then we avoid a trial. I've seen it happen dozens of times. Then nobody has to testify about anything. Might be better for everyone. I know that Price girl doesn't wanna talk about what she saw. She's been through a lot—I'd like to give her a break."

"What would happen to Grimes after that?" Ryan asked.

"Once he's at the bug farm, they'll probably give him a lobotomy. That calms a lot of them down."

I felt myself spinning and reeling, as if I were being sucked down a drain with water running around me. Now I just heard snippets.

"Thanks for calling us—"

"We gotta move outta this city—"

"I know what you mean. Those goddamn niggers—"

"A house in the country is all we want—"

"We'll put in a good word for you. That should do it."

I leaned against the sink and put my head down. My knees began to give way. I thought I was going to melt into a puddle on the floor as I glanced at the window and noticed the fire escape just outside.

"Whatsa matter, Grimes?" Valentine said. "Not such a hotshot anymore, are ya?"

"I'm gonna be sick," I said.

"Christ. Oh Christ."

I summoned coughing and gurgling sounds from somewhere deep within. Koenig bellowed from the living room, asking what the hell was going on back there.

"He's gonna puke!"

"Let him. But make sure you wash him off."

I hacked and spit and crawled to the toilet, which I opened as slowly as I could. Valentine said he was gonna be sick, too. I groaned, leaned over and pushed the door shut.

I kept coughing. Nothing came up. I stood quietly and flushed the toilet, then ran the water in the sink and the shower as loudly as I could. With water spraying all around, I hustled to the window and tried to jack it up.

It stuck. I jammed on it again. I hoped no one would hear the sound. The damn thing wouldn't budge. Finally I slammed on it as hard as I could. In the only small miracle I have ever observed, it popped up.

I shoved my coat through the fire escape before sliding through myself. It was still cold outside. I grabbed my coat. But before I hustled to the ground, I went through the pockets to make sure it was still there: the photograph that showed me with Sylvia Price on the one night I set foot in the Stork Club, the only time I was ever on the other side of the window, laughing and dancing and carrying on as if my life was joyful and carefree.

Epilogue

I started my journey west by taking a ferry that left me at a railroad terminal in New Jersey. I bought a ticket for as far as I could go. When I got off, I found a menial job. I stayed a few days until I got enough money to buy another ticket. Then I went west again. I kept doing this for I don't remember how long, becoming familiar with the Boweries across America, until I reached the desert and saw miles of empty land under a strong blue sky that was always warm. I found a shack and watched it for days. Nobody ever used it. Finally I brought in my bag and just started living there.

I let my hair and whiskers grow.

I gathered rainwater in a bucket.

I walked along the roads for hours looking for useful things.

Sometimes I'd hitch a ride to the nearest town, where I'd work a few days to make money. People tried to talk to me, but I said little. I'd had enough of people.

One day early in my stay, a newspaper story caught my eye. The article described the new skyscraper community on Manhattan's East Side that was now the home of the United Nations, the organization destined to bring peace to the planet. The world's leading architects had designed the buildings, which were gleaming and beautiful. The slums that blighted the area were being cleared. Soon the elevated railway that darkened Third Avenue would finally come down. Turtle Bay sparkled like a jewel. The best people on Earth wanted to live there.

I lifted the curtain and saw him again—a young Negro in a crisp shirt and an ironed tie, he and his clothes impervious to the sun that bakes everything brown in this part of the country.

I opened the door slightly. He smiled and asked if I remembered him. I may have nodded.

"I don't know how to say this, sir."

He paused, as if he expected a reply, then went on.

"My company has done a lot of research. We've gone through all the county's deed and title records since, well, since forever. And we have no record of this property ever being bought by you."

He smiled again, a little nervously. I said nothing.

"Do you have anything in here that indicates you own this place?"

I started to close the door.

"Sir?" he said.

I closed the door a little more.

"Men will be coming through in a week or two. They'll be doing surveys and stuff. The county is laying roads and water lines. My company plans to build homes and stores, even a golf course."

I shut the door and leaned against it.

"Did you hear me, sir?"

His voice was rising with the edgy indignation of a man who wasn't sure how to cope with silent defiance.

"I need an answer."

I walked to the back and thought about how I had ended up here. It was because I had tried to save an innocent man.

I had fought, as best I could, for justice, but nobody else was interested. There was business to be done, and that was more important.

Perhaps I had redeemed myself, but that is for the Almighty Whatever It Is to decide—if, in fact, judgments like that are ever made. I did all I could, but in the end, when it counted, I was just another ineffectual man who meant well.

I opened a drawer and looked at the picture I had kept for so many years. For all her flaws, the girl was forever beautiful. She had transported me, however briefly, to a world I had dreamed about.

For the first time in many years I summoned a prayer—not much of one, only a few words—forgiving Sylvia Price for transgressions both large and small, and offering my most sincere hope that everything had worked out for her.

Acknowledgments

Many people helped with the preparation of this book, and I apologize in advance to anyone I overlooked. In particular, I am indebted to Bill Contardi, John Paine, Tim Wendel, Melody Lawrence, Deborah Meghnagi and Kinneret Kra for their help with the manuscript. I'd also like to thank Matthew Miller for his support, and for his belief in this novel.

Mid-twentieth century New York was blessed with a number of strong chroniclers. Among the books I found most helpful were *A Song for Mary* by Dennis Smith, *The Stork Club* by Ralph Blumenthal and *Manhattan '45* by Jan Morris. David Kennedy's *Freedom from Fear* is a strong one-volume history of the travails and ultimate triumph of the United States in the Depression and World War II years. Neal Gabler's biography of Walter Winchell provided an illuminating look at the intersection of gossip and celebrity. *By the El* was a treasure trove, with Lawrence Stelter's text illuminating his father Lothar's brilliant photographs of the doomed Third Avenue line.

Most of all, I have to extend two special sets of thanks. The first goes to my wife, Jill, for too many things to list—but particularly for her forbearance. Finally, I want to thank my parents, for giving me the idea for this book so many years ago.

Tom Coffey

New York City, November 2007

About the Author

Tom Coffey is a writer and editor with an extensive background in journalism. A graduate of the Newhouse School of Communications at Syracuse University, Tom has been a reporter and editor for some of America's leading newspapers. A staff editor at the *New York Times* since 1997, he has also worked for *New York Newsday*, the *Los Angeles Herald-Examiner* and the *Miami Herald*.

His first novel, *The Serpent Club*, was published in 1999 to starred reviews. His second novel, *Miami Twilight*, was published in 2001. Tom has been a member of the Mystery Writers of America since 1999.

Tom lives in Lower Manhattan with his wife and daughter.

The fonts used in this book are from the Garamond family